T.S. Weaver

Published by Under the Moon, LLC
Pelican Rapids, MN

Hell's Own
System Wars
Frontier Wars Book 1
ISBN: 978-1-938339-43-1
Copyright © 2019 T.S. Weaver
Cover Art Copyright @ 2019 Samuel Pray
Editor in Chief: Terri Pray
All rights reserved.

Author's Note.

Hell's Own is book one in the Hell's Trilogy.

And a part of the System Wars: Frontier Wars setting.

All books in System Wars are clearly marked with their reading order to make the enjoyment of the series as easy as possible for readers.

Dedication

To my Sam, my Wolf, now and always.
And Rage, thank you for the extra set of eyes.

For Matt Jondar, one of my first readers so many years ago.
You'll never know how grateful I was for your support, and for
your willingness to listen to my tales.

Hell's Own

System Wars

Frontier Wars Book 1

T.S. Weaver

Prologue

"We got another series of malfunctions showing up." Zac Brusard brushed his fingers across the screen, then tapped it, then reached for the mug of cold coffee, or what passed for coffee out here. He grimaced but took two swallows and set the cup down. No lid. He glanced back over his shoulder. No sign of the supervisor, Laura. He didn't need another write up in his file. "I have to clean the display again, but I don't think this is dirt." He peered at the readout as he blindly searched for a lid and slapped it in place over the remains of his coffee. He rubbed at the screen with one thumb.

Nothing changed. Three blips flickered in and out as they made their way across the display. "Haden? You see anything in sector eight, right the on edge?"

"Give me a minute, bringing it up no-- oh. Yeah. Maybe we've got a couple of rogue asteroids coming in. I'll see what the long range shows me." Haden shoved himself, and the chair, across to the next set up, and keyed in the details. "Been a while since we had any excitement here. Could do with a change."

"If Laura hears you, she'll schedule a drill to keep us on our toes." Zac stared at the blips. If they were asteroids, they were large enough to cause a problem. He frowned as he worked out the destination if the unknowns kept to the same trajectory.

Pluto.

Heat drained from his face. He reran the numbers. Had to be a mistake. The long-range system would have informed them of the danger long before the objects appeared on his scanners. The navy would be on alert, ready to divert or destroy the approaching asteroids.

"Anything?" A system error? Had to be, he wasn't seeing three damn unknowns heading straight for them. Not on his watch. His mind reeled. Brandon, the man he'd taken over from, hadn't mentioned problems. Maybe the guy had spilled a drink, causing the glitch. Or one of the kids had hacked into the system to play a practical joke? Dangerous, considering the entire set up technically belonged to the navy. Naval Intelligence had no sense of humor, a teen caught up in hacking faced a tribunal. But any of those would be better than the reality of three large pieces of debris hitting the colony.

"Running scans on the system now."

Zac swallowed down a lump and fought against the urge to ask the man a hundred questions. Haden had seen them, or he wouldn't be running a check. His heart raced as he tried to bring his fears under control. If they were asteroids, they could move them out of the way or destroy them. Nothing to worry about. The navy would welcome the distraction. Not as if they had much else to do out here.

He turned his attention back to his screen. Haden would get to the bottom of it. The man knew what he was doing. Zac's lips parted, a strangled cry escaping as he stared at the display. "No possible." Had he spoken? The voice sounded like his, but he couldn't remember talking. "They're picking up speed." Couldn't be asteroids. Not even a comet would change speed without a massive increase in gravity. "Haden?"

"Not meteors. Or asteroids." Haden confirmed.

"Then what?"

"Sensors suggest they're ships. Readings are like nothing I've ever seen before. Energy source unknown, material unknown. Engines, least I can't imagine the energy flare being anything else, match on all three vessels. No transponders." Haden slid over to the first console, pulled on a headset and hit a series of keys. "Unknown ships, this is Pluto colony, please respond."

Ships? There were always explorers and miners who attempted to find the next big strike on the fringe, but they all carried transponders. Zac pulled up the list of vessels, checking against the data. Not one of the ones who had left the system slipped out to find a new mineral claim, matched the size of the three now blinking on the screen.

"Unknown ships, please respond and identify yourself. This is Pluto colony. Do you copy?"

Zac grabbed his headset and listened in.

Static.

"Please respond, or we will be forced to assume you're approaching with hostile intent. Do you copy?"

What was the drill if approached by a hostile? Zac punched up the information. They'd never dealt with a hostile, and if an SOP - Standard Operating Procedure - had been created, Zac didn't know it. Scrolling through the database produced a three-line basic outline. "No, there has to be more than this," he murmured as he brought up the search and keyed in the details. Another handful of lines. All right, this wasn't what he'd expected. "Why isn't there a blasted SOP for this situation."

"What situation?" A sleepy voice asked from behind him.

He didn't turn his attention away from the screen. "Possible hostiles."

"You drunk?"

"If he is, then it's contagious." Haden waved without turning toward the newcomer. "Laura, you know of anything else about dealing with unknown ships? Nothing in the handbook."

"Because we've never picked up signals before, let alone ships. It would be under unresponsive vessels, military and civilian. Pull up the section on communicating with approaching vessels, Haden." Laura leaned over Zac's shoulder. "Bring up the information on the ship, and zoom in, I want to see what we're dealing with."

Zac obeyed.

The screen shifted, and the three blips became elongated ovals. At this range, his scanners weren't designed to provide fine detail. "At the rate, they're approaching, they'll be here in ten minutes."

"From the edge of range? That's impossible. Has to be a computer glitch."

"Maybe for Terran vessels, but they aren't carrying transponders, or if they are, they're turned off. Haden's run the troubleshooting program our systems are fine. No problems reported." Zac tapped the screen. "They're jumping or moving so quickly our scanners aren't keeping track." Which didn't make sense, unless they had shields in place? Shields with the capability of masking their presence.

This wasn't happening. Not here. Not now. Zac pulled up all the information the sensors offered. It didn't make sense. Not with the way things had always worked. "Who are they?" His mind provided answers he wasn't willing to listen to. Aliens. Unknown ships, no communication, and readings which made no sense. Why weren't they responding to hails?

Sound the alert.

He couldn't. He didn't have the authority, not while Laura and Haden were present. They had rank and time on him.

"No damn idea, but they'll be in orbit soon enough if they don't change course and head for Earth." Laura slid into her seat. "Opening up a secure channel, I need to let the UTG know what's going on."

"Right, and they're going to accuse you of being in the hooch." It wouldn't be the first time someone had been drunk and opened the channel to Earth. Thankfully no one had realized it was him and had put it down to a kid playing a prank. "I'm pulling up extra data and-- God, I can't get a reading on lifeforms, or the type of metal used on the craft, if it is metal and not another material we don't recognize." Aliens. Freaking aliens. He wasn't ready for this. Command wasn't prepared for this, or there'd be an SOP in the damned system.

"I can't get the secure line to work." Laura cursed. "I've tried three different encryptions. Nothing but static." She yanked her headset off.

"They're jamming outgoing communications. It's not just the secure channels." Haden announced. "Trying to break through it."

"All of..." Zac's words faded as he reached for the alert.

"Incoming fire."

"Trigger the alarm."

Zac thumped the red button, his mind racing. Attack. They weren't supposed to be at risk out here, not from unknown ships which wouldn't respond to hails. This wasn't how things worked on the outer edge of the system.

The noise reached him before the first of the vibrations. Alerts sprang to life across the board, and he stared, unable to move.

"This is a colony-wide alert. We are under attack. Repeat, we are under attack." Laura's voice broke through his thoughts in the second before the building shuddered.

"We've got to move. Get down into the shelters." He darted for Laura.

"Not going anywhere. We stay at our posts," she snapped. "Get back to your station." She flicked the comm again. "Colony wide alert. Get to the shelters. All military are to report for duty. Repeat, this is a colony-wide alert."

Would the colony hear her? "If they're blocking all channels, they aren't going to get the warning. Not the verbal. Only the alerts." Which operated both on hard lines and channels.

"Get back to your post," Laura ordered.

"You're insane. You can't seriously expect us to stay here?" The ground trembled again, tipping him off balance as he reached for the back of a chair. His legs refused to hold him up, the grip on the chair doing nothing to keep him on his feet. He cried out, stumbling to the floor, the chair falling with him.

"It's our damn job, Zac. Get to your station." She didn't turn and made no attempt to look at him. "All section hands report to your supervisor. All civilians are to seek cover."

No reaction from her. Was she operating on automatic pilot?

Hell's Own

Why weren't the alarms sounding? He swore under his breath and avoided the temptation to return to his station to find out what was going on. Staying here was a fool's game. Like hell was he going to die at his post like a good little soldier.

The siren howled. Lights blinked into life. Patterns and sounds Zac had seen only once before, during a test drill.

"The dome." His throat tightened mouth dried as he tried to make his body work. "They've damaged the dome. We've got to get out of here." His suit. The emergency suit. He slapped his hands down on his belt, frantically searching for the small box which contained the emergency suit and mask. Not heavy enough to withstand a full spacewalk, but enough to keep him alive until he made it to a shelter.

"Then pull it on and get back to work."

No, he didn't belong here. Couldn't stay. Fear clawed at him, dark tendrils of terror wound their way up from his stomach and around his heart. Breathing stuttered, a tight band wrapped about his rib cage. He stood, one hand on the suit box. "I'm not staying here. You shouldn't either. Haden, come on."

"Run if you want, I'm not giving up," Haden growled. "Get out before she decides to shoot you for deserting your post."

Insane. They were both nuts. No one was paid enough to deal with this.

Zac took a step toward the door as the alarms continued to ring out. The suit, he couldn't leave the room without his suit in place. Air, protection for his skin, the cold would get to him, but he'd be safe, below ground, before it happened.

He scrambled to pull it on, sealing the thin gloves over his fingers, and connecting the suit to his boots before he smoothed glanced up again.

Laura stood in front of him. No longer at her console. Her flechette sidearm no longer in its holster. "You should have run when Haden told you to go."

"Laura, you don't have to do this." He took a step back. She wouldn't pull the trigger. It wasn't like her. They'd worked together for years now.

Above them, the dome shattered under the assault from the unknown ships, and the last thing Zac heard before the darkness claimed him was the alarm increasing in pitch and volume...

Chapter One

Glasses flew through the air as the table toppled, a body slammed into the black plastiwear, tipping the table over as the four who'd claimed it, grabbed their drinks and stepped to one side. One man growled as the rest found a safe place for their drinks before diving on the man who'd hit the floor. The man who'd started the fight grabbed one of the four men by the back of the neck and hauled him off his target.

Shouts and cries mingled. Complaints at knocked tables, spilled drinks, and disturbing the night. No one called for security to end the fight, nor would there be a point if they had. Jones' bar had many things, but men or women paid to bust up scraps wasn't one of them.

"Another dull night, I see." Cora Bloodlaw pulled out a chair and sat down, her gaze following the fight. "This is the first one I've seen since we arrived." She braced herself, half expecting the next rolling mess of humanity to collide with the table. With one hand wrapped around her drink, she didn't relax until she was confident the combatants had rolled the other way, shouts increasing as the men continued to tussle, yell insults and throw punches. "Won't be the last though." Not with the types who found their way to the *Get Away*.

Fights were normal, as were many other types of quasi-legal or illegal activities. Everyone knew about the bar, even if they didn't formally acknowledge its existence.

"You break it, you pay for it," Jones called out from behind the bar. "This means you, Norris. Hey, you listening to me?"

"He needs to learn how to throw a punch. Break his wrist or fingers if he isn't careful." He scraped his fingers through his short dirty blond hair, the movement made no difference to the brush cut. The style was not uncommon. Most of the men she worked with kept their hair short, not completely scalped but close enough to it. "Doesn't he know how to fight? Shit, he's an amateur," he continued.

Cora arched an eyebrow, a smile pulling at her lips. "Then why don't you join the fun and show them how it's done, Ready? Be interesting to see how you handle the fight before I have to walk in and drag you out to save your ass."

"If you're going to let him do this, at least give us enough warning to get a betting pool going." One of the other men sat down, beer in hand.

"Hah, as if you'd need to rescue my ass. They're civies, doubt it would be anything more than a waste of time. Civies don't listen to uniforms. Not around here anyway." PFC Jackson, better known as Ready, lifted his drink and drained half the remaining liquid, then flipped the other man the finger. "Bit like coming here and expecting decent beer, when we know they brew the stuff themselves."

"Would you prefer it if we hit the approved bars, and have to deal with the rules? The ones were we're watched every second, our drinks counted, and we're cut off long before any of us hit buzz level?" Cora set her glass down. "Go ahead. You're welcome to head out and see what they'd put up with. I'm not stopping you. Me, I'm going to stay here and enjoy the brew."

"Stop teasing Ready. He's still too wet behind the ears to understand when he has a good thing going here." Corporal Hudson claimed a chair and twisted it around before he swung a leg over and sat facing the back of his chair. "He's dreaming of those back home. And doesn't know how nice he has it here, he could be out on a backwater colony--oh, wait, he is."

"And you're any better, Lackey?" Ready snapped. "I've been here longer than you. This isn't my first trip to the edge."

"Like hell, you got in three days after me. Try your bullshit with someone else, not going to fly here." Lackey glowered, his body tensed, ready to tip the table or throw the nearest available object. "I've got just as much experience out here as you. Maybe more. And I have rank on you."

"Only because you kissed the right ass. Not like you earned it."

"Come here and say that." Lackey snarled.

"You'd like it, wouldn't you. Try and write me up for starting a fight." Ready sneered.

"You're both pups. If you want to fight, there's one ready and waiting for you, but it will have the locals called in, and we'll have to find a new bar. Jones wouldn't like it if we brought the MPs in. You make me give up my seat for anything but hitting the head, and I'll make you wish your momma never brought you into this world." Cora kept her voice calm, her emotions under control as she ran the tip of her finger over the rim of her glass. "Doubt me? Then try it, and you'll wake up in the infirmary." A quick kick or punch, and both men would be out for the count. Oh, the men were decent at their work, they had to be to make it out here, but they were still nothing more than children when it came to experience. But there was skilled, and there was sober and well trained, the two didn't always go hand in hand.

"Better listen to the Sarge. You should know by now she isn't going to take your shit, off duty, on duty, it's all the same." Gunny's low, steady voice carried and commanded everyone's attention. "And she isn't the only one. I came here for a decent drink, instead of hanging out with the stiff necks, and you're threatening to disturb my night."

"Don't need your backup, old man," she didn't glance at him, not when she had two men squaring off. "Are you two going to throw punches or go back to drinking like sane marines would?"

"Marines don't leave a man behind." Gunny lifted his glass. "Besides, no such thing as a sane marine. Against the rules."

Fine, she couldn't argue the point, they worked together, fought together, and you didn't fuck up a situation like this. Not when you'd spent half your life building up the respect and understanding from the men and women she worked with. "Didn't think I'd gone anywhere."

Gunner flicked the now empty glass. "Your round, Lawbook."

She didn't flinch at the name, not anymore. "You lost count, Gunny. It's your turn, I bought the last one."

"Must have blinked and missed it." Gunny shrugged and lifted his glass. "Hey, what does a man have to do to get a drink around here?"

"Pay for it, like everything else." Cora flashed a grin. "Nothing's for free. Especially for Marines." Didn't matter if they were in civilian dress, they'd always be marines.

"Except pussy. Shouldn't ever have to pay for private time with a willing partner. Flash them the uniform, and they're all over you." PFC Walker suggested. "It's what they told us back in--"

"You still believing all the lies the recruitment officer told you?" Lackey cut him off. "Damn man, you're dumber than you appear. You'd think after your first shipboard tour, you'd realize they spun you a crock of shit. No pussy on a ship. At least, none we're allowed to touch. No fraternization allowed. Bad for morale," said Lackey, a scowl furrowing his brow.

"Bad for moral my ass. The ship snobs want to keep them all to themselves. Not one of them knows how to catch the eye of a woman. And they wouldn't know what to do with one if they found themselves naked in the same damn room with one." Walker rolled his eyes. "Come on, you saw them. All stiff, like they hadn't been laid in a year, or longer."

"And what's it been for you, two years now? A date with your hand doesn't count."

"What the fuck, man. I had a girl back on earth. Real beauty too. With a sweet set of--"

"Yeah, of the automated kind." Walker laughed, cutting him off. "Only thing real about her would be the batteries you have to charge up. And maybe her hair, if you went for one of the deluxe models."

Cora leaned back in her chair and let the banter roll over her.

Hell's Own

It didn't matter to her how they talked, sex was sex, they used the terms without harm, and she'd seen more than one man, or woman, trip over themselves to gain the attention of the man or woman in uniform. It was the same anywhere she'd been, some loved a body in uniform, others, not so much. As for the talk, she'd joined the Marines, not the girl scouts. If she couldn't take a bit of swearing, or the way the men often openly lusted over a woman, real or imagined, then she was in the wrong place.

For them, it was a habit. For her, a test of how to keep her temper and learn to grow a thicker skin. Women were as bad, though normally not as obvious. And talking wasn't the same as doing. The men and women she'd served with over the years might bluster about the things they wanted to do, but the corp had a strict policy.

Consent.

Which could be withdrawn at any time.

By the way, this meant everyone.

Cross the line and the only uniforms you were likely to see in your lifetime was the prison garb you'd spend the rest of your life wearing, and the ones worn by the prison officers. And that was after you'd been *fixed.* Words were one thing, actions another.

First year it had been hard. Civilian life wasn't the same. Rules were different, the way you spoke to people wasn't the same as the way it was in the military. And after six months on a ship, surrounded by men and women who followed an old, weird code about marines being less than the fliers. Grunts, men and women who lacked intelligence, and couldn't make it through the basic training for the enlisted, let alone the officers.

Rich, considering she doubted one of them would be able to deal with the training marines went through. Too damn brutal for the majority of them.

She'd made the right choice, joining the marines. Sure, the other branches had been open to her, and her family had nudged for her to join one of the more respectable branches, but what did they know? She'd already broken the family rules by signing up. It went against the codes they lived by to resort to a life which included violence, death, and men who swore every third word.

Cora relaxed as she took in the bar. The building was three klicks outside of the base, accessed through the tunnels built initially when they first surveyed Pluto for the best place to build the base. A trek but worth it. There were tunnels the majority ignored, but everyone used them if they wanted to visit one of the underground chambers, bars, or storage holds without being tracked every step of the way. This didn't take into account the extra passageways known only to a rare few. Oh sure, there were sensors planted in the doors which opened into the tunnels. Officially no one entered or left the main colony without permission. Officially the bar wasn't a bar, but a storage facility for the miners making their way from the main settlement to the outlying claims and back again. A place to clean off, get themselves decent, then face the realities of what passed for civilization out here.

Screw civilization.

"Drinks. Remember. Party over here. Payment on delivery." Gunner called out as a server shimmied her way to the bar.

She paused and glanced back at the table, eyes narrowed until she took note of the group. "Be right there."

"Now what have you got that I don't?" Lackey grumbled and traced a line of condensation down the side of his glass. "I've been trying to get her attention for the past ten minutes."

"Age, maturity, experience, funds. Oh, yeah, and rank." Gunner tapped his arm where his insignia would typically sit. "Would have been the same if Lawbook had tried it. They know these stripes mean they'll get paid regardless of what else is going on."

Lackey glowered. "She knows you're going to pay her. The cash is what caught her attention."

"Earn the rank, and you'll be treated the same way, Lackey." Cora lifted her drink. "Money talks. Always has."

Hell's Own

"Don't call me that, Sarge. You know I don't like it. I didn't kiss my way to the rank. If I had, it would have been to jump into officer training. I mean, shit, who'd want to sit around drinking with you lot when they could be in the officer's lounge, being waited on hand and foot by the stewards."

"And be bored out of your skull. Why else do you think Gunny's here instead of hanging out at the base."

"The beer. It's better here. Still got a bite to it." Gunny hefted his still empty glass. "You wusses don't know what real beer tastes like. Obviously never had anyone drag you out to the old bars. No, you wet your whistle with the legit stuff, with no more than 3% alcohol. I pity you all. No understanding what it's like to hold a real beer and this is as close as we're going to get out here."

"Yeah, and occasionally you get extra chunky bits in the beer, added bonus," Ready smirked.

"You're kidding?" Lackey peered into the remains of his drink. "Bits? What the -- I ever get a mug of beer with bits in it, and I'm sending it back."

"Wuss."

"Hey, I like to drink my beer, not eat it."

"You wouldn't know a real drink if it bit you on the nose."

Cora glanced over her shoulder as she allowed the conversation to fade into the background. The server leaned over the bar, her tight pants making it clear she wore little or nothing beneath them, as the bartender added full glasses to her tray. Her mouth watering at the memory of a decent beer. A bar in Scotland, a trip ten years ago. The real bar hiding behind the facade of a tourist trap, but if they knew you, if you had a local to speak for you, then they showed you the hidden door, and you scooted your way in, found a table, and drank the nectar of the Gods, either in the form of beer, or single malt.

One day, when she had enough time back on earth, she'd take a trip and drown the dreams.

"Refill should be here in a few."

"Fantastic, a man could die of thirst around here." Gunny's dark brown gaze lowered to Cora's glass. "You're falling behind. Going to make people think you're not a real marine."

"Always do, fall behind I mean." It was one thing to drink and enjoy it, another to pass out. The only place she planned on face-planting herself was in her quarters where no one could see or take advantage of the situation. "Here to enjoy, not be carried out."

"They'd see you home, you know that, right?" Gunny leaned in, his voice lowering. "Have to learn to trust your people one day."

"I do, I mean, I will. Shit. You know what I'm saying." She shot a sideways glare at him. "One of us has to remain sober in case the Red Caps stumble our way." Military Police, the bane of their existence. Except when you needed them, then she'd buy them a drink and be polite until they were gone. At the end of the day, they were still brothers and sisters wearing a uniform and heaven help any civilian who got in the way. "Better one of us is able to handle the mess if it heads our way."

"Know what you're not saying, Cora. I'll make it clear, we'll talk tomorrow. When we're both awake, sober, and in clean uniforms."

She tensed, knuckles white as she cupped them around her glass. "Is that an order, Gunny?" Of all the men and women she'd served with, Gunny was one of the few she could and would listen to. The man had seen it all, taken care of everything ever thrown at him, and took care of those who served under him. It was the only way you lived long enough to make Gunnery Sergeant out here. Back home, it was different. Kiss the right asses, play within the rules, and in time you'd get promoted. Out here, you worked for it. Or you filled dead man's boots.

"Would it help if it was?"

She allowed herself a smile. "I doubt it. I'd still disobey. Personal reasons and all." She had her reasons, had her own experiences to draw on, and she'd take the step when she was ready, not before.

"Don't make me come looking for you tomorrow. You'll show up, at noon, at the door to my office. Got it." He caught and held her gaze.

"Yes, Gunny." Shit, there went any plans for the day.

"Glad you understand where I'm coming from. Now it's time to get drunk." He grinned and sat up, barely missing the server as she carried the tray over. "Sorry lass, nothing spilled, right?"

"It's all good, Gunny. You know I'd get replacements if there was an issue." She set the drinks down and rested a hand on his shoulder. "Anything else you need? Like some company? I'll be off in an hour." Her soft brown curls bobbed as she leaned in against Gunny.

"Ah, not today, lass. I'll be back in a few days. We can discuss matching up our free time then." He patted the server's ass with one large, tanned hand.

"You know where to find me."

Jakob Blyemon shifted in his seat. School functions, the last thing he wanted to spend his free time on, but at least it was almost finished. A few more minutes, and it would be over. Would he have enough time to catch Gail before he had to return home?

"Jakob, over here," she called out from across the room, her voice half muffled by the background noise from the gathered families.

"Gail wasn't certain you'd make it. I mean, not after yesterday. Didn't your family ground you?"

She snorted and pushed one hand through the wild dark curls as she joined him. "Yeah, well 'he' can't tell me what to do, and mom won't be back for two weeks. By the time she arrives, it'll be too late, and she'll brush it off. Maybe they'll fight, but then she'll drag him out to a bar or the bedroom to smooth things over."

Jakob grinned. "Think this one will last any longer than the last three? And why do always insist on calling them your stepdad?"

"He's made it six months, but I can see it's starting to wear thin. She's upfront about what she expects, the whole house husband or whatever you want to call it. But they always think it's going to be easier. And why bother to learn their names? They're never around long enough for it to matter." A single shrug as she turned away from him.

Did it hurt, having men wander in and out of her life as the various test periods for a house husband? He didn't ask, nor would he unless she gave him the right opening. "You have plans for the free day?"

"Not yet, depends on what happens tomorrow." She turned back to him. "What about you?"

"Figured I'd steal time for myself. Once the chores are done." Her gaze moved over the rest of the gathering. "The usual. But there's a new holo showing in the community center. If it all works, I should be able to catch the second showing." Would she take the offer, or make the casual suggestion she might be present, and he'd spend the rest of the night wondering if she'd turn up.

"Yeah, heard about it. Might give it a go and--"

A shrill siren echoed through the large room.

He grabbed Gail's upper arm. "Evacuation, we need to get to the lower levels." He didn't wait for her to reply, his grip tight as he turned and pulled her toward the doors. "We need to move. Before everyone starts to move." The doors weren't wide enough for a mass exit.

"Another drill, you know they pull one of these a month."

He wanted to believe her. Needed to. But it didn't fit with how things ran. "They always give a warning to the heads of department."

"And?"

"My Dad didn't say anything about a test." He tugged on her arm. "Come on, we have to get out of here. Might be nothing more than an explosion outside the dome, but better if we're down in the shelter before they announce what's going on." The words felt wrong. The alarm higher pitched and shriller than he'd experienced before.

Others now moved. Slow and uncertain. Confusion, protests, the request for answers, mingled in the room as people found their way to the doors. The floor trembled, sending vibrations up into his legs. Not a quake, there were no quakes on Pluto. Only the occasional tremor from an explosion, be it uncontrolled or an accident.

"Shit," Gail whispered.

"Not good, this isn't how things work." He darted through the door, heading for the top of the stairs.

"The elevator?"

"No, if we lose power, we'll be trapped in it." Think. He had to think. His mind raced as he went over everything he knew about the drills. Nothing fitted with what was happening now. Did it mean nothing like this had ever happened before? He wanted to push the idea into the deepest pit as his feet slapped against the steps, one hand resting on the rail. More footsteps above them. The mass finally moving now saner heads, or the drive to survive had kicked in.

"Where are we going?"

"The lower levels, there's a series of doors and ladders into the deep levels. The ones we only use in a dome emergency." His heart raced, sweat slicked his hands, but he didn't stop. Didn't look back at Gail.

"Dome emergency?"

"Where the dome has cracked." It was the only thing he could think of. And he didn't want to know what else could have happened.

"Cracked dome means no air. Shields. We have to get the suits on."

"Lower levels, then we'll have a chance. The building alerts will become active if the sensors pick up a loss of atmosphere."

Lights flickered and changed, no longer casting the soft illumination in the building to the red he had feared would follow.

"You mean like this?" Gail stopped on the landing before the next flight of stairs, one hand slapped the box holding the suit on her belt, opening it before she pulled it on. He did the same. No more questions. The suits would keep them safe for the short term, once they were in the bunkers, the lower levels, they would be safe. They had to be.

"Keep moving, kids. Don't block the stairs."

Gail turned as she secured her suit in place. "Get your suit on, unless you want to die." She gestured at the lights. "Dome problems."

"Another damned drill." The man complained, but those behind him pulled on their suits as the first full shake hit the building.

Walls cracked, dust spilled into the air. Screams rang out, men, women, and children, followed by sobs as reality set in. Jakob pushed away from the wall and ran. "Gail. Move!"

Chapter Two

Morgan Stone rested one arm on the bar, his free hand curled around the cold glass of amber beer. Foam, half an inch of the sweet stuff, topped the drink. Not enough to eat up a huge amount of space in the glass, but enough to allow him to enjoy the creamy texture. Only one thing threatened to spoil his time, the presence of a small group of military men and women, though they wore civvies, taking up one large table on the other side of the room. Military meant potential trouble, but not if he didn't catch their attention.

"You're in early, thought you wouldn't be back for another week." Jones, the bartender, wiped a cloth along the surface of the bar. "I'm not complaining. Always good to see you."

Stone shifted his weight, one eye on the rest of the bar. "It all worked out, and I finished ahead of schedule. The change in timing helps keep me on my toes." A lie, of course, he'd always planned on hitting the bar tonight. Tell a client you could manage things in a specific time, but add a buffer to the number, and they came to believe you were a miracle. Exactly the way he liked it. "Any problems?"

"Not of late. Been quiet, except for the occasional-- Hey, watch the chairs. You break it, you pay for it." He yelled out as the fists started flying. "Bloody hell, had hopes we'd go through a night without a fight breaking out."

"In this bar? Not going to happen." He turned his back to the bar. "The uniforms cause any issues."

"Normally no, but if they spill their drinks, all bets are off," Jones explained. "They're going to break tables if they keep this up, be right back." The man jumped the bar and hit the ground running.

Yeah, you go get them under control.

He sighed and grabbed his drink, uncomfortable with the bar behind him, but at least this way he'd have a warning if anyone came up behind him. His peripheral vision was better than average, which gave him an advantage if anyone approached him from either side or slightly behind him. A mouthful of beer chased away the dry mouth feeling as he continued to watch the fight. Nothing out of the norm there, a couple of prospectors blowing off steam, and the Marines appeared to be happy enough sitting down with their own beverages.

"You alright, Stone?" One of the servers, a slender young thing with a hint of curves in all the right places, set her tray on the bar.

"Doing fine. Woke up above ground today."

Her full lips shifted into a full, sensual smile. "You'd be missed if you didn't."

"Yeah, who'd help out on all those difficult requests?" He glanced at the woman but kept the majority of his attention on the rest of the bar. She was sweet enough and didn't, to his knowledge, offer extras like a few of the girls did. He didn't have a problem with it. A man, or woman, did what they had to to make their way in life. A few broke or bent the laws in order, but it was the way it was meant to be if you wanted to get through the day with enough money to keep a roof over your head and food in your stomach.

"Ah, there are others around who can help out."

"But do they have my connections?" He waggled his eyebrows and mock leered at her.

The server laughed, the bright, merry sound at odds with the fight. "You're a scoundrel, you know, right?"

He pressed his free hand over his heart. "You wound me, my lady. I'm cut to the core. Bleeding out here. Maybe you should kiss is better?"

"If I didn't know you were joking I'd have to slap you for that one, Stone." She inclined her head. "Better go clean up the mess." She turned, cloth and tray in hand as she sashayed across the room. "Don't go anywhere, I'll be back in a few."

He smiled and drank down the rest of his beer and set the empty glass down. The fight was continuing, but dying down. One man nursed a broken nose at a far table, two other men had gone from fighting to hugging, complete with back slaps, only the three primary trouble makers continued to throw fists, kicks and more than a few interesting words. He chuckled, shaking his head. Letting off steam, nothing more. No weapons drawn, no blood spilled, except by accident, and no need to call in for assistance to cart off the offending patrons.

Exactly the way he liked it.

Minus the uniforms.

Damned military. Always finding a way to spoil his plans, his day, his shipment. Papers, inspections, strangers rooting their way through his ship, or storage, or anything else they could get their grubby hands on. Documents, shipment orders, consignments, what did they know of what it took to make a living out here? They had a steady income, taken care of, three squares and a cot, all so they could fly around, claiming their rules were the ones everyone else had to follow. And they had nothing to be proud off, the military were his biggest customers. Quartermasters; he'd earned more money out of them than the civilians he still worked with. Always trading, making deals because an officer wanted a special bottle of whiskey, or a request for silk, the real stuff not the fake because a daughter or son was getting married. Medication occasionally made its way into his packs, from trading with the military. Things he could sell or barter out among the miners. Men and women who didn't come into the main base but once a year. Others hadn't visited the station since it was established a couple of years ago.

In the twenty years since Pluto had been settled, and the first of the mines opened, the colony had grown slowly. Once the main base had been rebuilt and expanded from the original half dozen buildings, the population had tripled with the influx of fortune hunters, or families seeking a better life. One where they could establish themselves away from the rules which governed Earth only to find the rules on Pluto could be equally restrictive and not always in better ways.

One of the uniforms moved, giving him a better look at the rest of them. Five at one table, a double check revealed two others sat at a booth, and another entered from the back of the bar. Nothing he needed to worry about, as long as the older man at the table didn't wander his way. The Gunny was a man he'd recognize anywhere, he didn't know what the man's real name was, had never bothered to find out, they all addressed him as Gunny.

His eyes narrowed. One of the men was a woman. One he'd seen in passing but had never dealt with, he tried to think back, to remember what he'd seen. Marine uniform with stripes. Sergeant stripes. He'd seen women in the fleet, pilots, navigators, and such like, but it was rare to see a woman wearing the uniform of a Marine out here. Not impossible, there were two others he'd come across, but rare enough he took notice. Sergeant stripes, which meant she had to be one of the unusual ones who fought their way up from the ranks. It shouldn't be this way, but as he understood it in some branches of the military, a woman had to work twice as hard as a man. Maybe he was wrong, but he didn't know enough about the service to accurately judge the situation.

Not that she, or the others, wore uniform out here. It was one thing to sneak off base, doing so in uniform meant trouble. A few were dumb enough to risk it, most weren't.

She was relaxed, at ease in the way a warrior could be, with one eye on the door and the other eye keeping track of the fight. Her pose matched the men at the table, but her eyes, oh they never stopped moving, taking in action, those who had entered, a small tightening around the eyes when it happened, not noticeable unless you searched for it. And he always watched for it. A man who reacted like this, who wasn't wearing a military uniform, he'd say was enforcement, scoping out the bar for a raid, but she wore pants and shirt he'd come to associate with men and women in service, and the Gunny he knew to be a Marine. Which is the only way he was able to identify which branch of the service this lot probably belonged to.

Military. He snorted and forced his attention away from the table.

He wasn't here to scope out those who snuck their way off base out into the wastes to places like this. The bar wasn't the only location men and women enjoyed out here, there were fight clubs, bare-knuckle, no holds barred, combat for whatever the current prize might be. More than one family had a holdout location out here, a place to stash their families if the shit hit the fan, and he was one of them. Sure, the base had its uses, but he avoided it whenever possible.

"Some people can't hold their drink." Jones eased back behind the bar with a sharp nod in the direction of the remaining fighters who now sat either at the table or were busy tending their wounds, then gestured to the empty glass. "Need another?"

"Sure, been a while." He tapped the glass. "It's all ready for you when you have the time."

"Usual?"

"Yup." He wasn't going to be foolish enough to haul the packages in here. Oh hell no, Jones and his friends could come and pick it up themselves.

"About the special?"

"Got it." Easy enough to find, though he wasn't going to tell Jones. "Tomorrow, right?"

"Usual time," Jones confirmed.

Sure, the odds of anyone hearing their conversation ranged between slim and none, but he wasn't about to take the risk. Not when he had carved out a decent living here and planned on keeping his business up and running for the next ten years and more. If it meant odd conversations, coached in terms of casual conversation in case things went wrong, so be it. He wasn't about to change when it had worked up to this point. "You got it."

"Glad to hear it as we're running low of a few things."

"Isn't it the way things work? You buy stuff, sell it, run out and need more. It's where I come in." He shifted his weight, taking in the bar and its occupants again. Enough patrons to keep the bar running, and he was happy enough to share in the profits in his own way.

"And it's always pleasant to see you here."

He felt it in the split second before the first of the shock waves rolled through the ground, shaking tables and chairs alike. A roaring, muffled, came from the heavy doors into the tunnels, but nothing from outside. No atmosphere, no sound. One of the joys of living on Pluto. Bottles clinked together on the shelves, liquid spilled, one of the servers stumbled, a full tray of drinks in hand. Stone moved without thinking, one hand snaking around the server's waist as he pulled her back up from the spread of broken glass. "Got you."

"Thanks, what the hell was that?" She turned toward the door. "I don't understand, Pluto doesn't have quakes."

No, it didn't, hadn't been one recorded in the entire time the planet, its status returned after valuable minerals were found beneath the icy surface, had been studied. Whatever happened, it wasn't a quake.

The second wave struck. Tables tipped over, men and women struggled to stay upright as the first of the screams rang out. Terror, not pain.

His jaw clenched as he pushed the server toward the bar and dug into his pocket. A small datapad, but with enough power to do the work he needed when he was away from his ship. He glanced up, his fingers dancing over the pad, demanding information from the base. Answers, they needed answers. Had a mine or building exploded? Possible. The rumble from the entrance into the tunnels carried sound, but details were missing, pieces of information he needed before he made a move.

The third set of rumbles tossed him, and everyone else, to the floor as the roar blasted against the heavy door separating them from the only known safe entrance and exit into the bar.

"Salla, grab your bag," Duncan called up the stairs as he clung to the banister. "We have to go. Need to move now." Where was the girl? The floor rattled, and he stumbled back into the wall, the breath knocked from his body. He groaned and pressed one hand to his ribs. "Getting too old for this."

"You're not too old, Pops. Just long on mileage."

He grinned, despite everything. His daughter was too young to know what it meant. So was he, but knowledge was never wasted. "Ready?"

"Yeah, and if I find out this is another damn drill, I'm shoving that alarm someplace the sun doesn't shine," Salla muttered her bugout bag slung across her shoulders. "Your supply dump?"

"No, we go where they want us to be this time. If we find out this is the real thing, we'll head to the dump." Supplies they would both need if they wanted to survive a real problem. The alert continued, the tone high and wailing, one he couldn't ignore. The lights shifted, turning from the normal welcoming hue to the red of warning. "Dome. Suit on. Now."

Salla didn't fight, didn't argue. One thing he could always be proud of was the way is daughter took things seriously. He slapped the box on his hip and pulled out his suit. With deft movements, long practiced, he sealed the suit in place before he looked at Salla again. Her own suit covered her from head to foot as she met his gaze. He nodded his approval and pointed to the stairs, then down. Silent communication from this point on, as they'd practiced.

Comms could be listened in on. Secrets shared. Or stolen. Either way, it wasn't a matter he had to deal with. Salla wouldn't complain, she knew how things worked. He gestured her to move ahead of him. Young legs, faster and more stamina, better to let her do the hard labor of opening the hatch. She hurried ahead of him, picking up the pace as they descended.

What the hell had caused the dome to crack?

No, he'd have time to find out later in the day, when the dome had been repaired, and he found the right people to ply with liquor to get the answers. There was always at least one tech with the willingness to spill secrets for the right price. Information. The real source of currency on Pluto, unless you were a trader dealing with the mercs and smugglers who dared to risk the rules governing the outer rim. Like Stone.

He grinned but kept silent. Yeah, Stone was one he'd dealt with regularly.

Salla reached the hatch, keyed in the passcode and pulled it open. With a sweep of one hand, she gestured for her father to go first.

Wahhhh Whoooo Wahhhh Whoooo.

The tone of the alert changed, taking on a sound he'd only heard once before. During his first year on Pluto.

Under attack.

The ground shuddered, and the walls cracked around them. Salla cried out as she stumbled away from the escape route, left shoulder hitting the wall with an audible slap. The hatch into the lower tunnels slammed shut before either of them could reach it.

Her suit. God, if it tore, she wouldn't be able to cope once the air seeped out and the heat joined it. "The hatch. Salla. Get the hatch." He activated his comm, breaking the rules he'd drummed into his daughter.

Nothing else mattered but Salla, getting her out in one piece, alive and able to survive whatever happened.

His Salla.

As bright and beautiful as her mother.

The mother he'd let down.

Interlude One
Unified Terran Government: Alpha Comms.

Sheila Cavanor settled into her seat and brought up the screens which would eat up the majority of her time and focus during her shift. She didn't look back, didn't need to in order to know the change of officer hadn't yet taken place. Another thirty minutes before the bane of her existence joined the crew and found a way, any way, of poking her.

"You look upset," tall, leggy and white blonde, Amanda leaned over the back of the display, her folded arms resting on top.

"He's changed shifts."

"Grant?"

"Yes." She kept her voice low enough to prevent it from carrying. "He does this at least once a week now I'm not officially a part of his team." Her skin crawled at the thought of him. "I can't keep this up much longer."

"Have you spoken to HR?"

"If I do, I have to put in a formal complaint." Sheila wiped her hands on her uniform pants. "Can't do that if I want a recommendation when I put in a request for a new posting." No, it would mean a hearing. SOP for any complaints which touched on harassment, sexual or otherwise. "If I can get the transfer it won't matter."

"Only places with openings are out on the rim. Pluto and Uranus."

Sheila groaned and rested her head in her hands. "I know, don't remind me." But if it meant putting a healthy distance between herself and Grant, then she'd take it. "Dumb, he has to be one of the last Neanderthals around."

"I don't know, there was one in basic training, but you're right, they're rare."

"With good reason." The punishments for sexual harassment

weren't pretty, and a career man like Grant had a lot to lose. Which didn't make sense. Did he want to be kicked out of the service? He'd been in the Navy for far more than his initial mandatory years. Ten years service to date, including a mandatory year as a private, to better understand how the Navy worked.

"Makes you wonder what's going on with him."

Sheila hit the sequence of keys to begin her initial sweep. "I don't know, just wish he'd take it elsewhere and leave me alone. I want to get on with my work." And he was careful. Nothing inappropriate, per the regs, when they were on duty. No, it was the way he looked at her, the small signs that he hadn't given up. A touch on the shoulder, that never roamed to her waist or ass, but lingered a heartbeat or two longer than it should. "Maybe I'm overreacting?"

"No, you're not." Amanda checked the time. "Damn, I've got to go. See you on Saturday? Girls night?"

"Last time I went on a girls night with you, I lost half my clothes and ended up giving the strippers lap dances."

"Which means we all had fun." Amanda grinned as she hurried away. "Later."

Shiela shook her head even as she fought against the urge to smile. Amanda was fun to be around, and letting off steam wouldn't do her any harm. She'd broken no rules, and with the others around her, she'd remain safe if Grant found out about their plans and shadowed them.

A red light flickered into life on the screen. She leaned closer and tapped the surface. The light blinked, went out, and returned five seconds later. "Run system scans, all areas." She brought her datapad up and pulled the information she needed during the scan. Last contacts had taken place on schedule, and nothing showed except one red light slowly blinking in and out of existence.

A new bug to work out. Great. Just what she needed at the start of a shift.

Chapter Three

Cora braced as the second wave hit, jaw set. "What the--"

"Explosions, either something big blew sky high, or we're in a whole lot of shit." Gunny pushed away from the table. "Eyes here, Marines."

They obeyed when the Gunny used his parade voice you didn't ignore it. No matter what rank you were. A lesson they all learned, or they paid for it.

"Information, injured personal, weapons, and equipment." The older man snapped out the order.

Cora nodded as the rest responded with an Oorah. Not that she expected anything else from them. She pushed back from the table, gaze moving as she checked the men and women around her. A few scratches and bumps, one woman had stumbled only to be caught by the man at the bar. She shifted her gaze back to the man. Tall, well built, dangerous eyes, an air of confidence she couldn't ignore and a face she knew. Couldn't put a name to, but knew nevertheless. "You heard the man, get moving."

Futile, they were already on the move, but she couldn't take back words she'd already given life to. She shook off her concerns and headed in the direction of the bar when the third one hit. The rumble struck the heavy door into the tunnels. The floor rippled beneath her feet, tipping her off balance as she bit back a cry and hit the ground. Her palms slapped the floor, knees a split second later. Shock knocked the breath from her body, pain replacing what was left as her mind struggled to catch up with the situation.

Explosion. The only thing which could cause a reaction of this nature. She grabbed for her comm, snagging it out of one of her pockets. Her hands trembled as she rolled onto her back and forced herself to sit up. "Sergeant Bloodlaw checking in. What's the status?"

Static.

"Ops, repeat, this is Sergeant Bloodlaw. Situation please."

Buzz and crackle of static.

Dust filled the air, mingled with soft cries, and whimpers. A scream, then a second as people realized they were injured.

"Ops?"

"Un-- ack. Unknown -- bers."

"Repeat Ops, only got half of your words."

"Under attack." The voice, male, trembling, broke through the background static. "Unknown numbers. Came from nowhere."

Her gaze found Gunny's as the older man shot a look her way. "Understood." Shit, there was nothing they could do from here, except getting their asses back to base. "You copy, Gunny?"

"Yeah, every damn word. What there was of it." He pushed to his feet, a small cut on his left cheek. "Up. Get on your feet. We've got a situation here. Don't know how bad, but we can't stand around doing nothing."

"Gunny, the civies?" Walker shoved the remains of two chairs out of the way as he dusted off his pants.

Cora rose, her gaze now scanning the interior of the bar. Broken bottles, glasses, men and women blinking in shock or uncertainty, all except the one by the bar. He'd moved after the second wave, catching a server before she'd hit the ground. Not military though. Still, she added him to the potential fighters list. "Need to get those who can't fight to a safer location. Hey, Jones, you alive."

The barman reappeared, holding a cloth against his chin. "Yeah, same can't be said for half my stock."

"Stock can be replaced. Need you to get the civies, those who can't or don't want to fight, to safety. You still have the bolt hole?"

Jones' eyes widened. "How the hell did you know about it? Never mind, yes, still have it."

"Get them into the tunnels and down to the bunker. Don't know who's behind this attack, but I don't want frightened civies in the way." Friendly fire was an all too real risk in any situation, but it doubled or tripled when you had civilians in the mix. Men and women who had no clue how to follow orders, and less of one when it came to using a gun.

"Shit means I'll have to--"

She cut off his complaints with a sharp stare. "Get it done."

"Yes, ma'am."

"Sergeant. I'm not an officer." No, she worked for a living.

"Listen up. Anyone who isn't coming back to base with us needs to follow Jones. If you're hurt, pair up with one who isn't." Gunny called out, but only a handful of the dust-covered men and women obeyed. "On your feet, now. Unless you want to be left behind. And I can't guarantee the seals will hold with another shock like the last one."

"He's right. The place isn't built for multiple shakes." The man at the bar called out. "Come on people, you want to live, you follow Jones." He helped two up to their feet before he turned his attention to the marines. "I'll be with you. I need to find out how bad the situation is, and I know how to handle myself."

"Fine, but can you also follow orders." Gunny pinned the man with a glare.

A wry smile claimed his features. "When I need to."

Well, shit. This was going to prove interesting.

Stone groaned as he sat up after the third shake, his back and ribs protesting at the way he'd hit the floor. Not quakes. He'd lived through the real thing several times, and the vibration and sound were both wrong. Had to be explosions. He scrambled for the handheld he'd lost when he'd hit the ground and swore. Cracked. But still working. Damn thing, it shouldn't have broken this easily, but Murphy's law was in full force, which meant he was lucky he hadn't broken something when he'd been sent tumbling with the last wave of ground shakes.

Data scrolled across the screen, the crack making it hard to read. Hard, but not impossible. Explosions, three points of attack, and it was an attack. Whatever had hit them, had done it from orbit. Ships? Or unmanned craft? Drones had been used on Earth from the late twentieth century, and full drone attack crafts weren't unknown, though there'd been little need for them in the last century. Not since the various governments on Earth had finally accepted, they needed to work together.

The uniforms were on the move, checking in with the men and women in the bar. More than a few were injured, but none of them appeared to be suffering from life-threatening injuries. It was a small blessing, but he'd take what he could get.

"Sergeant. I'm not an officer."

He smiled at the words, his attention fixed on the woman with her short cropped black hair. Strength rippled through her body, but she wasn't overly built. More like a woman who took care of her body and could match the men around her.

"You heard the Sergeant. Anyone who isn't coming back to base with us needs to follow Jones. If you're hurt, pair up with someone who isn't. On your feet, now. Unless you want to be left behind. And I can't guarantee the seals will hold with another shock like the last one."

"He's right. Place isn't built for multiple shakes." Stone rested one hand on the bar, mind racing. The bolt hole made sense. If the rest of the men and women followed Jones, there would be less to worry about. "Come on people, you want to live, you follow Jones." He helped two up to their feet before he turned his attention to the marines. "I'll be with you. I need to find out how bad the situation is, and I know how to handle myself."

"Fine, but can you also follow orders." The woman held his attention, her voice calm, focused.

"When I need to." Which meant only when it benefited him.

"It'll have to do." She glanced at the older man, silent communication passed between them with only the slight movement of eyebrows. "Sergeant Bloodlaw, Gunnery Sergeant Dobbs, Marine contingent."

"Stone," he nodded to the older man.

"Armed?" Gunny asked.

"Always." He patted his hip, hidden beneath the heavy duster he wore.

"Man after my own heart." Gunny turned back to the other Marines. "Weapons check, we're going to move out as soon as we can here people. Whatever else is waiting for us out there, we don't want to keep it waiting and miss all the fun."

He has an odd idea of fun. All right, it was one he could jump in on, but not until he knew what was going on. Details they all lacked and would continue to be without until they made contact with the colony. It didn't matter if the connection was via comm or in person. Information remained the key.

Jones grabbed his get out bag, a shotgun over his shoulder. Or what passed for one out here. You didn't fire the standard ammo here, or on the ship. Fast way of ending up with those around you dead or wishing they were. Flechettes or low energy weapons were the standard. But if the dome was damaged was there a point in keeping low impact weapons instead of grabbing more powerful options.

"You should come with us, could do with the help." Jones caught his gaze.

"You'll be fine. I've got things I need to see to back at the base." Or rather the stash he had inside the protective dome. A dome which had already been punctured. Had his stores been damaged? What about his ship? He shifted attention back to the room, seeking out the one who had made contact with the colony. "Bloodlaw, you get anything from the base?"

She didn't answer immediately, pausing long enough to catch Gunny's eye before she spoke. "They're under attack, but I've no idea who's behind it. Won't know unless they establish communication, or we see for ourselves." She was moving through the bar, helping those who still lingered, pushing the noncombatants toward Jones. With the other off duty marines he'd taken note of, and a handful other civilians ready to fight with them, they numbered fourteen, fifteen including himself. Not enough to fight off an invasion if one of the Earthbound governments had decided the agreements no longer applied to them, but more than enough to keep them safe as they moved through the tunnels.

"Three ships, according to the information I've been able to gather. Multiple strikes to the dome, which means it's likely fractured or punctured." He tapped the datapad, but nothing more appeared on the screen. "Either this thing is dead, or they've taken out the communications relay." Either was possible.

She paused long enough to try her comm, then shook her head. "Static. Barely got through last time." She paused, her grey eyes narrowed. "How did you get more information?"

"Lucky, I guess." If the marine believed he was going to share information, beyond what they all needed to survive, she didn't understand how things worked. "If anything else seeps through, I'll let you know." Or he would if it wasn't private, and the military needed the info to get them all safely out of this mess.

"We're on our own," said Stone. He slid the pan into a pocket. "Supplies?" How much would they need? "Going to need suits, even if we go back through the tunnels, we're going to hit spots which are no longer covered by the dome, and potential cracks in the tunnel walls." Collapses were a possibility. If anyone had been caught outside, beneath the dome, when the protection had given way, would they have had enough time to get into one of the housing units? Or shelters?

His mind raced. How many had died in the attack? Did he know any of them? Shit, of course, he would know at least a few of them. The colony wasn't big, but it was growing, the dome added to every six months or so, but he'd been here for a long time. Five years now. The odds of there being a friend or acquaintance caught up in the mix -- he shook the idea off. Better to think of the loss when they were safe.

"Gunny, we're going to need protection. Dome's cracked or worse. Might be the tunnels have been compromised."

"On it. Jones, the emergency suits?"

"Storeroom. I've got a handful of them. Not enough for everyone." Jones paused in organizing the men and women with him. "I'll run a scan see if the route down to the safehold is in one piece. Hey, anyone have suits with them?"

Most of the customers brought out the small boxes which held their suits. It was common practice to carry a suit with them at all times. The suits are enough to keep a person alive in the short term, moving from one area to another. Stone checked his belt, his was present, better quality, no doubt, than the backups Jones would have, or anyone but the military.

"I have oxygen cylinders in the storeroom. Big ones, enough to use to deal with any leaks if we're careful." Jones continued, "I can get a few extra face masks, add them with gloves and tape, might be enough to get this lot to safety."

"Show me what you've got." Stone gestured to the storeroom. Gloves over the thin suit would help if they had enough of them. Eventhen, it wouldn't be strong enough to keep the chill from seeping in.

"Hey, we're going to need full numbers. Walker, go with them." Bloodlaw gestured to one of the younger men.

"Yes, sergeant." The man inclined his head and joined Stone and Jones.

"And then what?" Jones asked. "You head out with the military and get yourself killed."

"Yes on heading out, no about dying. Have too much to do to die." He flashed a grin at the other man.

"You hate the military," Jones lowered his voice as he led the way to the storeroom. "Lug heads, obeying orders and not taking into account the lives of the others around them."

Walker growled. "We're nothing like that."

"Right, a wet behind the ears newbie is going to lecture me on what it's like?" Jones snapped back at the younger man. "And don't try and tell me you're not new here. You still have a shine to you, one which hasn't been knocked off by a couple of tours."

Walker didn't respond.

"Thought so. You can always tell the new ones."

Stone smiled but didn't add to the conversation as he followed Jones into the room, blinking as the lights turned on. Stacked shelves of stores, with some of the contents spilled across the floor, drew his attention but as Jones stepped over the worst of the mess and made his way deeper into the room, Stone caught sight of what the other man was heading for.

Three large wire baskets filled with military grade oxygen tanks, suits, first aid kits, food, and water. "You've been busy."

"Doesn't do any harm to be prepared."

He wasn't about to argue.

Chapter Four

Cora half glanced at the men as they vanished into the storage room, then dismissed what they were doing as she turned her attention to the rest of the occupants of the bar. The civilians mingled, their voices low, the occasional whimper of pain or fear filtered past their conversation to carry across the room. They'd be gone soon enough. She wouldn't have to worry about them. Jones would see them safe.

Or not.

Either way, there wasn't anything she could do about it.

"They'll be fine." Gunny **placed** one hand on her shoulder, the touch brief, vanishing before she had a chance to fully register it. "None of our people are injured, and we have enough, with a couple of civilians, to clear the path ahead of Jones and his people. We've got training on our side, and with Jones taking the majority of the civilians with him, we'll be able to move quickly through the tunnels."

"Agreed. Then what?" She checked off her equipment as they spoke. She had everything she needed unless you counted the lack of heavy weaponry. Sidearms were useful, but if they were going to run up against real trouble, they needed better weapons. Rifles. Flachette rifles packed a better punch than their sidearms. Whatever they were about to run into, they'd deal with it.

"We get to the base, see what the damage is, and kick ass. It's what we signed up to do."

Could he read her mind? No, he was an experienced Gunnery Sergeant. He'd seen it all, done it all, and would pull them through. As long as she had Gunny with her, they could tackle anything thrown at them. Kick ass. Sure, it was one of the reasons she'd joined the Marines. "Understood, Gunny. But we're going to have a problem without the right weapons. Don't know about you, but I didn't bring anything but the blazer." She tapped the small handgun.

"No, but there's the emergency dump half a klick out from the base. If the tunnels are safe, I'll be able to access it."

Emergency dump? Her eyes narrowed as she dug through the information she'd been given about the base and the supplies. "Something I didn't know about." If it wasn't intact, they'd find other ways of arming themselves. Sticks, stones, torn off limbs. It was the Marine way.

"Need to know basis, Sergeant. I need to know." He smiled, but it didn't last long. "If the tunnel is damaged, or the storage is breached, then we'll deal with it and find another way to grab weapons. If we have to go in with side arms and fists, then we do it. No one is taking our home from us, and we have civilians to protect."

Hadn't she decided the same thing? "Oorah."

"Weapons count, Sergeant. Get on it."

She didn't reply as she moved through the bar, collecting anything they could use to defend themselves with. Ice picks, knives, half a dozen sidearms, mostly from the rest of her team, though the bar had a shotgun beneath it. Not the type used on Earth, but the energy shotguns many a business, both on Pluto and other colonies, used. Could make a mess with a human body, but did little damage to the shields, domes, and other structures.

Not enough.

"Sergeant?"

"What is it, Corporal?"

"What are we facing?"

"You'll know when I do." She glanced over her shoulder at the man. Face pale, eyes wide, a nervous twitch beneath his left eye. Well shit, she was going into an unknown situation, facing attackers they had no information about, with a team who'd never encountered anything more than the occasional bar fight or rumble with a smuggler or two. "We've got this. Remember your training, listen to Gunny and me, and we'll get through this." The words should have offered comfort, but they remained hollow, echoing through her mind.

They'd pull through this.

She wouldn't allow it to be any other way.

"Understood, Sergeant."

"Work with Ready, sooner we get out of here, the better. I need numbers, how many of the civies have decent suits with them, injuries, and get me the information on the other marines here."

"Not all marines, one's navy. Shuttle pilot. Don't know what he's doing down here."

"Same as the rest of us, enjoying the downtime before the shit hit the fan." She took a long look around the bar. "When this is dealt with, we'll help Jones with the repairs. Otherwise, we could be waiting for months before we can use the place again."

"Sergeant?"

"Have to get our priorities straight, can't have the best bar on Pluto closed for too long. Where will we go to relax if it's closed for repairs?" She flashed a smile at the corporal. "Let's get this done."

"Damn, have you been preparing for the apocalypse back here? You've got enough supplies to support a small outpost." Walker whistled through his teeth.

Stone didn't disagree. He stepped past the marine, taking in items lining the shelves. The only thing they were missing were weapons. Sure, a few sidearms with the power packs stored to the left on the metal shelves. Metal, not plastiwear. Cost more due to the weight transporting them here, but less likely to crack under use. He ran his fingers over the edge of the nearest shelf. Small bumps, rough spots, not transported, but from here. Metal over heavy duty plastiwear? Interesting concept. Cheaper than he'd initially thought, but still out of the price range for most people. Had the mineral been mined here, or elsewhere?

He didn't have time to investigate, but noted the information, filing it away for a better time.

"Walker, grab the sidearms and power packs. Jones, take two for your group. But don't hand them out to anyone unless you know their skills and you trust them. You don't need to lose people because the wrong person has a gun." Friendly fire. Experienced troops could make a mistake, civies who didn't know their ass from their elbow were a hell of a lot more likely to make a mistake.

"On it."

Stone stuffed his pockets with food tubes, water pockets, and grabbed a pack of pain relief sticks for good measure.

"Hey, those aren't legal." Walker **asked**. "How did you get them?"

"This entire bar isn't legal, what did you expect?" Jones laughed, "geeze, you'd think people would think that one through. Of course, I'm going to carry the basics back here. All it takes is one small power out, or a dome crack, mining accident, and we're stuck out here. It's why I keep these shelves stocked, and why I had the bolt hold built."

"You're expecting marines to think. They only follow orders." Stone didn't look away from the shelves. "Wouldn't be safe to permit them a chance to make decisions for themselves."

"Hey." Walker took a step toward him. "Don't talk like that about the marines. We're trained for this."

"Yes, you are, but he's right, you're trained to follow orders. Nothing to be ashamed of. They aren't going to let a private do his own thinking. Too damn dangerous for everyone around you." Jones laughed as he pulled two of the tanks away from the wall. "These are going to be heavy to carry, but we can't leave without them. Not if we want to make it through the tunnels. You'll want one for your people, Walker."

"Yeah, sure, whatever." The words clipped and cold. Muttered words faded as the marine put distance between them.

Ah, the pride of young marines, if there was one thing guaranteed to hasten the death of a man in combat, it was pride. Sooner or later, it caught up with them. There were old soldiers and bold soldiers, but no old bold soldiers. Wasn't that the saying from old Earth? Before the collapse and what had passed for world war III?

The rumble caught him off guard. Ground shook. Items tumbled from the shelves as the three men tried to brace themselves. He flattened one hand against the wall as he dropped to his knees. The bottom shelf. Empty. He forced his body into the empty space. "Cover. Find cover. Now."

"Knew I shouldn't have come down here," Navy grumbled as he glanced around the bar. "Should have joined the others in the mess. Now I'm stuck down here with a bunch of Marines and civilians." He caught Cora's gaze and shrugged.

"You're here, and have a choice. Work with us, or take it up with me, or the Gunny. Once we have our... discussion... you'll still be faced with the same decision."

"Nice." He rolled his eyes.

"You have a name, or should I make one up?" Cora glanced at him.

"James Harvard."

"Rank?"

"Does it matter?"

Fantastic, she was dealing with an officer. "Pilot?"

"Been known to fly from time to time." A shrug. "Not that it matters down here."

"Sergeant Bloodlaw. Have you made up your mind?"

"Until I hear from my ship, I'm with you. So, what did you want me to do?" Another shrug.

She watched him, taking in the expressions, the small signs she'd been taught to watch for. Had to be careful about, especially when dealing with an officer. And she had no doubt. This man, Harvard, was an officer no matter what he might try to convince her of. "Weapons, supplies, and personal check."

Harvard grunted but moved away without another word.

Officer, one fighting his instincts to take over. She smiled, unwilling to waste the energy, preventing it from claiming her lips. The man would either do what they needed, or she'd have to deal with his officer side kicking in. One of the men she'd always keep one eye on, no matter what else he was doing. Her gaze remained on him as he walked through the bar, picking up chairs and tables as he went.

She felt it before she experienced it, a subtle vibration beneath her feet. Then the roar rolled through the tunnels, rattling chairs, bottles, and bodies alike. Cora darted beneath one of the bigger tables, one the owner had bolted to the floor. She didn't think if it was strong enough to offer protection. She took the shelter provided. "Cover. Now!" Men and women dived for cover or cowered in huddles. Pieces fell from the ceiling, dust and debris filled the air.

She peered out from her spot, tensed, her eyes narrowed. She swore and pushed out from the table before she had a chance to think things through. Instinct taking control. Cora hit the woman with her body, bowling her to the floor and covering her, protecting the other woman's head and upper torso with her own. "Don't move. I've got you." One of the servers or one of the customers?

Didn't matter.

A civilian in need of protection. This was how she'd been trained to react, and she wasn't about to question her own actions. Not in the moment at least.

Cora hissed as something struck her left calf. A man cried out in shock. A woman cried sobbing. But she didn't move. Not until the room stopped shaking. She waited, taking a deep breath, counting off to ten in slow, steady numbers before she lifted up from the cowering woman. "You hurt?"

The woman looked up, blinking, stunned, her face pale. "Don't think I am." She licked her bottom lip and swallowed. "You didn't have to do that."

"Yes, I did." Cora brushed dust and mess from her eyes and checked on the others. A few more injuries. Nothing major at first glance. A few cuts, and a shock of yet another explosion. "It's my job." Usually, the line would be enough to end the conversation. Not this time.

"Thank you." Tears glittered in the woman's eyes as she rose, still shaken by the vibrations and debris. "You're one of the rare ones."

"You're welcome." She glanced at her leg as the woman moved away. No blood. No sign of a cut. A bruise she could handle, though it might slow her down. "You'll be fine. Jones will get you out of here." He'd better, or she'd have more than words to exchange with the bartender. "Make sure you get your hands on a suit. You'll need it to travel through the tunnels."

The woman moved stiffly. No visible signs of injury, but adrenalin, plus being thrown to the floor, was enough to stiffen anyone's muscles.

"Everyone alright?" Gunny called out. "Injuries?"

A dozen voices replied. She didn't need to, knowing Gunny was only asking about real injuries, not a bruise she could walk off. Cora patted herself down as she scanned the bar, her gaze moving up over the walls to the ceiling. "Well, shit." A large crack marked the surface, spider-webbing across the once smooth surface. "Gunny, we're running out of time here."

The Gunny met her gaze, his eyes narrowing, brow furrowed. "You heard the Sergeant, get a move on. We leave in five, if not sooner."

Yeah, sooner would be better. She didn't like how the crack

spread, slowly now the rumbling had come to a halt, but still on the move. The next explosion would be it for the ceiling if it didn't collapse before.

Stone slid out from the cramped shelter, coughing as he brushed the fresh dust from his eyes. Had the structure been damaged? "Another one like that and the entire room will collapse."

"Best we're out of here before it happens." Jones pulled down a backpack and stuffed extra supplies into it. "Grab what you can, then we're out."

Stone followed suit, adding packages to his pockets and back up equipment to a pack he pulled from one of them. It expanded enough to fit most of what he wanted into the flexible confines. Still meant too much would be left behind for his mercenary tastes, but if the ceiling did collapse, there would be time to rebuild and supplies to claim from the ruins. Same could be said for the damage done to the buildings beneath the dome. A scavengers wet dream.

Or his.

Walker muttered under his breath and dragged one of the tanks toward the door, a pack slung over his left shoulder, pockets bulging.

Marines. One step up from mercs and scavengers. Not as if he'd tell Walker how he felt, wrong time and place for a full-on fight. "Times running out."

"Yeah, tell us something we don't know, trader." Walker snapped. "I'm not stupid."

Better to be identified as a trader than anything else. If Walker had any idea what he was, how he earned a living, his chances of heading out with the Marines would vanish. He nodded to the other men and pushed his way out through the debris and dust, one hand slamming against the closed door, slapping it open before he stepped into the main room.

"Was about to send a Marine to find you," the Gunny said.

"The last shock was interesting."

"I know." The older man pointed upward.

Stone followed the movement and swore in three different languages. Cracked walls and ceiling. It wasn't a welcome sign. "We don't have much time, do we?"

"No, we don't." Gunny took the pack from Walker and split up the items between the rest of the team. "Jones, you ready to go?"

"Halfway through the door."

"Wait, let us head out first." The sergeant spoke up. "If there's a problem, we're better equipped to handle it. We all have basic emergency masks, the civies masks aren't as reliable as ours, and they only have back up part masks, with goggles. They'll need a clear shot through before the lack of air, and the cold gets to their skin." She pulled on black gloves, skin tight, to protect her hands. Better than the thin covering offered by the suit. With the possibility of broken walls, the gloves had a better chance of standing up against the potential damage.

"Yeah, fine. Ladies first." Jones gestured to the small group of marines and smirked.

"Wanna watch what you say, might find yourself tripped up along the way," Lackey muttered, the words not designed to carry too far.

Jones flipped the Marine the bird.

Walker carried the tank and ended up in the middle of the group, where any of the Marines could access the precious supply of oxygen. Old fashioned, bulky, but lightweight tanks instead of the more modern small recyclers designed for use in limited oxygen areas. If the roof had collapsed, they'd lose all of the oxygen in the building, or tunnel. The recyclers would have made a decent backup, but useless in a true zero oxygen situation.

Gunny moved to the front of the group, mask, and gloves in place. "Let's get this done."

Chapter Five

Cora settled into place a step behind Gunny, checked on the rest of the team, then nodded once to the older man to indicate they were ready. Her marines knew what to do, and the three she wasn't as familiar with, kept pace with ease. The navy pilot listened, for now, though having an officer in the mix offered more potential trouble down the line. Still, he was military and knew enough not to fight to take control of a group made up mostly of marines. Men ready and willing to fight no matter what waited for them in the colony.

The civilians were another matter, but there were enough marines around to cover for any mistakes the civies might make. She knew the majority of the men in the group enough to trust them with her life. Now, with Gunny in charge, she fell back into the second in command position, she often assumed when there was an officer in the mix. Except she trusted Gunny a thousand times more than she would ever trust or respect the straight out of the academy second lieutenants they were often stuck with.

The door opened with a groan, instead of the near silent hiss which normally accompanied the action. She frowned and checked her sensors, the readings dancing into life across the back of her hand. They had backup oxygen ahead of them, and the supply from the bar which now seeped into the tunnels, would help, but she tapped her mask to indicate the fact they'd need the supplemental oxygen to make it through. She gestured turned and gestured to the tank, then back to the group with Jones, the message passed back without a word.

The Gunny nodded, a slight smile in place, and she inclined her head in thanks.

The older man eased into the passageway, scanners running. They didn't need to pull out anything else to know the area wasn't safe. The faster they made their way through the old byways, the better it would be for all of them. The tunnel was large enough to allow four men could walk abreast and tall, sufficient to prevent any of them from having to bow or duck under the flickering lights. That was one blessing; they hadn't lost power and weren't trying to make their way through the dark. Generators were still running, and the main lines, those she had seen lining the passageways, were intact.

For now.

Nothing was said as they picked up the pace, pausing only to check the civilians were keeping up or to clear rubble from their path. They could do this, yes walking wasn't the best way, but if you made it out to the bar, you weren't afraid of a little sweat and dust, you knew what you were getting into.

She did and offered no complaints.

Her mask kept her supplied with the required oxygen, gloves kept her hands warm, and the rest of her clothing enough to prevent major problems. She hadn't pulled on the full suit, opting to keep things light. Better to be able to move. It didn't take long to draw on the suit. Hah, pulling it on was the wrong term. A few instructions keyed in and it would slide out of place from belt and boots, covering her body and sealing itself to the gloves and facepiece within three seconds. All you had to do was smooth it over limbs before hitting the final seal.

Ten times faster than the civilian suits, and built to withstand bumps, scrapes and possible cuts.

Sweat beaded and froze against her skin, but the speed with which they moved countered the chill.

Noise filtered its way forward from Jones' group, and her jaw clenched. She signaled to Walker, who she knew would pass the instructions back, to be quiet. If the tunnels had been exposed, then the ones behind the attack might have discovered them, and they'd face more than rubble. More than a lack of heat and air. They didn't need a firefight with Jones' group still with them.

The chatter stopped, cut off mid-word.

Better. She wasn't going to have to go back and smack one of the civilians. Except it removed any chance to let off steam. Pressure built, tension tightened her shoulders and upper arms. Her skin itched with the need to fight, do something other than lead a bunch of civilians to safety.

What the hell was she thinking?

Fistfight, action, the need to act, to burn off the energy which now. These were things she could understand. It was a part of her, but it didn't mean she liked it.

Any more than she liked one of the civilians with them. The same man who'd caught her attention at the bar.

Mason Stone.

Smuggler? Merc? Who cared? He had a dangerous air, and trust was the last thing she felt toward him.

They reached one of the man areas where the tunnel branched off in three directions, and the Gunny signaled for them to stop. "Get Jones up here."

Cora didn't have to pass the order down the line, Walker took care of the issue. It took five minutes before the bartender made his way through the group as silently as a civilian was capable of.

"What's up?"

"Which way for your survival room?"

"Right, Gunny."

"We're heading left."

"Figured."

"Then this is where we part ways." Jones glanced back at the men and women waiting for him. "Thanks, you didn't have to do this. I mean, get us this far."

"And if we didn't need to get to the base, we'd see you all the way, but duty first." The older man clapped his free hand, the other holding his sidearm, on Jones' shoulder. "Stay safe. Keep your comm tunned to channel five, it's going to be the fastest way for you to get updates."

"Got it."

Cora checked the passageway each way. Both appeared to be clear, save for debris, though the one to the left had shown more signs of damage than the one Jones would follow. Made sense. The one to the right led away from the source of the explosions, the one to the left led toward it. At least the civilians would be safer, and they wouldn't get in the way if the shit hit the fan. For a moment she considered sending the two Marines she only knew in passing, with Jones, but shook off the idea. They'd need as many skilled fighters with them as possible. Whoever had attacked the colony would be well armed. You couldn't sneak up on one, possibly two naval vessels and attack Pluto unless you had numbers or better weapons on your side.

Three ships. Stone had shared enough information to suggest it had been coordinated attack. If the man was right, then there was a heap load of trouble building up out in the colony, and they didn't know if anyone else had survived. If the dome was damaged, then the loss of life--

No, she wasn't going to play keeper of the dead. Not unless there was no other choice.

"Good luck."

"Thanks, Sergeant." Jones flashed a smile and gathered the rest of his group together. Without words they split up, leaving the Marines and their civilians waited for word from the Gunny.

The older man paused for two minutes, allowing the civilians to vanish down the passageway, then gestured to the left. "Tight formation. We don't need to make any foolish mistakes here. Got it?"

"Oorah," the Marines replied, Cora, included, as one.

Cora swore, and she wasn't the only one. Rocks, pieces of wall and ceiling support blocked the passageway ahead, except for a small entrance at the top. Large enough to allow one person at a time through the debris, and only if it hadn't closed up out of line of sight. "We're going to have to make that opening larger if we're all going to get through." Especially with the equipment, they'd brought with them from Jones' supplies.

"Not before we check out what's going on out there, and see if the weapons stash is blocked." The Gunny rested one hand on her shoulder. "You up to it?"

"Yes," she said.

"Good, get on it. Keep radio silence unless there's a problem. Two clicks on the comm."

"Understood, Gunny." She eyeballed the gap and stripped off any equipment not essential to her immediate survival.

"Don't take any unnecessary risks out there. You might leave me in a position where I have to rely on Navy over there." His voice low, the comm set for personal communication only. "Harvard is a damn good pilot, but little full of himself. I've talked with him before, he'll follow orders when he needs to, and he knows the score. We all work together, or we die."

"Sounds normal for Navy." She took a moment to take in the faces of the men she was leaving behind. All men. The only other women in the bar had been patrons, but it wasn't the first time she'd been the lone female in a team. Marines tended to be top-heavy toward men, though more women joined the navy. "Too wrapped up in themselves."

"What do we expect from flyboys?" The Gunny smiled.

"Nothing but stuffed shirts, all ego, and no stamina." She completed the standard complaint. "First to the bar, last to pay."

If Harvard heard them, he didn't respond. Just as well, she didn't want an argument. She took a long look at the men, taking in the various suits they all wore. All but the two civilians wore military grade emergency suits. Strong enough to protect them from immediate damage, but they wouldn't take a full-on blast from an energy bolt, or a heavy flechette round. If her suit tore climbing through the gap, she'd hunt down the quartermaster who'd issued her damn supplies and remind him why the environmental gear was supposed to be better than those issued to the civilians.

Standing around, flapping her jaw with the Gunny wasn't getting the work done. No goodbyes, no long farewells, instead she did what was expected of her. She began the climb over the pile of debris toward the opening, a small light activated on her face mask, enough to give her a soft circle of light ahead of her and give her fair warning about potential hazards.

Her foot slipped once, but she didn't move a foot or hand until she had three other points of stability. A small slip would be enough to trigger a *rock* fall. Inch by inch she half crawled, half climbed her way toward the gap. If the men behind her were talking, it didn't reach her comm, suggesting either silence or personal communication between two or more.

Gunny, he'd be watching her until she was no longer in line of sight. Only then would he look away. She didn't need to see him to know what the older man would do. She'd served with him for five years now, enough time to learn his quirks and be grateful for them. It didn't matter if his behavior was from the core of the man, or the years spent in service, either way, it didn't matter. He was one of the best, and she was thankful he was here instead of trapped in the colony when the attack had begun.

Cora paused at the entrance to the gap.

Tunnel.

Fine, it was a blasted tunnel through who knew how deep a blockade it was. The light from her face mask only served to confirm she'd need to belly crawl through the gap and into the darkness. This wasn't going to be easy, but backing down, asking the Gunny to send another in her place, wasn't an option. Sure, the man might do it, but then her reputation would be shot. Not a risk she'd take. She closed her eyes for a moment, steadying her nerves. There were no other lifeforms on Pluto, not beyond the ones transported here to build the colony. No weird bugs or snakes she had to watch out for.

Small mercies, but she was glad of them.

Her skin crawled, heart raced as she peered into the distance. *Not claustrophobic.* She repeated the mantra in the back of her mind as she began the elbow, knee, elbow, knee crawl. Sharp points pressed against her suit. Enough to bruise, but not tear the military grade enviro-suit.

The knowledge didn't prevent the small voice of doubt or the larger one of fear competing away in the back of her mind.

Fear didn't mean you were a coward. It said you were human. Learning to work with fear was something you either managed, or you didn't. Each time was a new battle, one she never knew if she would win or lose.

To date, her wins outnumbered her losses, which was all she could ever wish for and remain human.

Jaw clenched as she made her way slowly through the tunnel, reaching out carefully to locate any problems. She could do this, would manage it. She'd get the answers they needed and return to the group. Then the real work would begin.

Her fingers found the small lip, which indicated where she needed to go. The exit. Or the tunnel widened. She lifted her head enough to allow the light to spill on the surroundings. Not a widening, but the end of the debris. She grinned and pulled herself through the gap.

What relief she'd felt at the knowledge of finding the end of the tunnel vanished. The markers which would have allowed her to find the storage was covered but for the first one.

Damn fall in had locked them out of the extra weapons they would need. Fine. They'd find a way around this. There were other storage points in the colony. Some military, some built up by civilians, such as the merc in their group. Stone. A man she didn't trust. Something about him, the way he moved, watched her or spoke, all of it added up to tell her the man was dangerous. He'd turn his back on them the first chance he had.

Hell's Own

She pushed the man to the back of her mind as she made her way down the far side of the debris, brushed off her suit, and allowed herself to calm before she approached the door. A quick check of the door showed minor damage, with the power supply still intact, except for the last lock. Not ideal, but she could operate it without power. Depending on what was waiting for her on the other side of the door. If they relied on energy, odds were they wouldn't look for the manual lock.

Cora deactivated the light before she ran her fingers over the control panel, listening as the soft sounds told her the security protocol was still active. She paused, taking a deep breath before she reached for the manual lock. Noise, this one had the potential to be louder than the others. If they heard her, whoever they were, it would be over. Just what she needed, a band of aliens or renegades using the cover of fake aliens, waiting for her on the other side of the door.

She pulled it open, taking care not to trigger any noise source, but eventhen the small sound scraped on her already raw nerves. When she had a gap wide enough to peer through, she listened, double checking for anything on the other side.

Nothing.

Not even the background noise she would expect from the colony.

Cora shifted position, settled her mind and did a visual sweep before she stepped back, giving her the chance to replay what she'd seen.

Damaged and destroyed buildings.

Destroyed transports.

Pieces of the dome scattered across the ground, yet the gravity remained. Whatever had happened, they hadn't taken out the machines producing the near earth gravity the colony maintained.

What she hadn't seen was any sign of survivors.

Or dead.

Movement, had she seen that over to the left? A distant

shadow? She pressed her mask against the gap. No moving, no giving a hint there was someone in the tunnel, or the tunnel existed at all. If someone looked close enough, they'd see the change in the wall, where she'd pushed the door open. Even a crack could then lead to her being spotted, but she had to take the risk.

Her gaze narrowed as she continued to watch the remains of the colony. Buildings destroyed, little more than crumbled heaps of once-sturdy homes, stores, and offices. At this time of day, based on colony time, the youngest of the children would have been in bed, unless taken out to an event by their parents. Lights flickered here and there, only to either die as she watched or expand into life.

How many had died?

If they were dead, what had happened to the bodies?

If she wanted more answers, it would mean stepping out into the remains of the colony and risk exposing herself to the dangers. Which was what she was paid to do, she reminded herself. She edged the door open another half inch, straining to hear what was going on, her senses on alert as she tried to take into account any and all vibrations beneath her feet.

A shape caught her attention. Large, on four legs. Bigger than five people put together. The size of an elephant? Yes, that was close to the mark. She'd only seen one elephant in her lifetime. The size and number of legs were the only things the creature had in common with the grey-skinned beast from Earth. A long head, with thick tendrils hanging down from all sides of the beings face. Eyes, if they had any, couldn't be seen. Teeth. A flash of light played off the long fangs glinting in its wide maw. The skin looked scale covered, light reflecting from not only the scales but a shimmering presence over its body, but not directly on the skin itself. She frowned, trying to understand what she was seeing.

A suit? Environmental suit?

Could be, but without moving close enough to get a precise

reading.

It lumbered further into view and shook its massive head, the thick cable like cords flapped around its head, but it wasn't the odd hair which caught her attention. Behind it, dragged by a harness attached to its back and chest, was a semi-clear cube filled with shapes.

Human shapes.

Moving, pressed against the walls of the cage.

Prisoners?

She swallowed. Hard.

Another shape walked into view. Four limbs, a strange creature with a crocodile-like shaped head. Teeth, sharp, ragged in appearance, pressed against its lips, but again there was something over its head and body. The same thin, shimmering bodysuit pulled against its form as it walked on two legs, the arms holding a substantial staff like object with handholds and nodules.

A weapon?

Instinct said yes.

Alright, two different types of aliens. Was the one pulling the cage a beast of burden or an equal who used its strength to help its comrades?

Cora shivered and pressed one hand against the inside of the door. All she had to do was close it and walk away. Take what she knew back to the men waiting for her. But she couldn't move. Her hands didn't obey her, legs refused to move as her heart raced. Fear traced cold fingers up and down the length of her spine as her mind adjusted to what she was seeing.

A third alien.

Six limbs. A triangle shaped head moving into a narrow chest and thick back legs. Like the second one, it held a long weapon, but also wore a belt with what could have been a sidearm. First one of the group she'd seen wear anything she could class as clothing. But it wasn't the legs, or weapons which held her attention.

Wings.

No, she couldn't be seeing this. She'd made a mistake, the creature couldn't have freaking wings.

It turned its head in her direction, small lights dancing in its three almond shaped eyes as its wings stretched out, scales glinting across their multicolored expanse.

Oh, hell no.

It took a step closer. Her heart threatened to burst from her chest, but still, she held position, grateful for the lack of oxygen. Nothing left to cause a ripple of hair, or clothing. No breeze, or fan moving to disrupt the air. Only stillness.

Whatever it sought, the moment was gone as the creature turned away and joined the others.

Sergeant Cora Bloodlaw waited until they were out of line of sight before she allowed herself a fresh breath. Her limbs trembled with the need to remain in place, the crack in the opening not enough for most humans to spot her, but they weren't dealing with humans.

This was the other. The unknown. And with them came dangers they had never before encountered.

With the door closed, she edged back through the opening, taking care not to make a sound as she crawled her way back to the others, mind racing. Aliens. Freaking aliens. Damn, it was one thing to dream of first contact, another to come face to face with it like this. Aliens. Not human. Monsters.

The other.

Jakob hit the floor, the breath knocked from his body, vision blurred from the crack of head against the floor. His ribs burned, back ached, and hips protested from the force which had sent him to the ground. He tried to breathe, struggling to deal with the pain in his chest. Move. He couldn't stay here forever. He'd die if he didn't move. The suit wouldn't protect him long term. If he were at risk, then the others would face the same danger. No one would be able to withstand the damage for long.

Low moans, soft cries, whimpers of pain, and fear reached him through the inbuilt comm as he blinked and tried to get his body to obey him. His legs didn't work, but he could feel them. Anything else was a blessing. He rolled onto his side and bit back a whimper. He wasn't going to allow his body to dictate to him what he could and couldn't do. Shake it off, wasn't that what the coach told him when he was knocked down during a game? Not a tussle this time but survival.

"Jakob?" A pain filled word.

He rose, unsteady, limbs trembling. His suit. Was it damaged? No, he'd feel it, or the internal alert would ring out.

"My suit. God, my suit." An older woman, a wail of fear. With the dome compromised, hiding the risk which came with a damaged suit would remain foremost in the minds of the colonists. "Help me, please, help me. I need a repair kit. Another suit. I'm losing air."

"It's alright, we'll make it. Trust me, we'll make it." The woman's husband? Friend? Lover? It didn't matter. The danger remained real, one he had to face and accept if he wanted a chance to survive.

"Gail?" He blinked, taking a precious moment to search for his friend. "Gail, answer me." Fear clenched his belly. Had she fallen? Hurt her head? He turned, searching for a sign of her amid the dust and chaos. He wouldn't leave her behind. "Gail?" His head swam. Small lights continued to dance across his vision as he tried to make sense of the mess. Bodies. The living and the dying pressed together, and only the dead were without fear.

"Here." She leaned against the wall, her breathing ragged as she straightened. She coughed, the sound carried across the personal commlink, then pressed her fingers to the headpiece, then smiled as she looked around. "That was interesting. Don't want to go through this again."

"Can't stay here. Need to get to the ground floor." He didn't disagree with her. The last thing he wanted to do was hang around for another shake or worse. "We'll be safer in the tunnels."

"Next shake might bring the building down. Not only this one but the others in the area. We have to keep moving."

"I know." He reached for her. Together. They'd make it out together. "We won't stay here, and I won't leave you behind." His fingers tangled with hers, and he squeezed. Reassurance, but he wasn't confident if he'd done it to soothe her nerves, or his. Either way, it didn't matter. They would remain together and find their way to the safety of the tunnels.

Nothing else was acceptable.

Stone frowned. What the hell was the Gunny doing, letting Jones head for safety without them? Foolish. Jones was a decent man. Calm enough to remain in control of a bunch of terrified colonists, sure. If there was enough money in it for him. Or he shot the first one who disobeyed him. Neither a recipe for success under the current circumstances. Stone rolled his eyes but kept silent. No matter what happened, he had to get to his ship, which meant working with the jarheads for the foreseeable future. Navy might be of use if he could get the man on his own long enough to present him with the idea. Besides, once he was close enough to the bay where his vessel was hidden, he'd slip away from the group and not look back. Why would he need to? He didn't need the idiot Marines on his tail, not with what he had stored in his cargo holds.

His gaze flicked to the Gunny, then away. His ship should be safe, far from the center of the colony, and on the opposite side to the military-run port.

Gunny caught his glance and inclined his head before he turned his attention elsewhere.

Did the man trust him?

Hell's Own

Hell no. Not a chance, no matter what he might want to believe. He didn't need the Gunny or his people. He needed to get the hell out of here before whoever was behind the attack decided to explore Pluto and pick off any survivors. People who attacked worlds, or small colonies like Pluto, didn't leave survivors. They wiped them out, or they collected them for whatever they had in mind.

He'd never heard of full-on attacks. Sure, the occasional raid to grab a specific person. A slave raid. Assassination. Nothing like this. Whatever this was.

Debris turned into a blockage five minutes down the corridor, with a small gap at the top. Not enough to allow anyone through. He swore, under his breath, and he wasn't the only one.

"Let's get this cleared, or as much as we can." Gunny glared at the mess. "And hope we don't have to deal with too much of this." With the low oxygen, it would mean burning through what they had in their masks and backups. The environmental gear they wore wouldn't be easily damaged, but it wouldn't keep out the cold the way full battle armor and built-in suits could. "Lackey and Walker, up there, get the first couple out of the way. Rest of you, form a chain to move the bigger pieces along the wall. If we can make it easier for Lawbook to return to us, so much the better."

Not the order he'd expected to hear, sending the woman through the hole when there were plenty of men around. Equality, he supposed. Or maybe he didn't see the Sergeant as a woman? It was possible but unlikely.

"On it."

Lawbook, odd name for a woman, had been gone too long for his comfort and his skin tightened, the urge to move, pace, be active, grew until his hands fisted and relaxed at his sides. The two men now working on the debris took care not to send pieces down in the direction of the men waiting at the bottom. Two other men, Ready and Harvard, took position to take the pieces when they were passed down.

"Stone."

He turned his attention back to Gunny. "Yeah?"

"Help them, no one gets to stand around here, admiring the scenery." The Gunny took position with the rest of the men, taking the first of the pieces, working alongside his people.

Arguing would waste oxygen, but it didn't mean he enjoyed lugging stone and rock around. Or pieces of whatever it was which had coated the walls. He hadn't been sent to the top of the pile to help shift the worst of the mess. Grunt labor. Hah. His mother would turn in her grave. If she was dead. As for the rest of his family, he didn't care what they believed he'd become, but the head of the family, she was another matter entirely. The damn female would never forgive him unless he came to her on bended knee and begged her forgiveness.

Never. Going. To. Happen.

He glanced up. No sign of Lawbook. How long had she been gone now? He growled and pushed all thoughts of the woman, and the length of time she'd been gone, to the back of his mind.

"I don't know what you're doing here, instead of going with Jones, but I'll get to the bottom of this, Stone. Don't think I won't." Gunny spoke in low tones, meant only for him. "If you do anything to put my people in danger, I'll rip your spine out. Got it?"

Stone smiled as he met the older man's gaze. "Oh, I understand, Gunny. I'm not out to do anything but survive and find out what's going." Not entirely a lie, he'd only missed out a few key details the marine didn't need to know. Such as the reason he'd been in the bar. And why he'd volunteered to come with the Marines when there was a softer option with Jones, the civilians and the stores the bar owner had squirreled away in the tunnels. "Your people are in no danger from me." Okay, that part was a lie. "Let me get on with life, and it's all good."

The man snorted. "If we make it. I don't know what's waiting out there for us, any more than you do. Three ships but we know nothing else about the situation. The colony attacked. And if you believe you have a chance of making it off planet while those bastards are out there, then you don't have the smarts I credited you with."

Stone bit back a growl. "I'm no fool. Getting off-world in one piece isn't a case of getting in a shuttle or whatever and heading out. We don't know why they attacked, who they are, the weapons they have, their goal, or anything other than the fact the base has been hit." Calm, he had to remain calm. "This isn't my first rodeo." Whatever the hell that was. "Laying low and gathering information is the wisest course of action, and only leaving Pluto when there's an actual chance of making it." He jerked his chin toward the rest of the Marines. "I'm here, working with you and this lot. If we're attacked, I'll fight."

"Unless someone offers you money to change sides, or for information."

"What do you think I am? A traitor." His heart raced, hands clenched. No matter what was going on, he'd never work with those who targeted paying clients. Waste of resources to blow up people who could offer you various items in trade or paid with colony recognized funds.

"Never said it, but you're a businessman. A merc or smuggler, maybe both. Means you'll protect your own skin first, and screw anyone who gets in your way."

He wanted to deny the words, but the lie stuck in his throat. Stone took a deep breath and forced his anger back under control. "Fine, under normal circumstances, you'd be right. This isn't normal. Unless it turns out this is being run by one of my contacts, one I trust, then I'm not about to switch sides. And to be honest, I can't see anyone I've ever worked with pulling shit like this." No, it would be bad for business to blow up a base and take on Earth's military. Didn't matter how powerful his contacts might be, not one of them had enough firepower to stand up against the combined forces of the military. "Whatever is going on, it's not mercs, couldn't be. Three ships of the size and with the firepower to take out the main base? No. Maybe a smaller settlement, on the other side of the planet. Or a station. Not something like this."

"We'll find out once we get through this. The base isn't far from here."

"Figured." Anger burned in his gut, but using it against the Marines wouldn't work. Holding onto it wasted energy. Letting it go was the only viable option, but not until the man got out of his face.

"Do I need to warn you we'll be watching you?"

"No." A smile crept across his lips. "Wouldn't expect anything else from you."

The Gunny inclined his head, eyes hard as he turned his attention back to the rubble, and the small gap the two at the top slowly enlarged. "Put your backs into it."

Silence, save for grunts and the occasional swearing, settled over the group as they worked together, hauling debris out of the way until the hole was comfortably large enough to get the team and their equipment through. Lawbook had pushed herself through the gap on her stomach. The space before the work had begun on the collapse had forced the woman to approach the tunnel on her belly. Tight confines, now widened on their side of the destruction, but there was still no sign of her.

What was keeping her? Were the others concerned? He glanced at the gathered men, searching their faces, what the masks didn't hide, for a hint of worry.

No one spoke, and all he could do was wait with the others, as his stomach knotted and writhed in a fear he refused to acknowledge.

Interlude Two
Unified Terran Government: Alpha Comms.

"Captain? We've got a problem with long range communications." Sheila Cavanor frowned at the screen as her fingers moved at a rapid pace across the controls. The last thing she wanted to do was call the man's attention her way, but in this she had no choice. He was in command, having swapped shifts with the woman initially assigned the duty, and as such she had no one else to turn to.

She kept her features neutral, back straight, shoulders back. He wouldn't find anything to correct her, not in her manner of address, or the way she sat. Everything by the book, it was the only way to keep him from dropping her into it or using her lapse as a reason to lean in close.

"What is it Lieutenant?" Captain Ulrich Grant moved with ease through the room until he stopped to the left of her chair.

"We've got a black out in communications at the edge of the system,. No, not only the edge, it's crawling out, heading toward the center of the system. Pluto is silent, as are the two ships assigned to the sector." To Earth, the block on communications spread out toward their home, or would if nothing was done to correct the situation. "I've run scans on the computers but everything's coming back clean." Five scans, more than enough to keep Grant from suggesting she'd missed the cause, forgotten to double check the backup systems, or had failed to run a particular program, designed to increase their communication range.

"Where did it begin?" He **set** one hand on the back of her chair and leaned in.

"Pluto. The routine check happened on time, both with the colony and the two navy vessels in the area." Three hours ago, nothing but the all clear and light chatter. Her jaw tightened as Grant shifted his weight until she couldn't shut out his presence. "I thought I caught a sound, a squelch, ninety minutes ago, but again the system came back clear. I checked in with the other colonies and ships, then worked my way back to Pluto, per regulations."

"And?"

"Nothing. No static." He didn't have to be this close to her. She didn't look at him, knowing it was what he was waiting for. Damn man wouldn't take no for an answer. She didn't date men she worked with, besides, there was the entire problem with him being her commanding officer. "I've run six different scans on the system, still nothing." She tapped the stream of data on the right-hand side of the screen. "See this? The energy flicker. I've never seen anything like it before."

"Sergeant Roberts, bring up everything we've got on the readings in and around Pluto." He squeezed her shoulder, the touch lingering a fraction longer than was acceptable. "Leave this to me, Sheila."

"Lieutenant Cavanor," she replied.

"Ah, always the formal one."

"This is work, Captain." No matter if he refused to accept it. "There's a problem. I know there is. It isn't a case of a system failure, or a hack job. We're being jammed."

"No one has the ability to jam our communications. Not with the back-ups in place." Scorn touched his words.

"I know that's how it's supposed to work, but I'm telling you our communications are being blocked. And this energy reading, it's appearance, matches the start of the problems with contacting the colony." Not only the colony, but the ships, vessels strong enough to deal with anything the local pirates would be able to throw at them. "We need to kick this up the chain."

"Are you telling me my job, Lieutenant?" Cold and crisp, the words slashed with a knife's edge.

"No sir, merely making a suggestion."

He grunted, straightened up and stalked across the room toward the Sergeant.

Hell's Own

Damn man, the vast majority of the men and women she worked with, as well as those who claimed no gender or were gender fluid, were decent people. But the Captain, she'd be relieved when he cycled out and was sent to his next station.

"The Lieutenant is right, Captain. We're being blocked. Signals aren't going through no matter how much we boost them. It's like hitting a brick wall a klick deep." Middle-aged, calm and one of the longest to serve at Comms Alpha, Roberts didn't take nonsense from anyone. No matter the rank. "The energy readings are coming in from three points, if I didn't know better I'd say ships, but this is like nothing in the database."

"Nonsense."

"Captain, it's right there on my screen. We need to send this up the line." Roberts insisted.

Silence, save for the low hum and occasional chirp from the consoles. Sheila held her breath. Either the captain would accept Roberts' words, or--

"Captain, if you don't inform command, then I will."

And there it was.

Grant turned on his heel and stormed his way back to his station. "Do it and be damned, Roberts. I'll be placing you on report for insubordination."

"Yes, Captain."

Chapter Six

"Salla, get the hatch open," Duncan ordered. Getting to safety had to be the first order of business. Gathering their get out bags and everything else they would need hadn't been easy. Each new shake of the ground had sent them into hiding, grabbing shelter in a doorway or beneath a large table. Now they were running out of time.

Shapes moved beyond the door, the windows, strange outlines which didn't fit with anything he'd seen before. One walked on all fours, another on hind legs, with six limbs, distinct through the hazy window in the door. Invaders. The alert had been right. They were no longer alone on Pluto. He swallowed. Hard. His daughter. She'd survive. No matter what happened, she'd make it.

"Dad?"

"Get it open and get down, away from here. You know where to go."

"I'm not leaving you."

"Yes, you are. I've trained you, raised you, and you know the rules mean you have to follow my commands if we're in an emergency situation. I think this counts." One of the shapes, the one with six limbs, turned toward their home. He shut down the comm, refusing to allow his daughter access to him, at least in one way. Salla. She'd live, she'd make it, no matter what it did to him. The risks. He knew them, understood them, and would never allow them to prevent what must be done. He blinked back a haze, refusing to acknowledge the liquid as tears.

The shape paused outside of the door, head tipped to the left.

Nails, claws, whatever it was, the sharp edges scraped over the door.

The enemy.

He didn't think, he reacted. With a cry of rage, he grabbed

the shotgun he kept close to the door, hidden behind a sliding panel. He had it out in a split second, raked the weapon, and took position between the door and his daughter.

"Dad, don't do this."

"I know what I'm doing. Get out of here. Go. Now." One of them would make it.

Salla. As long as she lived, he wouldn't be forgotten.

The door shattered, plasti coated shards sliced through the air. Shards struck him, digging into his suit. Pieces shredded through the covering. The inbuilt alarm rang out, warning him of the loss of integrity. Loss of air, and the limited warmth it offered. Damn suit, he'd been told it was close to military grade. Damn traders had sold him a dud. Hah, served the scum right of their own suits ceased to do its job.

Darkness, living darkness with a glimmering layer above the skin. A suit? Or a natural occurrence? It didn't matter. Not at this moment. "Get out of my store," he growled, widening his stance. Behind him, he heard it. The trapdoor opening. Salla obeyed him. No matter what she wanted, or how afraid she was, she continued to follow him. Pride rushed through him, claimed him as his fingers tightened on the trigger as the creature approached.

No weapons.

No, it held a rifle or a weapon that looked like one, if you ignored the jagged design, the glistening material, and the dangerous hands holding it. Hands with eight fingers, digits, whatever. Long claws tipped each one, a deep red, almost black in color until the light caught it.

It hissed. Teeth, fangs, a long split tongue. Eyes, four of them. No nose above the dripping maw. Not human.

Alien.

The enemy.

And it wasn't getting his daughter.

With a scream of rage, he charged, pulling the trigger as he moved, knowing it would be the last thing he ever did.

*****

Stone scowled and turned away, refusing to stare at the pile of rubble. She'd return or she wouldn't, either way, watching wouldn't make it happen any faster. Blasted Marines, for all he knew she'd found one of the new arrivals to start a fight with. Wasn't that how they reacted? How the military worked when they didn't have an officer or senior NCO around to keep them under control.

"She'll be back," one of the men spoke up.

"Yeah, you can't knock the Sarg down, she always comes back up throwing punches and taking names." The youngest of the Marines grinned. What was his name again? Walker?

"Better hope she doesn't start throwing punches." Stone pinned the man with a glare. "A fight draws attention, and we don't need eyes on us. Not until we know what's happened."

"The man's right," said Gunny. "We have to get to the bottom of what's going on. Who's behind the attack. How many are injured."

"Never thought I'd see the day when I'd agree with you, Gunny. Or any other member of the military, but yeah. We need information before we move." Stone rolled out his shoulders and rubbed the back of his neck. This wasn't a time or place to pick an argument, but talking helped him, it gave him something to do, even if it wasn't productive. "If she starts a fight, we're dead, or captured."

"Lawbook wouldn't give us up. She'd die first." The youngest protested. What was his name? Walker? "She's tough. She'd bite off her own tongue before she gave us up."

"No, she wouldn't." Gunny reached out and slapped the back of Walker's head. "Dumbass. She'd die fighting, lie, cheat, escape, and find a way of getting word to us."

Stone rolled his eyes. Military. She was a woman on her own. Didn't matter how tough they believed her to be, she was human, female, and had weaknesses, like every other woman out there.

Fine, every human being. Women had a few extra issues, but he'd seen enough of them to know they could be equally as deadly in a fight as a man. And this one had been trained, survived long enough in the Marines to gain a decent rank. If she returned, he'd give her the benefit of the doubt. Marines, from what he knew, didn't hand out rank to keep up numbers.

You earned the rank.

Nothing but the heavy sound of breathing as they recovered from shifting the often heavy pieces around. If they'd been outside, beyond the artificial gravity maintained through the passageways and structures on Pluto, it wouldn't have been as difficult to clear the space.

Couldn't have everything.

A soft scraping noise drew his attention back to the hole as a small pebble skittered down the pile of rubble. One hand, then another, glove-covered, appeared before Lawbook crawled into view. She edged her way down from the opening and brushed herself off as she walked down to the Gunny. "We have a problem." Her voice calm and clear.

"Another?" The older man replied.

"The invasion, they've got boots on the ground, and they're not what we expected." Stone waited, his gaze flicking back and forth to the gap, the hole the Sergeant had wriggled through. Was she safe? Where there other survivors? Information, he needed the same information the Gunny now waited for. Only then would he have a chance to make his way to his ship and get out before it was too late.

Unless it already was.

Invasion. He frowned, taking in her words. She wasn't talking about a hit from pirates or mercs out of control, but a military presence.

He shifted his weight, gaze drawn back to the gap, eyes narrowed. Hands first, then a face as she appeared and carefully made her way down. No one spoke, no one moved, but he didn't have to check in order to know she was the center of everyone's attention.

"We have a problem, Gunny." Bloodlaw dusted herself off. "Yes, it's a full attack, but it's not the real issue." She took a deep breath, pausing to put her words in order.

The Gunny didn't press, giving the woman time to continue.

"The attackers aren't human."

Indrawn breaths, low exclamations, and a shuffle of feet followed her announcement.

"Describe what you saw," said Gunny. "Don't leave anything out."

"Only counted three, but there have to be more. Two walked on all four limbs, one of them pulling a large box-like cell, containing captives. Living ones from the movement inside. I couldn't see clearly enough to know the status of the people in the cell. Luckily the power was still on in places, enough to provide light. The third had six limbs, walked on the back two, had a weapon. This one I got a closer look at. Head was weird, and it appeared as if it was wearing a type of environmental suit. Its head," she paused and ran the tip of her tongue over her bottom lip, "appeared to be like something I've seen in old books. A crocodile. By the shape. But with prominent fangs."

"You're joking, Sarg, right? Come on, you're kidding with us."

"Wish I was, Walker. Damn, I wish I was. Always wanted to be involved in first contact, but not like this." Her face grim, despite the clear mask providing her with much-needed oxygen. "Dome is compromised, very little oxygen, far less than we have here. Lot of destruction. Buildings hit, if there were fires, they've gone out through lack of fuel. I didn't venture into the colony, only took in what I could see from the entrance, but it was more than enough to understand how bad the situation is."

Stone tried to focus on the rest of the words, knowing he needed as much intelligence as the woman could provide, but his mind raced. Aliens. God damn freaking aliens. Humans he could deal with, buy them off, a bribe to the right person, but this? How did you deal with aliens? Did they speak a language he'd be able to understand? What did they want with the captives they'd taken?

"Always believed aliens would be like us." One of the Marines murmured.

"Think we all did. Arrogant assumption, but no one ever said humans were smart," the Gunny replied.

"So, now what?" Walker asked.

"Recon, help the survivors, and get word back home," said Gunny.

"They need to know what happened out here," Lawbook added, her pale grey gaze swept over the group. "Doesn't matter what happens to us, if Earth is alerted they might have a chance. We've no idea about the weapons these creatures are using, what they want, only that they've hit the base and have taken prisoners."

"Well, shit," Stone muttered.

"No arguments from me," Lawbook agreed.

"Check your gear, everyone. I need exact numbers of weapons, what equipment we have, food, water, oxygen, everything. Lawbook, with me. Corporal, you're in charge of getting our equipment list." The Gunny gestured for the woman to follow him down the passageway, away from the rest of the group.

Stone's eyes narrowed as he watched the two talk in low tones. He didn't wait for the Corporal, jaw set he followed the couple, stopping only when the Gunny turned a cold gaze on him.

"Yes?"

"You'll need my assistance."

"What makes you believe we need you?" The older man arched an eyebrow.

"Because I know more about the ins and outs of the colony, ways around checkpoints. Passageways which were built after the mapping was completed, and bolt holes we might be able to use."

How much could he risk telling them? "And supply dumps built up by those who prefer to keep such things hidden away from the prying eyes of the military. I don't know all of them, no one does, but enough to perhaps tip the odds in our favor." Some of the equipment he'd need if he was going to get out of here. "If the shuttles and navy craft are gone, damaged, destroyed, whatever, then you'll need another way off world."

"And you know of one?" Lawblood's lips curled into a cynical smile.

"I do."

"Might be useful for the civilians." The Gunny inclined his head.

"Only the civies?" A cold hand wrapped around Stone's heart.

"We get them out, odds are most of us won't make it off world. Not if the navy ship is gone. But you and the civies are another matter."

"If they aren't already all rounded up in those cages." Stone met and held the older man's gaze.

"We'll get as many of them out as we can."

How big did they think his ship was? A fricking cruiser? He couldn't fit everyone in his ship, and if it was the only one they could get to, people would be left behind. Not his problem. He wasn't in the business of rescuing people. Not unless there was money in it for him. "And then?"

"We do what Marines are supposed to do. We provide cover for the escape and take out as many of the bastards as we can."

Chapter Seven

Cora paused and waited at the closed door, allowing the others in the team to ready themselves. Despite the usual eagerness, she had come to expect from the men she worked with, this time they were silent. Fear and doubt clung to Walker, any desire to make a name for himself now squashed with the knowledge of what waited for them on the other side of the door.

She didn't blame him.

As for the others, they cast the occasional glance in the direction of the door but said nothing. She didn't have to be a mind reader to know the doubts they dealt with, nor could she blame them. Facing aliens, with unknown tech and weaponry wasn't her idea of fun, but it had to be done. They owed their service and loyalty to those who called the colony home.

If she took the time to think about it, she'd acknowledge the fear whispering in the back of her mind, but there were other things to focus on. The route to the barracks. The equipment they needed. The people she'd seen in the cage. No, she wasn't going to think about the aliens. Or what they wanted with the captive humans. Cora closed her eyes, focused on her breathing, and counted to twenty before she risked opening them again.

She glanced back at the rest of the group. Down by one as Jackson, one of the men who'd been in the bar, but hadn't joined the rest of the Marines at their table, had been sent to the bolt hole to let Jones and his group know what was going on. With aliens in the mix, neither Cora or Gunny could be confident if the comms, including the secured channels, were safe to use. Jackson's equipment had been shared among the others, the oxygen packs refilled from the larger tank. A tank which they would leave behind. They couldn't allow themselves to be burdened once they were beyond the door.

Aliens. Blasted aliens. Not remotely human. She swallowed down a lump from her throat. Fear had its place, as long as she didn't allow herself to become paralyzed by it. She'd been through training, had clawed her way to her stripes over the last fifteen years, and had no intention of freezing, putting her people at risk.

"Ready?" Cora asked.

"Yes, check for targets," Gunny replied.

She inclined her head and turned her attention to the door. As she had the first time, she pressed one ear against the metal, straining to hear. Distant, muffled sounds. The rumble of a small explosion in the distance. Not big enough to cause more damage to the tunnel, but she had no desire to wait around and be crushed if the enemy decided to blow up the rest of the colony. Cora held up a hand to indicate they needed to stop and continued to listen.

The noise faded, and she waited until she heard nothing, only then did she pull the door open and peer through the crack. Her muscles tensed, adrenaline rushing through her body as she took the time to search the area for any sign of the aliens.

Nothing.

She tugged the door open and slipped out, leaving it open wide enough for the others to follow as she crouched low, sidearm in her right hand, and ran to the nearest set of rubble. Cora dropped down on one knee scanning the area, weapon ready. One by one the others joined her, Gunny the last to make the crossing, Stone in the middle of the group, along with Walker.

Her gaze flickered to Stone, then away.

Dangerous man, one they would typically be watching as a potential problem, a suspected smuggler and merc. No, more than suspected. He'd admitted it. Spoken of the caches and contacts. Her fingers tightened around the grip of her sidearm, then relaxed. They'd use him, but it didn't mean they'd trust him. She certainly didn't. He'd turn on them the first chance he had. Not to be trusted no matter what he said.

A detail she wouldn't forget.

*****

"Move. Don't slow down. We have to keep moving no matter what we hear. Or what happens behind us. We need to make it to the tunnels."

Jakob didn't turn, didn't look back at the one calling out. Ground floor, the escape hatches were here. He knew where at least two of them lay.

Walls trembled, dust and debris filled the atmosphere, or what remained. He brushed his face mask clear, needing to see where they were going, what dangers lay ahead of them. And Gail. He wasn't going to let go of Gail. His hand tightened on her arm, but she didn't complain.

"They're coming in!"

Who?

It didn't matter. Once he was safe, he could find out, ask the questions he didn't have the time to ask now.

Gail pulled back out of his grasp. "Wait, I see someone. It's Pippa."

Pippa? He frowned, allowing himself to turn and see what was happening. A girl, four, maybe five, wailed as she sat on the floor, knees hugged to her chest as she wept. Her suit in place, protecting her for now. He wanted to yell at Gail to come back, but the woman wouldn't listen. He knew without trying, she would continue to try and help Pippa. Gail reached the child first. In one smooth move, she scooped her up, and hugged Pippa to her chest, one hand cupping the back of the girl's head.

He knew the girl, had seen her before, but the where evaded him.

"Gail, come on, we're running out of time."

"What are they?" A strangers voice across the comm. One of the men with the survivors. A man without a name or face as they hurried toward the escape hatches.

"Aliens." Another voice, a woman's.

Aliens? What were they talking about? The dome had cracked. Had there been a gas leak or contamination from the broken dome which triggered hallucinations?

"Move, we can't stay here." Gail hurried to join them, Pippa clenched to her body.

Invaders. He couldn't believe real invaders now caused havoc in the colony, but what else could have caused the dome to shatter? If they destroyed all of it. Maybe it was cracked? But by what? An explosion? Mining? Terrorists? He moved, feet taking him away from the source of the danger. Hard and fast a hand slammed against the small of his back. He half stumbled, left leg giving out beneath him before he was grabbed by the upper arms and tugged him back to his feet.

Not one, but two. A man and a woman he knew but couldn't put a name to them.

"Don't stop. No matter what you hear, what happens, you don't stop." The man instructed. "Keep moving, keep going."

He nodded, mouth dry, heart racing. He swallowed and didn't pause. Feet slapping against the ground.

In front of him, a woman opened the hatch, waving for people to go down the ladder. They were going to make it. They'd get out of here, then they'd be able to find out what was going on.

A scream.

Gail.

He turned, eyes wide as he searched for her. She'd been with him only a moment before.

"Don't stop. You can't save her."

He darted toward the last place he'd seen Gail, but the grips on his arms returned as he was turned and forced back toward the trapdoor. He screamed and struggled, fighting against the hold. "I can't leave her. I have to help. Let me go. Please. Let me go." Jakob kicked and fought, desperate to escape, to find her, to grab Gail and Pippa. This wasn't right. He could help. He had to find her.

"It's too late."

Hell's Own

A movement. Tall, winged. Monstrous. Not human. Not alone. A scream caught in the back of his throat. Panic seized his limbs, locking him in place as the two grips lifted and hauled him toward the ladder. Aliens. Not real. Couldn't be real.

"Get to safety, if she's still alive, she'll find you in the shelters." The woman holding him explained as she released her grasp. The man didn't let him go until he had one foot on the ladder. "You have to survive."

Gail. Pippa. He tried to climb back up, but the man stood in his way. "Don't put yourself at risk. It'll only add more captives or dead to the numbers. Go, before I send you down the hard way."

Heart torn in two Jakob began his climb down into the darkness, away from the cries, screams, and pleas for help. Only when he was halfway down did he realize his face was wet.

Stone followed the group, scanning the area as he ran, half crouched to the protected area Lawbook had chosen. Light fell in small pools, but the full illumination he'd become used no longer existed. Power sources, a few appeared to still be online, others no longer worked. He frowned, it was to be expected with the devastation which greeted them. Few buildings, in this area, remained untouched. In the distance movement, the suggestion of an attack still in progress toward the center of the colony. But around their current location, scorch marks decorated the half-destroyed walls, blast marks, the distinctive rubble which came from explosions. But on first glance, something was missing.

He closed his eyes and replayed the last time he'd been in the dome. Realization struck as he opened his eyes and double checked what lay in front of him. "Where are the bodies?" He kept his voice low. "There should be bodies with this level of damage to the buildings. But I don't see any."

The Gunny joined them and frowned. "I see your point. There should be bodies everywhere. Wounded, dead, survivor signs.

Nothing. Doesn't make sense."

"I didn't have the chance to take it in when I checked the area out. Damn. Maybe they were engaged in a running firefight? Or the bodies could have been removed, pulled elsewhere."

"Why would they move them?" Stone pressed.

"No damn idea. They're aliens. We don't know why they're here, what they're doing or if we can communicate with them." Lawbook shifted her weight and edged back from the wall, stepping into the extra cover created by the shadows. "We could be anything from a food source, to fuel, to fertilizer. We don't have enough information to work it out yet."

Information, the one currency you never had enough of, no matter what was going on, or who you were dealing with.

"We need to find out as much as we can. Earth will need the data in case these creatures decide to hit home," said Gunny, his voice steady despite his words. "And my gut tells me they're going to head for earth. We can't allow them to be hit without warning, or assume Comms got the word out before they were destroyed."

"Destroyed?"

"Only thing that makes sense. It had to have been hit, or the entire base would have been warned. Full details of the situation. No, however this happened, it was fast. Too fast to get things into place. Not so much as an alert sent to the military." Gunny turned his attention to their surroundings. "We're screwed, but only as long as we lack information. Our first order of business, other than reaching a supply dump or safe area, has to be gathering information to send to Earth."

"If we survive long enough to transmit the data." The Corporal muttered as he turned to brush one hand over the marks in the rubble. "Energy weapons. Couldn't tell you what type."

"We can't stay here, need to get moving." Gunny gestured to the back of the crumpled building. "Lawbook, check we're in the clear."

"Yes, Gunny." She turned and edged her way through the

building, sidearm in her right hand.

He didn't envy the woman or the rest of the Marines. Not with the Gunny in charge. Better than Lawbook, she'd have something to prove being the only woman in the group. Still, they were walking dead men. Not his problem. He tried to shut out the idea, but the worry continued to niggle away in the back of his mind. Did choosing to go with Gunny mean he'd end up yet another name in the list of the dead? Hell no, not if he had anything to do about it. At least one man had to escape this mess, live to tell the tale. Maybe come out a hero.

No, heroes were too well known for his tastes.

"We're clear, Gunny."

Cora leaned against the wall before taking the chance to peer out. She didn't linger, risking only a quick glance, then pulled back, her eyes closing as she went over the information. No sign of the creatures, or anything else. Nothing living or dead. Where the hell were the bodies? Now Stone had brought up the issue, she couldn't help but see the lack everywhere. She risked a second glance, following the same pattern.

Nothing.

"We're clear, Gunny."

She felt, more than heard the rest of the group move through the rubble. She waited long enough to know there was someone behind her, ready to cover her if the need arose. Cora ran, keeping low to the ground, gaze sweeping the area before she made it to the next round of cover. Two minutes later, the rest were with her. "Which way?"

The Gunny pulled out a datapad. "This should be living quarters for two families, here." He tapped the display. "Left, two blocks. Then right three."

Blocks. Sure, she could figure out blocks if the damage hadn't leveled everything, and blocked off walkways. "It's a mess. Like leaving a city and coming back to a pile of kids bricks scattered where the buildings should be. All we're missing are the bright, primary colors."

Walker snorted, the sound turning into a giggle before Gunny smacked Walker across the back of the head.

"I remember those things. My niece has a set. Or did, the last time I saw her." Lackey flashed a grin. "Hurt like hell if you step on them barefooted."

Tension eased from her shoulders. "I'll check to see what we're facing for the next leg." Her gaze found the Gunny's before she met Stone's. "You, with me. Keep close."

The man scowled but nodded his agreement. Good, she didn't need an argument. Not until they were safe. She clambered through the rubble and rested on the far side. One wall stood, or the remains of it, no more than two meters up, and seven across. A support beam propped up the second floor or would have done if it hadn't been reduced to a handful of reinforced plastiboards. A small pink and blue toy horse hung from one of the beams, its long silver-blue mane caught on a ragged board.

Children.

Her gut tightened and rolled.

What did they do to the kids?

Dead, or taken captive?

She forced herself to turn away from the toy. How many people had been taken, or were dead? Men, women, and children. God, the kids. Grief, she didn't have the time for it now. She shoved the emotion into a box, locked it, and mentally buried it under six feet of fastcrete.

"Sergeant?"

Cora forced her features into a cold mask before she risked a reply. "Give me a minute, need to make sure we're safe." Not entirely a lie, but the man didn't need to crawl around through her mind, and she wasn't going to open the door for him.

She dropped down onto her belly and crawled forward on her

elbows enough to peer around the corner. Left, then right, left again.

Movement.

A shape.

A survivor? They'd been kept safe because of where they'd been when the attack had hit but was it possible for others to have found their way into the shelters and tunnels? If so, could this be one of the colonists searching for other survivors?

Hope surged and died in the same heartbeat.

Human's didn't have wings.

He followed the woman, keeping close and dropped to one knee as she moved belly crawled into position. Stone didn't stop himself when the urge struck him to look over the woman's body. He was human. Male. And she was attractive, but definitely off limits. The woman had a weapon, knew how to use it, and Lawbook wasn't the type to let unwanted contact go unanswered. Stone smiled. He could respect a woman who didn't allow other's to walk over them.

She tensed, and he followed her gaze, eyes narrowed. A shape. Human? It was on two feet, but that didn't mean they'd found a survivor. If they tracked down another fighter, there might be new information they could use against the enemy. Or at least details about survivors, ships and weapons.

The figure took a step into a pool of light, vanishing a moment later when it moved into the darkness once more. His heart threatened to climb out of his chest. A band tightened around his ribs. Warmth drained from his body, and he pressed his lips into a tight, thin line to keep from making a sound.

Wings.

Black wings glinted as they lay folded against the creature's back.

He closed his eyes, but he could still see the alien. The image imprinted in his mind. Tall, slender-bodied, over two meters tall, the body closer to a squat triangle, its head attached to the highest point of the *triangle.* The word didn't fit the shape of the alien, but it was the only thing his mind was willing to offer him. Geometrical shapes, instead of the softer forms he'd come to expect in living beings. Harsh lines instead of gentle curves, or well-rounded muscle. The wings. Not reptilian or feathered but there'd been an odd glint to the folded shapes against the alien's back. A glimmer. Colors. Scales? On wings? Every depiction he'd seen of winged creatures had been either the delicate membranes insects used, or the thin skin stretched between the finger-like structures within a bat's wings. Feather, he'd have accepted feathers as standard, more than enough birds existed on Earth.

But scales?

The more he learned, the harder the blow from reality struck his gut.

Aliens.

Freaking aliens. With wings. Had anyone mentioned the wings?

His fingers trembled.

No, he wasn't going to lose it, but damn. Wings.

Jakob trembled as he stumbled down the tunnels, one man behind him, teenagers in front of him, but no sign of Gail. The hatch closed. Secured. It wasn't what he'd expected. Gail. She should be with him and Pippa. He had to get to them, but the hatch had closed before she'd had the chance to join them.

Anger bubbled into life. Hands clenched as he glared at those around him. Nothing changed. The trapdoor remained locked above them. He closed his eyes and turned away. She didn't deserve to be locked out. Nor did the others. They were friends, family, people he'd grown up with. People he should have helped. But he didn't stop. None of them did.

Hell's Own

"The attacks are still going on, mostly toward the center of the colony. A few signals, broken though. Scans say they're running blocking tech, preventing messages from getting out. If we're close enough to the signal, then we hear it, but anything else is nothing but static." A male voice, calm and confident despite the situation.

Hoods down, masks off, they saved what they had left of their back up oxygen. He frowned as he glared at the speaker. A teen like him. One he knew from school. He tried to put names to faces, but his mind refused to obey him, half lost in the shock of what they'd all been through. Simon? Frank? No, those names didn't fit the face. He swiped his hands down his legs then shook them out. "What about the others? We left a lot of people behind. We have to wait for them."

"They'll either join us through one of the other hatches, or they're lost. We can't risk being snatched up by those things, not when we don't know what they're doing with the captives, or if they're killing anyone they get their hands on."

"No," he said, steps faltering. Claws, he'd seen a flash of long, claw-like appendages, hadn't he? "We can't leave them behind. It's wrong. They're people, like us. We have to be able to get to them, to help them. They're dying. A second longer and it could have been you, me, any one of us on the wrong side of the door. Now you expect us to wait as they kill everyone we've ever known or loved?"

"Are they? We don't know that. We haven't seen anyone killed yet."

"What else do you think is happening?" A new voice, a woman's. One from the stairs.

"I don't know."

His heart sank at the answer.

"None of us do. But we will. We'll find out." The male continued.

Doors opened and closed behind them. Sealed, locked. No way of others behind able to follow them. They'd be dead. Or prisoners. Same thing when they didn't know what was going on. Men, women, children. All lost. No going back.

"We've got to get I contact with other survivors. We can't be the only ones." Jakob forced himself to think clearly, to go over their options, however slim they might be. But what if they were the only ones left? If the aliens had already captured or killed the rest of the colony and only this small group remained? He didn't voice his concern, he didn't have to, he saw it reflected in the faces all around him, but no one expressed the doubt.

Not this time.

Chapter Eight

Cora didn't move, she didn't dare, not with the all too close presence of the alien. She forced her breathing to remain normal, slow, in through the mouth, and out through the nose. Her mask silenced the sound of breathing, but the cold seeped its way past the thin layers of cloth and protective gear. The emergency suits weren't designed for heavy use, it wouldn't tear easily, but it could be cut. Not a risk any of them could take.

Wings. Okay, after everything else she'd seen she could accept a weird ass monster alien with its odd body and the way it walked. Graceful and ugly all rolled into one. She didn't need this, any of this. All she'd wanted was one night in the bar, relaxing and shit talking before she caught up with work, sorted through papers, reports, and any personal messages. Not this.

A small noise drew her attention and allowed herself a brief glimpse at the merc before she turned away.

Paler than he had been, through the mask shielded his features, it did nothing to mask the color. When you first had alien life thrown in your face, it was bound to have an effect on you. He reached out, fingers brushing her arm. She shifted enough to meet his gaze and still be able to watch for problems, then arched an eyebrow.

"You saw that?" His voice carried through the comm channel, a tremble in the words.

"Yes."

"Fuck."

"Not in the mood, but thanks." She turned away, searching for sins of the aliens. How many had landed? Three ships involved in the attack but they knew nothing more. Size? Weapons? Reason for the attack? Cora tried to focus on one thing at a time, but it didn't come easily. She'd seen weapons in the grasp of both of the aliens who'd walked on hind legs. Were there other aliens? She'd seen three types so far. How had they reached the colony? Dropships? Shuttles? Or however, they'd made their way into the territory. Unless they had a means of transporting their people without ships? Who knew exactly what they were capable of doing?

Stone laughed, the sound muffled, barely audible despite the comm. "I like your sense of humor, Sergeant."

"Can't say the same about yours." Was the damn man flirting? If he believed this was time to hook up and bonk like bunnies, he was insane.

"Yeah, well I'm used to being on my own." He edged closer to her position. "What do you think about them?" His head almost touching hers.

"Not human. Anything else I don't have enough information to be able to give you an answer." What did he think, she could take a peek at something and know it all? She wasn't a wet behind the ears second lieutenant.

"Sorry, didn't think. Not like me. Guess this is getting to me, the idea of aliens invading." He shook his head and eased back from her, moving near silently. Only the occasional shifting of rubble beneath his feet gaze away what he was doing.

Cora ignored him. The aliens. It didn't matter if she remained still or not, they were still out there, and the chill now seeped into her skin, down to the muscle beneath. Soon enough, it would enter her bones. They'd all face the same issue. These were emergency suits, not designed for long term use in zero atmosphere situations even if they were military grade. If they used them for too long, without being able to step into sealed units and refresh both their oxygen requirements and warm up, the cold would become too much for them, and hypothermia would set in.

A change in equipment. Refresh the oxygen. Build other supplies. And go over what they knew, information wise. Then move. Get to a place where they could restock, find better environmental suits, or at this point full military suit. With all of the added extras which went with their issued gear. Her jaw clenched. Did any of the hidden caches the merc had mentioned, contain stolen suits? This one time, she'd let the owner off with a warning, if they were still around or alive.

"What are they doing with the bodies?" Her grip tightened and relaxed around the hilt of her sidearm. "It doesn't make sense." She was missing something here. Hell, she was missing a lot, but the lack of bodies or survivors played on her mind.

"Experiments." Gunny settled down behind her. "Food. Fuel. Information. Could be any of the four or for a reason we haven't come up with yet. They're aliens. We can't think of them as human, with the same drive and desires as us. Treat everything as new, unknown, watch, learn, report. It's about all we can do at this point."

"And stay alive." She closed her eyes, then blinked back the unwanted emotions. She'd have time to react when they were safe. Or she wouldn't live long enough to deal with the mental fall out. Either was fine by her as long as the information reached the Unified Terran government.

"Goes without saying, Lawbook."

Silence settled over the group, with only the occasional shuffle of weight, changing location or position to prevent muscles from cramping, but still, they waited. Three more sets of aliens appeared and disappeared in and out of the remains of the colony.

Her limbs ached, head pounded, and she knew she wasn't the only one. With the suits, how the oxygen was recycled as much as the rescue suits allowed, they were all suffering. "We can't stay here much longer." Her mouth protested the sudden need to work, dry, the familiar pull between tissues as the gummy sensation was brought under control.

The Gunny grunted.

Cora opened up her comm, after holding up one finger and pointing to the implant, and listened. If there was anything out there. A survivor, beacon, military alert, anything at all, she'd hear it unless it came from off planet, as long as they weren't out of orbit she had a chance to listen to them. In silence, she moved through the channels, listening to each one for five minutes before she moved to the next. In a perfect situation, she'd have listened for fifteen to twenty minutes, but they didn't have enough time. By channel seven, frustration set in, but she continued to watch the time as she listened.

Nothing.

A planet load of nothing, piled on top of her shoulders.

She moved to change the channel.

"--survivors?" Male voice, young, trembling, and only one damn word.

She gestured at Gunny, then pointed to the comm and held up seven fingers.

The older man nodded and tapped his own implant.

Cora waited. Had she misheard? Imagined it? No, she was too focused on the situation to have allowed her imagination to stray.

"Pleas----we n--d help. Survivors..." static swamped the words.

Gunny caught her attention and indicated she should reply.

"This is Sergeant Cora Bloodlaw, do you copy?"

A crackle. Silence. Crackle. "Repeat please." Hope filtered through the words.

"Sergeant Cora Bloodlaw, Marines. Do you copy?"

"Thank the stars." The young man gasped. "Thought we were all alone here."

"Where are you? We're from the colony, you can stick to local names, not the formal." Most of the busy places in the colony had gained nicknames, which people used instead of the assigned name. "We're no longer on our own here."

"S-- them." Crackles flared up and settled once more. "Under the rooster. Three down."

Three floors down. "Bolt hole?"

"Yes, s--led. Safe."

The Rooster. She closed her eyes, letting her mind bring up the layout of the colony. "We'll be there in under an hour unless we run into problems. Don't broadcast but listen for us. Bloodlaw out."

"We'll need supplies before we reach the Rooster," said Gunny.

"Figured that one out. We might be able to hit one of the dumps along the way, but it's going to be tight."

"Just the way we like it." The older man flashed a grin, mischief dancing in his chocolate eyes. "Time to get moving."

"We have contact."

Jakob took a deep breath at the news. Marines. People who knew what they were doing. He could think, take a breath, calm himself down. No matter what else happened, they were no longer alone. Hope. A slender thread, but it was one he could cling to. "Once they get to us we'll be safe, right?"

"No idea." One of the women leaned back against a wall. "We might be. We could be in a worse mess if those things listen in. They might be able to trace the signal and find us."

"Which is why we're not going to open communications again. We listen, send nothing unless we're told its safe. It's the only way we can have a chance to remain hidden."

A door on the far side of the chamber opened up, a woman, too older to be in school, but a face he recognized. Hope surged to life as he pushed himself to move. "Salla?"

"Jakob?" Relief chased the worry from her features. "God, I didn't know who else would make it down here. I didn't see anyone on the way down, not since I left the shop. It's chaos up there."

Salla, which meant Duncan would be with her. He peered behind Salla, but of the older man didn't appear. "Where's your dad?"

Her jaw set. "Gone. They took him. I couldn't stop them. He wouldn't let me. Told me to go. Made me leave him."

"Not dead?"

"He was alive when they pulled him out of the store." Emotions vanished, her face a mask. "Don't know what else they've done, or if his suit is in one piece. I don't have enough information to say if he's alive or dead. But if he's dead, I hope it was quick."

"God. I'm sorry." How many more were either dead or in the hands, claws, tentacles, whatever, of the aliens? "I don't know how many we've lost. Or will lose." The entire colony? Everyone he knew and loved? "They attacked without warning."

"Yeah, I guess, or we'd have been warned." Salla looked back over her shoulder at the closed door. Sealed, protecting them against anyone else entering unless they had the right codes, or had someone with them who knew how to get them to work. "Your parents?"

"No idea, they weren't with us tonight. Should have been but you know how things work." Or had worked. If his parents were alive, they'd find their way into the tunnels. Either here or elsewhere in the colony. Safe rooms, bunkers, the rest of the options, there had to be others who would be huddled in their own shelters, unable to let people know where they had fled to. If Duncan hadn't escaped, hadn't made it to the tunnels in time, how could his parents have a chance. They were soft. Not weak, but not fighters. Educated, scientists but not soldiers.

Nor was he.

Real, the aliens were real. No matter how he tried to push past the revelation, he couldn't turn his thoughts away from the glimpses he'd caught of the enemy. He didn't move, but at least his heart no longer pounded against his ribs with the fanatical beat of a man trying to escape death.

He half listened to the conversation or the Marine's end of it. Lawbook was Bloodlaw, alright, he could adapt. Nicknames were commonplace with the military or had been from his dealings with them. But the Rooster? Which building did they mean? He frowned, trying to remember the layout of the colony, the buildings. Why call one a rooster? Unless... the crest. One structure had a ridge, or close to it, the school. It made sense, as much as anything else did in the middle of a damned alien invasion.

Who would be among the survivors? Children, teenagers, maybe a few teachers. Not fighters. The odds of there being anyone else from the military in the shelter were slim at best. They needed others who could fight alongside them, not kids they'd have to protect and damn civilian teachers. If they were lucky, one or two might know how to use a weapon, but he wasn't holding out hope. He rubbed his hands, fingers cold enough he was beginning to lose feeling in them.

"If we don't resupply, we'll be looking at frostbite and slowing down to the point we won't stand a chance. Our bodies won't take the exposure to lower temperatures for much longer. But I know where there are supplies." He leaned down in the rubble and sketched out a path. Using pieces of plastiboard to mark outbuildings. "It's a ten-minute walk, under normal circumstances. If we're lucky, we can be there in twenty, maybe thirty." Destroyed buildings, the lack of proper suits, and the aliens all combined into potentially dangerous delays.

The Gunny and Lawbook drew close, studying the makeshift map between them.

"Doable. If there are full suits in storage, it will help. If not, extra layers. Pressurized gloves and boots will keep the extremities going, and we'll have a chance to warm up," said Gunny.

"From the supply dump to the Rooster is a short run. We'll need to alert the kids once we're in place, so they don't panic due to the delay of us pausing to collect what we need, but other than that, it should work." She tapped the rock, indicating the supply dump, then moved three buildings over and touched one finger there. "Gunny, isn't this where you live?"

He peered in. "Yes, and if it's **still standing**, there are a few backup pieces we can collect, but we hit Stone's supplies first. I know I have two combat-ready suits stashed away."

What else did the Gunny have at his place? His armored suit? If that's what he meant by combat ready, it gave them a slight edge. At least one man would have the armor needed to face these things. "Time we moved then. I don't think we've seen any sign of the aliens in what, twenty minutes? Thirty?"

"Sounds about right." Gunny turned to take in the rest of the group. "You heard the man, we're heading out. You have one minute to check your gear and--"

The rumble hit without warning. Stone flung out one gloved hand to grab the nearest wall. Boards creaked and cracked. Dust danced along the ground as more than one man threw himself into a corner or doorway. Anything they could use to keep the rubble from landing on them. Lawbook forced her body into a tight space which should have been a window, one which belonged on the second story but had been brought down to the ground floor in an earlier shake, or from the weapons, the aliens had used to breach the dome.

Crack.

The noise overhead forced him to look up. The remains of the second floor, what hadn't yet hit the ground, now shook and rattled above them. A large board, the last of the significant supports, shattered above them.

"Watch out!" He pushed himself away from the wall, half jumping, half diving through the opening they'd used to observe the aliens. The board and the walls it had held up, caved in on them. A cloud of dust and debris tossed into the 'air,' blocking out his view of the rest of the group as he did his best to protect his face and mask from damage. All he wanted to do was survive and get out of here.

Was it really too much to ask for?

"Gunny? Walker? Lackey?" Cora struggled free of the plastiboard, her bruised leg offering a running commentary on the pain levels, despite her attempts to ignore it. "Report."

"Here." One by one they answered, except for the merc, Stone, and the Gunny.

"Gunny?" She limped through the debris, searching for signs of the older man. Gunny had to be alive, safe, ready to fight. He was the Gunnery Sergeant. The man was a walking legend. "Answer me, Gunny. Don't make me dig your ass out of here, you'll never live it down." Here, he'd been around the last time she'd seen him. Stone could wait, she needed to get Gunny out to prevent the rest of the group from losing heart.

A groan followed the tumbling of rubble in the corner of the building. Movement meant life. Hope surged, and she grabbed the biggest piece of plastiboard and hauled it out of the way. More followed as the other men joined her, digging through the debris, pulling wires out of the way. Cloth, the remains of toys, bedding. It all joined the pile in the far corner. He had to be safe, alive, and ready to fight. Nothing else would be acceptable.

She yanked a wide piece of plaster and board away.

A human-shaped form. No, not just a shape. Gunny's unmoving body.

Her heart caught in her throat as she cleared the debris from his head. Closed eyes, dust coated mask which she cleaned off with a swipe of her hand. She reached down to his neck and pressed two fingers beneath his chin, watching for signs of life. It wouldn't be easy to feel the man's pulse with her gloves on, but it was better than nothing.

A faint movement beneath her fingers.

"We've got a pulse. All right, let's get this cleared off. Need to see if he's injured." His eyes moved, a flicker of lashes. Life. He was going to make it. Nothing else was allowed. She glanced at the men working with her. One was missing. She still worked, shifting, lifting, easing things out of the way as they dug the Gunny free. The missing man, her thoughts kept returning to him. Stone. Had something happened to him?

Her stomach rolled.

"Walker, where's Stone?" She didn't pause, her gloved hands wrapped around the largest piece of debris left.

"Who?"

"The civilian in the trench coat." How the hell he managed to justify wearing the trench coat over his suit was beyond her. Cora brushed the dust from Gunny's face. His eyes moved, a flicker of eyelashes. But not enough to ease her concerns. "We move him now, on three." She waited until the others were in place. "One. Two... Three." As one they lifted him up and away from the remains, shifting him onto a flat surface. "Who has a working med scanner to hand? We need to find out what's going on, injuries, internal and external. Won't be safe to move him until we know what type of damage we're dealing with."

"Here," said Lackey as he shoved the unit into her hand.

"Thanks. Stone, anyone got eyes on him?" She ran her fingers over the screen, waking it up before the information scrolled into sight.

"Wasn't he with you."

"No, he was close but not right by me." Her mind raced. Had he been blown out of the ruins? No, it hadn't been an explosion, the tremors had damaged the already crumbling structure. "Check outside."

"On it."

She didn't turn away from the screen. "He's alive, heartbeat is building back up. Blood pressure above normal, but within range if you take pain into account." She scowled, fingers tightening on the thin reader. "Bruised, battered, broken ribs." She flinched. The ribs could be a significant issue. "Lungs aren't compromised, but the suit is. Torn in places, but his mask is intact." The cold would build up faster with the tears in the suit. She moved the med scan over his body again and frowned. No, she wasn't seeing this. Maybe she was misinterpreting it the wrong way. She wasn't a medic, it wasn't in her training to patch things up beyond the basics of making a man stable before getting him to real medical care. "Shit, alright, we need to get him ready to move."

"Be easy if he was awake." Walker murmured.

"Yeah, I know." Moving the older man would prove interesting. "Gunny? Can you hear me?" She patted the side of his face, taking care not to damage the mask. No cracks in it, which was a blessing. You couldn't truly touch his face with the protection in place, but it was still the best chance she had. "Open your eyes, old man. I need you up and moving. Don't want to let the side down, or have these young 'uns think you fell asleep on the job." Her hand trembled as she tried to wake him again. "Hey, you don't wake up, you won't get the chance to kill one of those monsters, then you'll never hear the end of it."

His lips parted, a crack, then more as his eyes moved beneath the closed lids.

"Come on, almost there. Open up, you can't leave me on my own to keep this lot in order." She didn't need him, not in that way, she knew how to handle a team. But with Gunny it would be easier, she'd have a reliable man at her back she could trust to make a balanced decision. Hell, her training had never prepared her for an alien invasion.

He groaned the sound muffled through the mask, eyes open but unfocused.

"He's going to make it." Walker reached out and clapped her on the shoulder.

"We all are unless I decide to remove your hand, at the shoulder."

Walker pulled his hand back quickly enough she swore she could hear the pop of a vacuum.

"Must be in hell, no way he'd let you lot into heaven," Gunny groaned as he tried to lift his head. "Purgatory. Yeah, we could be stuck in the void, waiting for a decision to be made by whoever is in charge."

"Good to see you back with us." Relief washed over her, a chill seeping into her muscles now the immediate danger had passed. "I was beginning to wonder if you'd found a bar to hide out in and had left a clone as a replacement."

"Like I'd pull a shit move like that." The older man reached out his hand, blood bubbled on his lips.

Lung damage? No, she didn't want to think about the possibility as she took the offered hand, clasping his lower arm as she felt his fingers close around hers. "Hey, we have aliens here, who knows how you'd react to their presence. Personally, I'd hoped first contact would include sexy humanoid alien types, all oiled up and wearing little more than loin cloths. But no, we had to pick the monster aliens with crocodile heads and scaled wings."

"We're Marines, Sergeant. We never take things the easy way."

"Fair point."

"Maybe they keep the sexy ones away from the fighting?" Gunny coughed, his skin graying out around his lips. "For the parties. All dolled up in silk and stuff. Yeah, I can go with that idea. Once we deal with this mess, we'll have a celebration of our own, and see how they can dance."

"We can hope." He couldn't die. She needed his help, his experience to get them out of this.

"All a marine ever has at the end of the day is the hope he'll die in bed with a deliciously curved piece of sweet company."

"Alien company? Your telling me dancing aliens is on your bucket list?"

"Hey, didn't you ever hear about the old vids, the ones where the captain of the ship kissed and slept his way through a hundred alien babes? Well, if a captain can do it, why not a Gunny?"

She didn't argue.

Dust and debris clouded his vision. Blades of bitter cold stabbed through his chest and into the muscles in his thighs. His bones ached as he tried to move, joints creaking with the effort as he tried to get his eyes to work. Everything remained fuzzy, out of focus as he blinked. His mouth worked, but his brain refused to catch up with the orders to work. If he hadn't known better, he'd have sworn he'd woken up after a heavy night on the town, and sinking into the depths of a freshly cracked barrel of beer.

"Stone, you with us?"

Male. One of the Marines? He turned in the direction of the sound and tried to bring the image of the man into focus. His brain refused to latch onto the figure for more than a heartbeat. "Yeah, mostly."

"Wasn't sure where you'd got to but it looks like you half fell out of the doorway."

Stone forced his body to comply as he sat up. Pain rippled through his body, ribs crackled as he tried to stand, thighs ached, bones complained. His jaw clenched. The last thing he needed was to stumble in front of the marines. "Will take me a bit to get back up and moving fully. Took a tumble, but the suit is…" he paused as he ran his hands over the suit, "so much for that idea, two tears. Over my thighs." Explained the cold. How many other tears would he find? He could patch these two. He ran his fingers over his mask, checking for damage. One piece. The last thing he needed was to deal with a cracked mask. A hand grabbed him by the upper arm, helping him to his feet, and the two men returned to the scant shelter of the damaged home.

The others had gathered around a man. The Gunny. Voices low as concern hung in the air.

"Going to be hard work, with your cracked ribs. But we'll

manage. Not going to leave you behind, don't even suggest it."

"Not behind, but as a rear guard." The Gunny insisted. "You can't drag me half across the colony. We don't know what else you're going to be facing out here."

"No, you'll be in the center of the group, same as we'd do with an injured man." Lawbook insisted, her voice cold and lacking leeway. "We don't leave our people behind. Not you, not anyone."

Ah, there was a woman he could admire or at least respect. Hard-nosed, to the point, taking charge of the situation. Not one he'd encourage into his bed, but to fight alongside. Business partner, fighter, anything but sharing his bed. Not a chance. When it came to partners of the intimate nature, his preference ran to the softer curves, gentle eyes, and the need to please. One he didn't have to fight with to show who was in charge. Love them, leave them, move onto the next woman when he needed company. Nothing permanent, and Lawbook wasn't the type of woman you walked away from, not unless it was her choice.

He shook off the idea.

"I'm not an invalid."

"No, but you're injured. We'll do this by the book. No arguments. Until you're back on your feet, you follow orders." Her voice hardened. "Same as the rest of the team."

Gunny laughed, wincing as he did so. "You're one stubborn woman, Lawbook."

"And it's never going to change. Wouldn't be much of a Marine if I couldn't get a stubborn man see sense now, would I?" She patted the man on the shoulder, then turned away, her gaze catching Stone's. "Good to see you're still with us."

"Because you wouldn't get into the supply dump without me. No need to butter me up, Sergeant. I know where I stand." Useful only as long as they needed him, then he could be left at the wayside. Those were rules he could live with.

"You're under our care, same as any other civie we run into. And Marines don't leave people behind." She jerked her head back at the Gunny. "You heard me tell him the same thing, and I don't want to waste time getting into the same argument with you. Got it?"

"Yes, Sergeant." He inclined his head. Words, nothing but words. Actions proved what people meant, where they heart lay. Words could be spoken and never followed through on. "Whatever you say, Lawbook. No arguments from me." No, arguments wasted air. Once he had new equipment, he'd reevaluate traveling with the Marines. He didn't have to stay with them, and sooner or later they'd run into trouble with the aliens. Not a firefight he wanted to be dragged into. Better to find a safe place and wait out the worst than act too quickly and die in the middle of a firefight with the invaders.

Survival.

Nothing else mattered but getting out of this mess in one piece.

Chapter Nine

"Gunny, I want Stone with you."

"What?" Stone took a step toward her.

"You're someone who's skills I don't know, putting you with Gunny makes sense. He's going to need an extra hand staying upright with those cracked ribs. And he knows when to call out if there's an issue."

"Don't go treating me like an invalid, Lawbook." The older man growled.

The growl did nothing to convince her Gunny would manage without assistance. The scan had told her more than she wanted to know, and they had no medics in their group. Unless they stumbled into a civilian medic among the survivors, he wasn't going to make it. The internal damage was far more than she'd expected to see. And the shadows around one lung, how the hell was she supposed to be able to decode those? Emotions rose, and she took a deep breath and kept her feelings under control. She wouldn't allow them to see what was going on behind her eyes. Have the breakdown, if it came, when they were safe, and she knew no one else was watching her. Or she could do what most Marines did, either find a fight, find a bed partner for a night, or drink herself into a sound sleep when time allowed. "I'm not, this is about getting us all to the supply drop. Stone isn't injured, nothing beyond the bruises and shake up most of us have dealt with. He can act as a stabilizer for you if the pain slows you down. He might be able to fight, be a decent shot, but I don't know how good, or bad he is with a sidearm." She glanced from Stone to the Gunny and back again.

Did he know how badly he was injured? The man wasn't a fool, he had to understand it wasn't a quick fix situation.

She didn't meet his gaze, unwilling to show him the truth, or see it reflected in his eyes.

"Well, shit, girl. You're acting like you're the one in charge." Gunny laughed and pressed one hand against his ribs. He swore, pain stripping color from his features. The hand pressed against his ribs trembled. "Alright, makes sense. You heard the Sergeant, I'm in the middle with Stone." His gaze moved to the civilian. "No arguments from you. If I'm going to let her treat me as if I can't fight, then you can do the sane thing and accept when you're beaten."

The civilian's jaw clenched, his words clipped. "Understood."

Cora bit back a laugh. Exchange male for female and the word would have been fine, with all the dangers and challenges the single word statement could offer. "On your feet. Lackey, you're with me, everyone else, cross two at a time, but not until you're given the signal. Eyes open, we're not alone out here, and the party guests aren't friendly." She gestured to the corporal and made her way into the opening of the building, where she'd waited and watched for the aliens. Watching for danger allowed the rest of the group to fall into position. Time was running out. With damaged suits, oxygen on the low end, and the cold seeping in, they either made it to the supply dump or died along the way. There was no third option.

She signaled Lackey, inclining her head in the direction of the next building across the pedestrian way. She lifted her hand and counted down from five before she moved, knowing he would wait for five before following her. She kept low to the ground as she hurried, sidearm in place as she scrambled for cover and turned to watch as the corporal followed her. In twos, the group joined them, and when the last two began their escape from the building, she edged her way around the rubble, searching for the next set of cover they'd use.

Time had no meaning, and her world narrowed down to finding the safest place to move, the next area where she and her people could rest, repeated until Stone edged closer to her.

"There it is."

"The dump?"

"Three floors down, but we should be able to make it. Most of the building appears to be intact. Might have to clear debris, but it's in better condition than expected."

The deeper they'd moved into the colony, the less damage there appeared to be. But still no bodies. It didn't make sense. There had to be a reason behind the lack of casualties. Information they'd need to pass it onto the Unified Terran Government.

"You're with me, Stone. Lackey, take Stone's place with Gunny."

"Yes, Sergeant."

She didn't need to watch to know Lackey obeyed. Following orders became second nature after a time in the Marines. No doubt it was the same, or close, with the other branches of service. "Stay close, Stone. You follow me after a count of five. Same way you saw me cross with Lackey. Got it?"

"Understood." A single harsh, clipped word.

Still holding a grudge at being put with Gunny? She neither knew nor had the time to find out. If he had an issue with her, they'd deal with it when they were less likely to be spotted by the invaders. Luck had been on their side for the majority of the trip. They'd seen signs of the aliens in the distance, but none had glanced their way. She counted down, then darted across the clearing, one hand pressed against the front door, still intact, and pushed it open enough to allow easy entrance for those who'd follow. Dust fell from the ceiling, debris scattered across the floor, but for the most part, the building was in one piece. She listened, visually scanning the room before she turned her attention back to the door in time to see Stone barreling through the door.

"I'll take the door, you find the entrance into the dump."

"Whatever you say." Stone didn't look at her but continued through the structure.

Hell's Own

If he shot her or slipped free, there was nothing she could do about it. Her attention had to be on those making their way into the building before the enemy spotted them. It didn't stop the itch between her shoulder blades. The man wasn't to be trusted, not with a weapon at her back. She pushed back the thought and continued to provide cover for the remaining members of the group.

Gunny needed help, she didn't like it, but it was how things had worked out. And she wasn't about to let him down.

Zac groaned as he rolled onto his back and stared up into the darkness.

Odd, should have been lights. Faint, distant, but lights. Maybe from the consoles or datapads. Emergency lights.

Nothing.

He lifted one hand in front of his face. He knew he'd moved the hand, knew where he'd tried to place it, but he couldn't see it.

The suit crinkled, giving him another piece of information. He'd pulled his suit on before the dome had shattered. Activated it when the first warning of a dome crack had rung out. Was it intact? He listened, but there was nothing. No alert rang out. Not even the low buzz which would tell him the suit had been stressed but hadn't torn.

Their suits were military grade.

Their?

Laura. Haden. They'd been with him. He sat up and stared into the darkness.

A distant light, faint, a small red slow blink.

How long had he been out? Minutes? Hours? Days?

Not days, his suit didn't have enough power or air to keep him alive for days. Panic, fear, he knew they surged through his body, and there was nothing he could do about it. He wasn't trained for this shit. No one was. Aliens. No pirates could cause this amount of damage to the dome, or the colony as a whole. The energy readings. Shapes which jumped from the outer edge of their sensor readings to right on top of them faster than anything human-built could do it.

Sure, the idea of traveling at unknown speeds, folding space, stable wormholes, and a dozen other theories, remained a part of the talk whenever you got a group of pilots together. But his job was here, operating a console, not dreaming of planets unknown and first contact with peaceful alien worlds. The reality was different, and it sucked.

I didn't sign up for this.

Except he had, even if he hadn't realized it at the time.

Zac stood but didn't move. Without a source of real illumination, he couldn't be certain the floor remained steady beneath him. Had to be a way of seeing what was going on. He patted down his suit. A torch. Handheld. He had something, didn't he?

Head.

He reached up and tapped his face mask. Lights flickered into life, and he blinked to give his eyes time to adjust. Shapes. Fallen walls. He looked up and wished he hadn't. No ceiling. How bad was the damage to the dome? The colony as a whole?

He tapped his comm into life.

Static. A soft buzz barely audible. The majority of the systems had to be down or jammed. He frowned. Yes, jammed, Laura had tried to contact Earth, but the signal had bounced back on them. Blocked.

They were on their own unless the UTG realized there was a problem. And they would, in time.

Time they didn't have.

Zac turned, slowly, allowing the lights on his mask to sweep around the room. He hadn't been on his own when the attack had come, and he'd been the nearest one to the door. Laura and Haden wouldn't have moved far from where he'd last seen them.

Hell's Own

He tried to place the memory of the room with the now destroyed remains. The walls were mostly in the same place, which gave him a frame of reference.

Laura. She'd pulled a sidearm on him, but she'd been the closest.

Uncertain, and careful not to rush, he moved further into the room. Work stations, a crushed line of them, stood in front of him. His station would have been to the right. Laura's to the left, but she'd approached him when he'd made a move to leave. He edged closer to where he'd last seen the woman, head half bowed as he watched the floor.

A boot stuck out from beneath a pile of rubble. Small, not a man's foot. Not Haden's.

Alive? Dead? He shuddered, knowing there was only one way to be sure.

Zac lifted the rubble, broken plastiboard and plaster, away from the foot, revealing the leg an inch at a time. He tossed the pieces aside, it didn't matter if he threw things. Not as if there was anyone else in the way. If the enemy was close to the comm center; they'd either kill him, ignore him, or take him, prisoner. Odds were in his favor he'd survive their arrival if they chose to investigate the noise. If they heard him. Without a true atmosphere, sound wouldn't carry as clearly. If they were aliens, they might not hear anything, but rely on other senses.

First contact.

He laughed, tears hazing his vision as he continued to remove the remains of the ceiling from Laura's body until he found her leg. No suit.

He frowned. Hadn't she activated her suit when the alert had rung out? He tried to remember, to put the shards of the events together, but his mind refused to cooperate. Without a suit, she'd die if the crushing debris hadn't killed her. No air. No protection.

Zac pushed her pant leg up enough to touch her leg, feeling along it to locate an area to check her pulse. With fingers pressed against her leg, he waited.

Nothing.

"Come on, there has to be a pulse." He shifted his hold, searching for a better place to check. Three times he tried to find a pulse, three times the veins beneath his touch remained still and silent. Zac swallowed and released his grip on the woman's leg. Gone. Dead. He couldn't do anything for Laura. No more than he could for anyone else unless there was a flicker of life in the body, then he might have a chance, a hope of bringing them back to life.

Laura was dead.

He should be upset with her loss, but after the way she'd waved a sidearm at him, he wasn't going to grieve.

Haden.

Was the other man still alive? Laura hadn't pulled her suit on, but Haden might have had the time to activate his before the roof caved in.

He glanced up again, taking note of the extent of the damage. Bad. Nothing he'd be able to repair. The deterioration in the rest of the colony might be as bad, or less, depending on how the aliens had approached the attack. Survivors. Yeah, once he'd found out if Haden were still alive, he'd search for other survivors. With the tunnels beneath the colony, the bolt holes, supply dumps, and emergency shelters, there had to be other survivors.

Unless the aliens were now on the ground and hunting them down.

He paled, a shiver worked through his body, stomach rolled, the bitter taste of bile in the back of his throat. He didn't want to throw up. The idea of being sick with a mask in place didn't appeal to him. His nose wrinkled. If he vomited in the suit, he'd be stuck with the smell, and worse.

It didn't take long to find Haden. Like Laura, he hadn't activated his suit in time.

Zac stepped back from the destruction, reality sinking in as he turned toward the door or the large gap where the door had been.

Hell's Own

Until he found survivors, he was alone.

Completely alone.

Something he hadn't been in as long as he could remember.

Stone didn't say a word as he made it into the building, one glance at Lawbook was enough to send him deeper into the structure to find the door. It took only a moment for him to get his bearings. Dust, debris, pieces of art knocked from the walls, the things he would have stopped to take note of if the colony wasn't currently playing host to aliens. His mind raced until he forced his thoughts to calm, settle into order long enough to allow him to dig out the information he needed. He counted the doors inside, each one leading to a new room, a corridor, storage. The last one opened up onto a supply room.

Footsteps rang out. New people headed his way. It had to be the other members of the group. Men, as the only woman in the group, was the stubborn Sergeant he'd been stuck with, the one he knew didn't trust him. It didn't matter, he didn't trust her either. She'd turn him in the first chance she had. No matter, they'd part ways soon enough, and he'd be able to get on with his life, slip free from Pluto without drawing attention to himself. He glanced at the woman. She wasn't aware of his movements, for now. In theory, he could vanish through the trapdoor and hideout. Except she'd come and deal with him, pin him against the wall, or throw him out into the street where the aliens would find him. This wasn't a woman who would allow him to get away with dumping her and the rest of the team, and if he tried, he'd pay for it in more ways than he wanted to imagine.

All in all, it wasn't his idea of a good plan.

If he could earn her trust, it would be easier to break away from them when the time came. She had the manpower on her side, weapons, and she'd have more once they were down in the supply dump. A small point in her favor, but she already held all the cards no matter what he might like to believe.

He yanked up the trapdoor. "Clear back here."

She nodded, casting a quick glance his way. "Lackey, get Gunny down into the supply room, make sure he gets in ahead of the rest of us. He needs the rest. Walker, need you here, rest of you follow them down. Make sure there's enough room for the rest of us.

"There will be." What did she think? He didn't know the size of the room or what had been stored in the secure chamber. Damn the woman, she pushed with the simplest of statements. He swung himself down onto the top of the ladder, his feet finding the first rung as he climbed down the ladder. The others wouldn't be able to enter, not unless he went ahead of them. Without the right code, the door wouldn't open. At least there would be extra weapons, along with better suits. His legs would appreciate the warmth. If his thighs didn't warm up soon, he'd face injury he'd need treatment to recover from, and he wouldn't be able to keep up with the rest of the group.

Why did he need to?

He frowned and jumped the last four steps, wincing as he hit the ground and turned his attention to the locked door. Sixty seconds is all it took to unlock the secured door and step into the airlock.

"Wait up," said Lackey. "Need to get Gunny in there with you. Airlock, right?"

"Yes." He swore under his breath. "All right, he can come in with me, should be enough room." Better if he'd entered on his own, but if he needed to keep the others out of the secure room it was already too late. His mind raced, options to rid himself of the marines. All he had to do was hide out until the coast was clear. They couldn't make him leave. Perhaps it was as simple as refusing to move out with them.

"Gunny, you holding up?"

"I'll be fine, you worry about the rest of them." The man half walked, half stumbled into the airlock and rested one hand against the wall. "Time for you to show us what you've got hidden." The color drained from beneath his olive touched skin, leaving it gray, but the man didn't ask for help or display any other sign of the weakness caused by the injury.

More than weakness if the glazed look in the other man's eyes was anything to go by. Did Lawbook know how badly the Gunny had been injured? If she did, she hadn't said a damn word to him or her marines. Did she cling to the hope there would be enough in the way of supplies to be able to save the older man? A dozen questions bubbled into life, and he crammed them down into a box, to be dealt with when there was time.

Stone didn't talk to the Gunny as he punched in the security code and closed the airlock. A soft thump and hiss confirmed the door was secure. The floor trembled beneath their feet, a barely felt vibration before the door out of the chamber opened behind them.

"Nice setup," said Gunny, his voice weak. All the strength the man had shown before, now gone, leaving only a husk of a soldier in its wake.

"Not my design, but I won't argue." Stone stepped out first, the fleeting idea of shoving the injured man back into the airlock and slamming the doors shut, flashed through his mind. Even injured he doubted the Gunny had lost any of his edges. An experienced marine wouldn't allow himself to be taken off guard, not in an enclosed space. Torn between wanting to be rid of the Gunny and knowing it was a fool's game, he let Gunny step out and hit the right sequence of keys to shut the airlock and allow the next two entry into the storage room.

He watched the man as he stumbled, steps wooden before he sat down, back against a wall.

"Full airlock set up, awesome." Walker grinned as he appeared a few minutes later. "True bolt hole. Could have done with something like this out at the bar."

"It's meant to make it harder for people to get in as well as keep the air in here from escaping." The bolt hole Jones had built was along the same lines. Not that Walker needed to know the details. Or how much Stone knew about the various hideaways scattered beneath the colony.

"The code."

"What?"

"You'll need to share the code with those in the airlock."

"I can let them out from my side." The code was one of the few weapons he had.

"Now, Stone." Gunny didn't move to touch his sidearm. He didn't need to, his appearance said it all. On death's door, the man might be, but until the final breath left his body, Gunny remained dangerous.

"Fine. You can relay it to them." He ran off the series of numbers and stepped away from the airlock. His last, potential, leverage yanked out from beneath him. Gunny's voice continued behind him as the other man shared the code with the remainder of the group. He didn't glance back at the door, or Gunny, as he moved further into the supply room.

Boxes sat on shelves, others on the floor. Tanks of oxygen lay on their sides in racks. Food supplies. A few weapons in immediate line of sight, but nowhere near enough to be effective against the aliens. Still, the Marines would be content. Water, medical supplies, parts for machines, ships, and others. And with the way the room had been set up, they wouldn't run out of oxygen quickly. At the back, if his memory served him, was a small washroom and shower set up. Making it easier for a handful of people to hide out.

And for one person the supplies would be enough for a year.

He didn't have to leave. Not if he didn't want to. Perhaps hiding out would be safer than making for his ship? Not a decision he would make until he knew more about what was going on with the aliens. If all went according to plan, the creatures would grab what they wanted, and leave. Never to be seen again. If they took a few captives with them, who cared as long as he remained free to continue his work.

So, why did the idea leave him unsettled?

"Keep moving," Cora ordered the last two down the ladder. They'd made it this far. No aliens, no screams, no one firing on the group. She opened up her comm and checked she had it on the right channel. "Sergeant Bloodlaw, update. We've found a supply dump and will be restocking. Will advise when we're on our way."

Static filtered through the airway. "Understood." A single word, it was all she needed.

The kids were still alive. Another point in their favor. She could do this. They could. But it didn't prevent the weight of doubt from dropping onto her shoulder if she let her focus slip away from the work at hand. Cora waited until she knew the last of her people would be by the airlock, only then did she pull the front door closed and followed them, making certain the door to the closet was closed behind them, and she tugged the entrance to the ladder shut before she joined them at the bottom of the ladder. Because of the size of the airlock, she let the two ahead go in, then took her turn when the airlock was empty.

"Not a bad bolt hole." Lackey grinned as she stepped out into view.

"Give me a few to get my bearings, but as long as those creatures don't find us, we'll be fine." She shook out her hands, then pulled the gloves off and rubbed them. Heat, oxygen, light, and supplies. Not everything they needed, but close enough for Government work. She tugged the mask off, setting it on her head as the others had done. "Gives us a chance to warm up. If there are replacement suits in here, our bodies still require time to recover if we're to be effective." She'd take back up suits, but if they could find one full suit, they could shove Gunny into it, giving his body a chance to recover.

Won't be enough. Need to stop lying to myself.

She pushed back the thought, it was one thing to know Gunny was dying, another to admit to it, and keep the idea at the forefront of her mind.

"Welcome relief." Lackey agreed.

"Take stock." She rolled out her shoulders, then arms, getting the circulation moving. Her toes tingled, heat seeping into them, and she fought against the urge to whimper. Sergeant's didn't bloody whimper. Not where her people would hear them.

"On it." The corporal hurried away, catching the attention of the rest of the men.

Orders rang out as she found the Gunny. "How you holding up?"

"Could be better, could be worse." A small shrug, followed by a wince. "Ribs don't like this. Took more of a beating than I expected." He glanced up at her, then away.

"Don't imagine they do." She moved to his side. Nothing said about the real danger, the fact his coloring spoke of death, and his body was failing him as they tried to find a way of extending his life. Such conversations weren't needed until there was no other choice. "Need to check what's going on with you." She slid the medical unit into her hand and ran it up and down the Gunny. Her heart sank. Punctured organs, internal bleeding. Her vision hazed and she blinked unshed tears away. She wasn't going to cry, the one damn thing she'd never been able to get rid of was the foolish need to scream out her frustration at the wrong time. Better to let it out when she was alone, where no one could see her and call it a weakness. Real marines didn't cry. Buck it up, Marine. Oh, she'd heard those lines more often than she cared to count. "Appears to be more like cracked than broken, not that it makes much a difference. Pain is pain." How long did he have?

"Cracked hurts, broken offers more problems. As long as I don't do any more damage to them, I should be alright for a few hours." Color didn't return to his face, and blood bubbled at his nose and mouth. "We've got a decent place to hold up here. You contact the kids?"

"Yes, let them know we're delayed." She slid the unit into a pocket. Change in topic. She couldn't blame him, not with what she saw on the scanner. "Shit, Gunny, you pick the worst times to want a vacation." A few hours? Would he last that long? She glanced at the medical unit. No, not if this was anything to go by. He wasn't going to make it, not without a full medical bay, and it wasn't an option they had to hand. "I can give you something for the pain."

"Hey, I'll grab a vacation when I can get one. We kick these aliens hard enough, and they'll be throwing us parties back home." His gaze shifted in the direction of Stone. "Watch him. We need him, but..." he let the last word trail off.

"Understood. Don't much trust him either." As in she didn't trust him as far as she could throw him, with gravity at double strength. "But he got us here, and we haven't lost anyone."

The Gunny lifted his gaze. "Yet. He won't follow orders for long, and you'll have to remind him who's in charge." He coughed, flecks of blood spread with the push of air from his damaged lungs. "If it means a beat down, you do it. Think of him as a recruit with a chip on his shoulder. If you can get his respect, you're halfway there."

She inclined her head, not willing to say more on the subject. "I'll check on the others." On Stone. The rest she could trust to get on with the assignment. Even the other two civilians knew better than to argue, they'd complied and worked alongside her team, with Gunny, and hadn't caused a problem. Stone was another matter. "I'll be back soon, don't go anywhere."

"I'll be here."

She exchanged a handful of words with the Marines before she found Stone. The man had half disappeared in among the shelving and stacked supplies. He ran his hands over a stack of food packs and turned as she approached.

"Something I can do for you, Sergeant?"

"How many more dumps like this are in the colony?"

"You don't really expect me to answer, do you? Give all my secrets away without anything in return?" He arched an eyebrow. Like the others, he'd taken off his gloves and pushed the mask back, revealing his features. No one wanted to waste oxygen, you didn't have to be military to know when it was best to use the atmosphere supplied in the bolt hole. "No, I didn't think so. You know how the world works."

"Can't blame me for trying." She leaned against the nearest set of racks, allowing her body to relax.

"I suppose not, and if you're attempting to appear less threatening, it doesn't work. Anyone looking at you can see you're military. The fact you've climbed the ladder to Sergeant in the Marines, says you're skilled enough to be dangerous. I'm not going to pretend otherwise." He rested one hand on an unopened box. "We'll need to open this one. It has pressure bandages, and rib wraps. I don't know if there's a bone fuser in here, but I'll keep searching."

The bone fuser had a technical name, but the only people who used it were doctors and the clerk in charge of ordering replacements. "Thanks." Fine, trying to relax around Stone wasn't going to work. She'd find other ways of managing the smuggler. "We'll need as much information as we can, supply wise before we head out for the kids." The space here was large enough to bring half a dozen survivors in, more would be a stretch, but doable. "And we'll need to know about the other locations to have enough shelter for the kids, and whoever else hid in the destroyed remains of the colony.

His top lip curled. "Good attempt, but no."

"You think I threw you a line?"

"Yes."

"You're insane. This isn't about getting you or anyone else in trouble. We don't know how many survivors are hiding outside and are now running out of air." Warmth was the same problem. If they didn't have full suits, they'd be feeling the cold. Places like this would provide them with a better chance of staying alive.

"Doesn't change a damn thing. If they're still alive, they'll be fine. They've got air and--"

"They might be in the same situation we are, with basic suits, and no long term supply of air. Food, water, medical supplies, they're going to need all of it. Or they'll die. Either killed or through hypothermia, dehydration, injury."

"Not my problem. When you go for the kids, I'm staying here. And you won't be bringing them back."

Her muscles clenched, eyes narrowed. "You agreed to follow orders."

"I didn't say how long, and I agreed to follow Gunny's orders."

"I see." She flexed the fingers in her right hand.

"It's got nothing to do with you being a woman. You know what you're doing, or you wouldn't be wearing stripes."

"Then what?" Cora shifted her weight a fraction, never turned away from him.

"This isn't my fight. I'm a survivor, Lawbook. Not a marine. A merc, not a soldier."

She moved, closing the gap between them, one hand locked around the man's throat as she shoved him back against the racks. Items slammed together, clinking and rustling filled the air as she held the man in place. "You're either with us, or you're dead. No middle ground. If you're with us, you take orders. If not, I'll strip you of anything useful and shove you in front of the next damned alien myself."

He didn't reach for her hand. Didn't attempt to break free. The only reaction to her grasp was the increase of his pulse beneath her fingers. "You're strong, I'll give you that much. And I'm outnumbered, but you won't kill me unless I openly threaten you."

She closed her grasp enough to make each breath a struggle. "Don't confuse me with Gunny. He'll give you a chance. I won't."

She leaned in, her face inches from his, eyes never leaving his gaze. Chances were a luxury she could no longer afford.

One hand rose, fingers touching the hand around his throat. "Persuasive."

"Which is it to be. With us or not. Make your choice."

He swallowed, pulse rapid. His voice calm, but strained with the way she held him. "What makes you believe I'll stick to my choice?"

"You'll search for loopholes, you're a merc. But betray your given word? Oh, you might, the odds are against it as time progresses, unless there's a profit in it for you. But somehow I don't think these creatures will be open for trading anytime soon." She eased back on her hold, then tightened. "Choose."

His eyes widened under the new pressure, then narrowed, lines furrowing across his brow. "Fine, I'll follow your damned orders, Sergeant, but this isn't over. When we're safe, no longer at risk from being discovered, you and I will *discuss* how you handled this." He rubbed his throat as she released her grip and stepped out of his immediate reach.

Jakob leaned against the wall, relief at knowing they weren't on their own resulted in a welcome change of pace. The Marines had found another bolt hole, undamaged by the attack. If there was one, there'd be others, which meant a chance at finding other survivors. His parents. Salla's father. Pippa. Gail. Maybe they found a way of breaking free from the enemy? And marines. If marines had survived, then the navy might be on their way.

They wouldn't be alone.

He wanted to believe, to hope the rest of their families and friends were still alive. A prisoner had a chance. A corpse didn't.

"You holding up?"

"I think. Maybe." He glanced at the ceiling. "Not really in the headspace to be able to think straight."

"I get you." She paused for a moment, long enough to glance back at the others before she continued. "We can't stay here much longer. Be safer if we move deeper into the caverns. Seal everything up behind us. Make it harder for them to find us." Salla followed his gaze. "They will be coming for us, sooner or later."

"Why?" What was she getting at?

"I don't know why they hit the colony, but they were grabbing people. Not outright killing them. We can't sit back and fool ourselves into believing we're safe when we know we're not." She scrubbed a hand over her face. "They aren't going to give up at the first roadblock. Shit, they cracked the dome. Blasted the military base. Destroyed the navy presence and--"

"Wait, what? How do you know they destroyed the base and the navy?"

"Because they didn't meet any resistance. Must have blown them out of existence. Either that or the navy saw what was coming our way and got out fast. But I don't think they pulled a coward's retreat. Not without sending word to the colony." Her eyes half closed. "No, they hit hard, fast, took out the most dangerous targets first. Like the Navy ships. Only then did they attack the dome. It's how Dad would have handled it if he'd been in charge of an attack."

Jakob should have been afraid, but there was a tone about the way Salla explained things. She didn't panic. Her voice calm as she continued to watch him. He smiled, then wrapped his arms about his body and shivered. "Alright, how do we get this lot moving? Not like they're going to listen to us."

"Yes, they will. Someone has to take charge, might as well be those who've thought things through." She pushed away from the wall and marched to the largest group.

His gaze narrowed. Where were the adults? He could see three of four, but the rest of them were teenagers, with a few younger kids in the mix.

"We need to keep moving. They'll search for survivors, and we don't want to make it easy for them." Salla announced, her voice carrying clearly through the chamber.

She had the right idea, but would the others agree? He hurried, joining the group. "Who's in charge now?"

Salla rolled her eyes. "No one, that's the problem. It's why we're all standing around waiting for one person to step up and tell us what to do. We can't take the risk. Not with our lives at stake."

"The military will be here soon. Then we'll be safe. They'll get us out of here, and more will be on the way to deal with those things."

"If you mean the small group heading out way, it won't be fast. They're stocking up, and we don't know how far away they are." Salla gestured to the rest of the teens. "We have to step up. Make decisions. I suggest we head deeper into the system, down to the supply rooms, where we have a chance of hiding or scattering through the tunnels if they break through."

"Supplies might have weapons if we have to make a stand to let the younger kids escape," Jakob added.

"Make a stand? We're not military." A pre-teen complained. "You can't be serious about this."

"Never said you were, but we all know how to point and pull." He mimed holding a sidearm and pulling the trigger. "Don't have to kill them, fire enough their way and it's bound to do damage. If we can buy enough time for the little ones to get clear, it's all that matters." Had those words come out of his mouth? He straightened, pushing his shoulders back. He wasn't a kid. So what if he was a teenager, he was seventeen, old enough to make a few decisions himself, and he'd been on Pluto for ten years. "Come on, people, what choice do we have?"

"We could, you know, surrender?" Freckle-faced with a mess of red-blond hair, the girl rested one hand on her hip as she glared at Jakob.

"Sure, go ahead. You give up. Let me know what it's like being turned into food." Black haired with an upturned nose, the older girl smirked.

"Helena, you don't know they're going to eat us."

"You don't know they won't either, Felicia."

"It's Fee, you know I hate Felicia."

"What you going to do about it?" Helena took a step toward the redhead.

"Enough. If you want to fight, save it for the aliens." Salla moved in between the two girls. "This isn't school. You can flex your social muscles when things return to normal."

If they ever did.

Stone didn't turn away from the woman, one he now counted as far more dangerous than he had moments ago. The way she'd gone for his neck, with a grip strong enough to put pressure on his ability to breathe? Impressive. Not an action he'd have believed she'd take. Now he knew better.

"A talk? Only thing you'll be doing is following orders until we're safe, then we'll part ways." Her voice remained calm.

"Is that right?" His hands itched to do something, anything to be rid of the tension. His temper bubbled, and he took a step away from the racks. "You won't always be in charge. Flex your temporary muscles all you want, we both know it won't do any good. Sooner or later we'll find a Marine of higher rank, and you'll have to answer for your actions." The same ones he would have taken had the roles been reversed. Not information he'd share with Lawbook anytime soon.

"I don't doubt my command is short term. When the Gunny is back to full strength, he'll be in charge unless we run into an officer." Her voice cold.

Gunny.

The older man had a core of steel, but he was no fool. He'd seen the way the man lost his color, the blood at his lips and nose.

If he made it another hour, Stone would be surprised. "I'm human, remember? Means I have rights. Ones you can't strip from me."

"I'm aware." The two words bland, emotionless. She knew. The way she spoke, the lack of emotion, oh, she was aware Gunny was dying.

"I haven't signed with the military." He watched her, searching for a sign of what was going on behind her eyes. "And I don't have any plans to change. Happy enough with my life, or was until these visitors arrived."

"I know."

"Which means you don't have the right to tell me what to do."

"Right now I do, you gave me the right by agreeing to follow orders." Her lips twitched into a smile which vanished a moment later. "Or are you saying you lied? Never intended to keep your word?"

He growled. If there was one thing he held to, it was his oath. A merc who couldn't be trusted to finish the assignment or a trader who didn't follow through with their load, couldn't be trusted. If people believed you'd take their money and run, you didn't get the chance at the bigger packages or working for the man with the deepest pockets. His word was all he had. "No, I didn't lie. Not something I'm in the habit of doing."

"Then there's no problem. I want you to work with the others, take inventory. If you know where a ready-made one is kept, it'll cut into the work we have ahead of us. I want to be out of here in the hour. We've no idea how much air and heat those kids have, and they can't stay hidden for much longer, not with the way those things are acting."

Kids. What the hell did he want to do with a gaggle of kids? Teachers might know how to use a gun and would be able to keep the brats in line, but he wanted nothing to do with them. "Got it."

"When this is over if you still want to throw a punch at me, go for it." She turned and walked away from him.

What made her think he wanted to hit her? He didn't hit

women. Alright, most of the time, he didn't. If there was a woman in the middle of a fight, she was treated the same as the rest of them. But throwing a punch at her without being in the middle of a brawl? Not an action he could see himself committing. Stone allowed himself a smile. Crafty female, she had him questioning himself.

Inventory. Yeah, he knew where there should be one.

At least if he found it, she'd leave him alone for a time.

Muttering to himself, Stone made his way through the storage shelves in search of the data pad the original owner of the supply dump, kept hidden.

Chapter Ten

"How you holding up, Gunny?" Cora settled on her knees next to the Gunny, the older man propped up against a shelving unit. Gray, blood at the lips and nose, his breathing a loud rattle which couldn't be ignored. Time. It was slipping through her fingers, and no matter how she grabbed for it, the moments would continue to escape her hold.

"Well, as I can ask for." He grimaced as he shifted his weight.

"Have something here which should help." She held out the bone fuser Walker had found. "Between the scanner and this, we'll have you back on your feet." Lies fell from her lips without hesitation.

"Give me the scanner." He held out one hand. "Need to see for myself."

She swore under her breath but handed him the unit. Once he saw the data for himself, there would be no more hiding the truth. "Might show bruising there."

"Yeah, around my lungs, right?" He pinned her with a stare.

"Maybe, I didn't have long to go over the data, not after I saw the issue with your ribs." Not entirely a lie. How was she supposed to tell him he was dying?

He knows.

"Right." He turned his attention to the unit and brought up the information. His eyes narrowed before he shot her a glare, then returned to take in the data. "Dealing with the cracks will help. The rest, shit I don't know. I'm not a doctor. Or Corpsman. But it didn't appear to be good news." He let the unit drop into his lap. "No point in playing games. I'm dying, we both see it written across this damn thing." He took a deep breath only to wince. "Alright, Sergeant, get it done. If we can buy me more time, brilliant. If not, don't stress it."

"I'm not going to let you die." A fierce determination claimed her voice. "You're not allowed to give up on us."

He smiled, a light dancing within his pain-filled eyes. "You're an experienced Marine, Lawbook, but no one is strong enough to fix what's wrong with me, not without a medic and full suite to hand. We both know what those readings mean. At most I've got a day, but odds are it's closer to an hour, maybe less. I couldn't tell you exactly what's wrong, what needs to be fixed, but the swelling, blood loss, internal bleeding, blood pressure dropping, then there's this cloud thing around my lung." He shook his head, the movement weak. "Less than an hour, and so much I want to say, to do. Should have taken the option to return to Earth three months ago. Nice sweet duty on a cushy station, but no, I opted to stay out here with this lot." He coughed again, the sound wet. "Jones and his beer. All his fault. You tell him that when you get the chance. I stayed for his crappy beer."

"Gunny." Her grip tightened on the fuzer. They all knew the basics of using one, even if they couldn't manage anything else other than clot blocker, and synth skin patches. They weren't trained in anything in-depth when it came to patching up bodies. Each one of them could tear a body apart with weapons, some with bare hands, depending on the situation, but healers they weren't. "I'm sorry. I should know what to do here."

"You didn't cause the injury. You're not a healer, or you'd be in a different unit. All dressed in white and green. No, our unwanted visitors are responsible. Bury the pain. Use it to deal with Stone." He gestured upward and coughed. "Shit, this is getting worse." He pressed against his ribs. "Should tell you to save the fuser for another time. Someone with a chance."

"Like hell. You're the Gunny. You've got this. A little rest and you'll be kicking the rest of us to get moving, and calling us out for dragging heels. When this is over with, I'll buy you all the beer you can drink, from Jones I mean. Not wasting money on the crap they serve in the Sergeants Mess."

"I wish." He met her gaze and shifted to sit upright, away from the wall, his face a mask of pain. "Arguing wastes energy. Let's get this done, see if it buys me an hour. Or at least ease the discomfort."

"Discomfort my ass. You're allowed to say if you're hurting, Gunny."

"What, and ruin my rep. Not going to happen."

Cora lifted his shirt out of the way, grateful Gunny was in civies instead of uniform and body armor, an activated the fuser. Would body armor have protected Gunny enough to have saved his life? The idea danced through her mind, stripping away all other thoughts until it spun, naked, through her mind. Her jaw set. No changing what had happened, not unless she stumbled across a means to step back in time, and have them all in fighting gear when the attack had struck.

She turned the fuser over in her hand as it hummed to life in her hand as she ran it over the area she'd seen indicated by the scanner. The urge to move quickly niggled away in the back of her mind, but she forced herself to keep the movement slow and steady. Rushing wouldn't help with either the injury or pain.

Gunny hissed but kept an eye on the medical scanner. "Move left, around closer to the spine."

"On it." Under the Gunny's guidance, she moved the fuser where it needed to be, letting him tell her where to move it to next and what needed longer or shorter attention to heal. Sweat beaded over his skin, muscles trembling from the effort of remaining in position. "Almost done here, a minute more." She moved around to his other side and worked the fuser along the ribs. It had to be enough, even with the swelling, bruising, and potentially other problems the injury had caused. "I'll be heading out soon, thinking it will be best to leave you here, don't want to strain those ribs."

"You won't be coming back for me." The Gunny smiled.

"Say's you. I'll be back, then we find a way off world." She kept her gaze on the fuser. "Once we've found the rest of the navy, we'll kick these bastards off our world." The lie tried to stick in her throat, but she forced it into life. "Then we're going to ask for time off, and if you've nothing better to do, I'll drag you to this place in Scotland. Best damn beer and single malts you've ever tasted."

Gunny rested one hand on her arm. "Listen to me, Lawbook. You get out, get those kids, and find a way to keep them safe. If you can get off-world, fantastic. If not, head for one of the bunkers outside the dome. Find Jones, he'll know if there are other tunnels heading away from the colony. Stone might know, but..."

"She bossing you around now?" Stone stepped into view, found the one clear spot where he could lean against a wall, and claimed it. "And yeah, I know about the tunnels."

"Bossing people around goes with the stripes." He didn't turn to look at the man. He didn't need to. "You have a problem with the sergeant here?"

"More like she has a problem with me, but we'll sort it out, smooth out the rough spots." He lifted the datapad. "Information you wanted is here, Lawbook."

"I'll take it, and you can go help the others." She held out one hand for the list. Sooner he was out her line of sight, the better. "We need to get a few things sorted before we head out and get the kids."

"She's enjoying the power too much." Stone didn't move, didn't hand her the tablet.

"Not from where I'm sitting."

Cora closed her eyes and took a deep breath. No matter what the man said, she wasn't going to rise to the bait. "Do I have to take the list from you, or are you going to hand it over?"

Zac pressed his back against the wall. They were out there, shadows lacking human shape. Beasts on four legs, ones with wings. Monstrous features and limbs. His heart raced as he remained hidden. What did they want with him? With the colony? Why hadn't they answered the hail? Questions clouded his mind. No real information. He couldn't act without details. Data. Pieces of the puzzle.

His jaw clenched as he forced himself out of the mental spiral. This wasn't the comm room, with it's cooling cups of coffee, laid back manner, and the knowledge they were on the edge of the system, with little or nothing to disturb them. Only a handful of vessels approached Pluto each month. Mostly navy, smugglers and private vessels. All moving in and out with no trouble. His life could never have changed and he'd have been fine with that.

First contact.

God, this was so not the way he'd imagined it would be. It should have been peaceful, not an introduction to hell. The human race hadn't been faced with a hostile nation in over three hundred years. He didn't know enough to recall the exact time and reasons for the last conflict, but the point remained. Earth and its colonies had known peace, and they had no one experienced in the arts of war to call upon.

Had anyone been prepared for first contact? The Unified Terran Government? Had they known of the risks? Picked up signals and not shared the information with the colony? Or maybe they had passed it along, and he was too low on the totem pole to be included? Laura didn't like him. Hadn't liked him. Whatever. Had she pushed him out of the information loop?

Don't think ill of the dead.

Dead. They were all dead. Laura. Haden. Others. But the only bodies he'd seen belonged to the two in the comm room. Signs of violence, sure, he'd seen those. Marks on the walls. A smudge of dried liquid. Blood? He didn't know. Had no handheld to scan the mark.

The ground trembled beneath his feet. Not the shakes he'd experienced earlier, but smaller, closer to him.

The big alien. Had to be the beast pulling things. Boxes.

People. Prisoners.

He groaned and slid down onto his haunches. They'd find him. Kill him. Eat him.

No where to hide. No one to protect him.

With hands pressed over his mask covered face, Zac whimpered and rocked on his heels.

Energy struck the wall to the left. Sharp shards tore through the air as he flattened himself to the ground. Another rumble, followed by an explosion of dust and debris in front of him. He shook, arms over his head, as he curled into ball.

A marine or pilot would know what to do. They'd fight back. Save the day. Not him. His bladder threatened to lose control as he whimpered.

Not here. I'm not here. Leave me alone.

The vibrations jarred his body, finding each bruise and scrape marked across his body. His teeth clenched. Pain. Shame. It didn't matter, as long as the aliens left him alone. He didn't have anything for them. He was only a comm tech. No one important.

It didn't matter. They were coming for him and there was no where left to hide.

Shivers tore through his body as he clenched his jaw in an attempt to remain silent. Would they hear him? These shadows turned into living nightmares? He swallowed but didn't move from the ground. They didn't need him. He couldn't tell them anything and--

A hand grabbed him by the arm and yanked him up, the new arrival touching his helmet to Zac's, the voice a shock after only his own thoughts since waking amid the rubble. "Get up. You stay here, you're caught. Or dead. Get the hell up."

He didn't resist as the man pulled him to his feet. "Who are you?" Had he managed to speak, or was it nothing more than the echo of a mental cry?

"Run now. Talk later." Cold blue eyes met his gaze.

Violent vibrations rolled through him. A sound he felt more

than heard before a bolt of energy struck the remains of the wall Zac had hidden behind. The wall exploded, shards sliced at him. Thumps which threatened to knock him to the ground. If the other man hadn't held him in place, he would have been flattened, left whimpering in terror.

"They're coming."

He wanted to demand information. To turn and look at the invaders. Find a way of putting the pieces together, gather date and file it away for when he had the time to deal with it. His throat dried out. Heart raced. This wasn't happening to him. He couldn't be caught in a mess like this. No, his job was supposed to be safe. A desk jocky, not a pilot who would risk his life to explore the outer rim.

The stranger kept a tight hold of Zac's arm as they ran.They didn't look back, didn't pause to check how close the enemy might be. Nothing mattered except putting one foot in front of the other as they ran until his ribs hurt and each breath scraped its way into his lungs. They were going to do it, would escape, find a safe place and then he'd be able to ask his questions.

The blow came without warning. Something struck him in the small of his back. He cried out, pain and shock tumbling him to the ground. The grip holding him to the stranger, lost as he rolled. Bruises. Sore muscles. Damage he needed time to heal before he'd be able to return to work.

Zac rolled onto his back, blinking as he tried to force his body to adjust to the blow.

A shadow, taller than any human, crept across his chest, forcing him to turn and search for the owner, only to regret his choice a moment later. Fear tightened a band around his heart, cold terror seized his mind as he stared up into the grotesque features of the winged alien with three eyes, and a large weapon carried in both hands. A weapon the creature shifted in his grip until the butt of the rifle like implement slammed down toward his head, sending him spinning into the darkness.

Stone grinned, the pad in hand. Oh, she didn't like this, did she? "I think I'll keep hold of it for a time, not as if there's any hurry."

Her eyes flashed, cold and hard. "Fine."

And there it was, one of the most dangerous words in a woman's vocabulary.

"Until I'm back on my feet, Lawbook's in charge."

"He already knows this." Cora's clipped cold response did nothing to change his decision. "I believe he has an issue with me, on a personal level, but it won't damage my ability to lead the group."

"What did you do?"

"Pinned him against the racks with my hand." She put the medical reader away. "Around his throat. He decided he didn't have to follow my orders. We discussed the matter and came to an understanding." A small shrug.

He studied her features. No hint of being ashamed of what she'd done, or the desire to apologize. Strong. Determined. If the Sergeant ever wanted to leave the military, she'd do well as security for hire. "She threatened to kill me."

"A promise, not a threat, if I know Lawbook." The Gunny leaned back against the shelving. "Best if you follow her orders, she's going to be busy, but she's a woman of her word."

"I suggest you rein your girl in before someone decides to teach her a lesson." Stone straightened. "She's going to be in a lot of trouble if she doesn't watch her back." He glanced at Lawbook. "No offense, but you're fighting out of your league. Maybe if you learn to smile, you'd get better responses."

Small lines tightened around her eyes, her jaw clenched, but she didn't explode. Didn't give in to the anger he poked at.

"What would you do with a new recruit who pulled this crap, Lawbook?"

"A quick lesson. With five points." Her gaze never moved from his.

Stone flipped the datapad in his hand, catching it with ease before he flipped it again. "I'm supposed to be impressed by this? Doesn't work. She held me by my throat." He'd deal with the sergeant when time allowed. The idea didn't sit well with him. She was doing her job. Damn the woman. Did he want something else from her? Sex? No, his body didn't react to her presence, not in a sexual way.

"Then, why are you waiting?" Gunny asked as he tried to prop himself up. He coughed, violently then wiped the blood away with the back of his hand.

"She's all bluster, like most." He offered the data pad out, then snatched it back before Lawbook could grab it. "I've no doubt she's a strong fighter, one of the troops, but anything else?" When would she explode, go into the rant and rave, with tears, he was used to when he challenged a woman. It didn't matter how professional they were, they caved. Emotions got the better of them.

Never work with women, children, or animals. Shit, better off working on my own whenever I get the chance.

"Gunny?" She flicked a glance at the older man. Her gaze lingered on the Gunny.

Did she see his health was failing? The blood on his lips, the lack of focus in his gaze. It wouldn't be long now, and he'd be able to deal with Lawbook without the Gunny getting in the way.

"Your choice, Sergeant. I believe I know what I'd do." His voice faint.

Stone took a step toward the Gunny. "Look, I know you're a decent man, and we both know you're not going to make it out of here. Your lungs are screwed, who knows what else is damaged and--"

She moved without warning. Her right hand fisted and she lashed out, her punch landed with bruising force against his cheek.

Hell's Own

He stumbled, lights dancing in front of his eyes, balance shifting as his vision spun. Stone struggled to find his balance, one hand reaching out for the racks, shelves, wall, anything to stop him from hitting the floor. "What the hell?" He spat, blood frothing across his lips.

Oh, hell no, she hadn't hit him. He growled and took a step toward her.

"A single punch, same as I'd use if anyone insisted on disrespecting my sergeants." The Gunny smiled. "Now, is there anything else you two need to talk about? No, I thought not. Matter over and done with. I'm ready for a decent nap if you can find me something to rest my head on. Getting a bit old for hard floors and no relief."

Stone ran his fingers over his cheek. Tender but it would pass. "I don't believe you did to me."

She didn't answer, without a word she turned her back on him and walked away.

"Hey, answer me."

"She doesn't have to, and I recommend you leave her alone unless you want another introduction to her fist." The Gunny slid down onto his back, then rolled onto his side. "Damn ribs, fuser worked, but does nothing for the bruising or anything else."

"I can't let her get away with punching me. Are you out of your mind?" The words escaped before he had the wit to prevent them. "If this gets out I'll be a laughing stock." Not entirely true, but there were those who would make his life interesting. He frowned, only now realizing the other man was lying down. "You're looking worse."

"Why, because she's a woman?" Gunny didn't rise to the bait.

"Hell no, because I didn't strike back. I let her walk away." He worked his jaw, checking his teeth hadn't been loosened. "She's the first person I've let walk away from me after hitting me."

"You in the habit of being punched?"

"It happens from time to time, but as I said, she's a first when it comes to getting off without payback."

"And why did you do that?"

He opened his mouth to answer, but the words refused to come. For once in his life, he didn't have an answer.

"I'll tell you why. You need her, and the others. Doesn't matter how strong or smart you are, you're going to need her skills and the others will turn to her for guidance when I'm gone." He coughed again. "Which won't be long now. Blasted ribs. I wouldn't mind if it didn't hurt like a son of a bitch."

Stone turned away, his gaze searching the shelves. Without another word, he grabbed a tote, yanked it open and pulled out two folded blankets. One he balled up, placing it beneath the Gunny's head, the other he spread over the man.

"Knew you'd see sense. You don't live long in your line of work unless you've learned to keep your temper under control and make the smart choices. Not always the right ones, but the smart ones." Gunny closed his eyes. "Shit, this wasn't the way I wanted to go out. Crushed by a building because alien bug monsters decided to pay an unscheduled visit wasn't anywhere on my list."

"You have a list. How many options did you come up with?"

"Several. All of them involved an aged scotch, a willing woman, and a warm bed."

"Not a blaze of glory then?"

"That's for the young bucks, not old-timers like me."

Old? The Gunny couldn't be more than ten years his senior.

"Years in service can age a man, especially if he doesn't have a wife and family waiting for him. Shit, any decent woman wouldn't want a part of the life I've led. Away more than I'd ever been home. She'd have to be willing to make a home on one of the colonies if she wanted to see me more than once every two or three years. Who wants to deal with the shit passed down to dependents, or be the one waiting at home for the knock on the door. No, better this way. No one to complain about the paperwork and disposal of remains." The Gunny's voice faded until it trailed off, and only the rattle of his breathing remained.

They were running out of time.

Jakob brought up the rear, hurrying those who lingered to follow Salla and the others through the doors. Only when the last of them were safe on the other side did he step through and secured the door behind him. They'd followed the same routine with each cavern they'd passed through. Six chambers, two tunnels, each with multiple offshoots, now lay behind them. Enough to buy them time, at least long enough to wait for the Marines to arrive.

It wasn't much of a plan, but it beat doing nothing.

"We should be able to rest for a time here. Maybe long enough for the rescue team to reach us." Keeval settled down onto an upturned box.

"Rescue? Is that what you believe they're here to do?" Jakob pulled out his handheld as he walked over to the racks stacked with supplies. Boxes, sealed bundles, a few marked with their contents, others missing the labels.

"What else would they be up to? And what are you doing?"

"Inventory. We need to see what we have here. Items we'll need if we have to move." Most of the items still had a barcode in place. Scanning the packages would make it easier than tearing them open and adding the data by hand. "And they're survivors, like us. Didn't sound like a full squad, which means they won't have the ability to get us off world. Not unless there are pieces of information they haven't shared with us." Which was entirely possible. He hadn't had much to do with the military. Sure, he'd seen a few in passing, run into one around the colony at a store, or event. But by and large, the civilians and military didn't mix, not when it came to minors.

He snorted at the idea. There were no minors anymore, not in that sense. They'd all had a shock, been introduced to a situation no one expected, there were children, those too young to fully understand the impact of the attack, and everyone else. Where the line was drawn depended on the individual. Under five, yeah, children. Between five and ten, it varied, mostly children, but some now had a dull light in their eyes, the one which warned they'd seen too much and their world had changed.

"Shit, I hadn't thought of that. I mean, if there were any real troops left, they'd be out in the colony, fighting. Not wandering around to help us."

For all, they knew the small group headed their way comprised of the only members of the military left who were on their feet and ready to work. "It's like here, look around you. How many adults do you see?"

"Five, at least by current standards. Add in the upper teens and the amount triples."

"Right. Then why didn't more adults make it with us?" He ran the handheld over the containers as his mind continued to put the pieces together. The silence which had settled in over the group as they'd traveled through the tunnels had given him plenty of time to put the pieces together, and he didn't like what it suggested.

Keeval fell silent.

"Because they were picked off first. The adults were protecting us kids, making them an easier target. Stop for a minute and take the time to watch Salla, her father was taken, she wasn't. She was deemed the lesser threat like we were." He moved to the next set of boxes. "We're weaker. Which means the aliens are intelligent."

"Well, obviously, or they wouldn't have attacked without being seen first."

Jakob bit back the impulse to jump Keeval. He took a deep breath and continued. "This has been thought out. They knew there are children here, pre-teens, teens, babies. They could have chosen the soft targets first, but did the sensible thing and took out the adults, the men, and women who might build a resistance, who might fight back, first."

"Resistance? What do you think this is, a long term invasion?"

"I don't know, but it would make sense. You don't come all this way, from wherever they live, for a hit and run. Fuel, time, manpower, all the resources involved, it all adds up to a lot more than a casual, hey look over there, let's go blow shit up."

"How does a nerd like you figure this out? You're not a fighter, you're one of the chess kids."

Jakob turned away from the shelves and leaned against them. "Chess includes tactics. You have to be able to see the long and short term goals, think at least five moves in advance, longer if you're able. And spot the weaknesses in your opponent's strategy." He gestured to Keeval. "You do the same in a team game, but you've got a coach figuring the majority of it out, sending signals to the quarterback, or team captain."

"Yeah, alright, makes sense. So being a nerd has advantages?"

"As does being a jock. Strengths and weaknesses." He shrugged. "I can't run as fast as you, but you're not able to see as far ahead as I can, at least for now."

"You saying I'm not smart?" Keeval stood, darkness flashing across his eyes.

"No, I'm saying you have skills I don't and vice versa." *Never get involved in a discussion like this with a jock.* "If I needed a man to figure out how fast the ball needs to move to strike the right target, I'd come to you."

"Ball, right. What good is it now?"

"If you can throw a ball with accuracy, and you can, then you can throw a grenade or another weapon with a better chance of it hitting the right place than I'd have."

"Oh, right. I get it."

"Jakob?" Salla waved from the other end of the chamber.

"Be right there." With more than a measure of relief, Jakob slid the handheld away. "Be back later. Need to get these all checked."

"Send me the file, and I'll pick up where you left off."

The offer, from a jock he'd spent most of his time in high

school avoiding, paused Jakob in his tracks. He blinked, then grinned, pulling the pad out. "Thanks, it'll help. A lot." A day ago Keeval wouldn't have offered, but their world, their home, had been turned on its head, and if Keeval was anything to go by, they were all reassessing their roles and status. School was out. Not for the summer, but for as long as they faced their current situation.

Interlude Three
Unified Terran Government: Alpha Comms.

He'd been gone longer than expected, but Sheila didn't risk voicing the question rattling through her mind. Whatever was going on, they'd find out soon enough when and if Grant returned. He'd been summoned minutes after the information had been passed up the line and now, several hours later, he hadn't returned. She wanted to know what was happening, why the meeting was taking this long, but like others in Alpha Comms, she lacked the rank and connections to find out.

Unable to do anything else, Sheila forced herself to focus on her work, but it only added to her growing tension.

The dead zone remained in place. No signals escaped Pluto, neither did they respond to any attempts to hail them.

Could be a malfunction they're trying to fix.

She rolled her eyes at the idea. A malfunction which prevented the two ships, *December Rain* and *Wendal* should be within comfortable hailing range of the Pluto colony. Close enough to send a shuttle to find out what was happening, if the block stopped communication between the ships and the base. Yet there'd been nothing. As far as she could make out, the vessels remained close to the planet, but it was guesswork as neither ship had reported in as moving away from their assignment to send a signal back to Earth.

They were blind to whatever was happening out on the edge of their solar system. Something they hadn't been in two hundred years.

The door slammed open, crashing against the wall before it bounced back into place with a dull clang.

Sheila flinched as Grant stormed his way back into Ops. She didn't need to ask him what was happening to know he'd been overruled, and she watched her screens to make sure she didn't miss the message. It flashed up on her display. Orders to alert every ship in the system. The nearest one to Pluto flashed up, along with the transponder information.

Her fingers moved with practiced ease over the keys, details punched in and compressed. The message burst would reach the ship with the smallest of delays.

Grant stalked behind her chair and leaned in, his voice a hiss of fury. "You won't get away with this. You and that fucking Sergeant. Believe me, once this is over, I'll have your guts."

She didn't look back, refused to say anything to him, and refrained from smiling when he stepped back to continue with his shift.

If she was wrong, so be it.

But if she was right, then there would be nothing he could do to her.

Chapter Eleven

Cora didn't look back at the man, despite his words. Instead, she walked away with her head held high, back straight, features schooled into an emotionless mask. Only once she was out of sight did she shake out her hand to ease the sting from the punch. No broken knuckles or fingers, a bruise later, but nothing she needed to worry about. Hitting him had made sense, though she should have shifted her stance before punching him. The pain wasn't a problem, the lack of skill behind the blow was. She knew better. Still, the man deserved it. *Arrogant.* The idea caught her off guard. Was she the arrogant one? Or him? The urge to turn around and confront him again surged into life, but she ignored it. If she was arrogant, it was with a damn fine reason, and she didn't allow it to rule her decisions, or how she worked. Her time in the Marines had taught her several valuable lessons. Including the fact you didn't reach the rank of sergeant unless you were ready to go toe to toe with anyone who got in your way.

It didn't mean throwing punches anytime a fellow Marine decided to flex their muscles. But being willing to knock down the occasional recruit prevented the rest from determining you weren't worth listening to.

Marines respected strength, the ability to command, and a calm head in the middle of chaos.

Like Gunny.

Her throat tightened. The Gunny wasn't long for this world, and walking away from him wouldn't change a damn thing. They had to leave, and soon if they wanted to reach the other survivors. Could she risk waiting for Gunny to pass?

Have to. We don't leave a man behind. Especially not to die alone, on a world not their own. He'd have waited for her, or anyone else in the small group and she'd do no less. Only a handful of colonists had been born on Pluto, maybe twenty children since she'd arrived. Not that she kept a close eye on the birth announcements. Not her family. Not her problem.

Except they were her problem now. If there were young children in the mix, it would slow them down. No, she wouldn't think about it, not until she could see the situation for herself.

"Sergeant?" Lackey lifted his gaze. "What next?"

"Gunny." She didn't glance back at where she'd left the older man.

"He's doing better?" Hope flickered across the corporal's eyes.

"No, this is..." her words trailed off. Damn it, she wasn't going to cry. "He's not going to make it, internal bleeding. All we can do is make him comfortable."

"No, you're wrong. You didn't pay attention to the readouts," Lackey took a step toward Gunny.

She reached out and grabbed Lackey's arm. "Don't. This isn't a joke. Or a mistake. Both lungs punctured. Internal bleeding. There's another problem, a shadow around one lung. I don't know what it means, but it's not good. I'm sorry, Lackey. I don't want him to lose him either, but we don't get to choose who lives and who dies. It's in the hands of fate, god, or whoever you believe in." She could drag it out, she had options, a means of keeping him around for a few more hours, but the end result would be the same. Selfish idea. No one deserved their final hours being dragged out, increasing the pain. Different if he demanded it, but she wasn't about to make the offer. A shot of pain reliever, a boost shot, and he might make it for another two hours, three if she was lucky. But then he'd die alone. They couldn't wait, not with the civilians huddled in the shelters.

Duty.

Yeah, she fuckin' hated duty, but it wouldn't prevent her from doing what was right.

"You get the kids." Gunny's voice, strained but audible, carried through the room.

"Not yet, but it's the plan, Gunny." She pasted on a smile and turned back to watch him. "You need anything?" His eyes closed as she watched him.

Silence.

"Gunny?" She took a step, then three before the movement turned into a half run. "Gunny?"

A rattle. His lungs working, but barely.

She dropped to her knees and reached for his hands. Cool, clammy.

"Here," a whispered rumble of a word, "for now."

"Gunny, stay with us." Damnit, she'd convinced herself she was ready to say farewell, but now her heart said otherwise. It wanted him to stay, to live, to do anything he needed to remain with them. "You don't have to leave."

"No choice." His eyes moved beneath the closed lids. "Going off duty, Sergeant Bloodlaw. You have command."

No, she didn't want to deal with him dying on her. *Don't always get what you want.* "Understood, Gunny." She squeezed his hand. He wouldn't go into the darkness alone.

"Sergeant?" Lackey asked from behind her.

"Few more minutes. Walker is grabbing the rifles, they appeared to be in decent shape when I found them. Plenty of power packs and magazines." She didn't turn to address him.

"How's Gunny?"

She shook her head. The hand she held was now limp and lacking the strength she'd always associated with the Gunnery Sergeant. With her free hand, she touched his wrist, finding his pulse. Slow. The gaps between the beats increased each time. Her throat tightened, but she didn't leave his side. "I won't let you down, Gunny." Had she spoken the words out loud, or had they been in her mind? Not that it mattered, either way, he'd have heard her.

A hand touched her shoulder. Lackey. A small squeeze as the corporal stood at her side, waiting in silence.

A sigh, long, marked with the rattle she now understood marked his death, the Gunny released his last breath and moved no more.

How long she knelt at the older man's side, she neither knew nor cared. Lackey remained with her, neither speaking as she folded the Gunny's arms over his chest, took his tags, then pulled the blanket over his face. Only then did she stand and turn to glance around the room.

Everyone, including Stone, watched her. Faces sober.

"We have a job to do, and he wouldn't want us to linger. Not on his behalf. He's no longer with us in body, but you can bet, no matter what your beliefs, he's watching us. I, for one, have no desire to have a disappointed Gunnery Sergeant chasing me down because we let him down." A band wrapped itself around her heart, tears tried to spill, but her voice remained steady. "Let's get this done."

"Oorah." The reply came from all of them, including the civilians.

"Got the rifles, Sergeant." Walker held up the bundle.

"It's a start." The weapons would give them an edge. Under normal circumstances, anything which might damage the dome wouldn't be used, but it no longer mattered. The dome no longer held oxygen in place, and the only reason they hadn't floated off into space, or at least were still able to run, move and hide with their rate of pace was because the gravity units worked, at least for now. Not being a tech, she had no clue how it worked when the dome had been damaged, she merely accepted it did and continued on with her work. She activated her comm and double checked the channel. "We're heading out in ten minutes. Will be there soon. Stay tight."

"Understood."

She closed the channel. The kids were smart enough not to engage in chit chat on the open line. Better than many adults she'd dealt with.

"John Clarkson?" Had she remembered the name?

The pale skinned, nervous civilian lifted one trembling hand. "Yes, Sergeant?"

"I need you to stay with Walker, he's trained with the rifle, and can help you if you need assistance." She inclined her head in Walker's direction. "Stone, you're with me."

"Oh, thank God," he said as relief chased away the shadows across his eyes. "Thought I'd have to figure it out on my own."

"Not how we work, Clarkson." No one else needed special assistance, not from the small amount of information she'd been able to gather from the civilians. Liam Somner had weapons and explosives experience, and Virgil Power had time spent in private security, though going by his gut he was more a desk man of late. Harvard inclined his head and tapped the rifle he held. Navy or not, the man had enough training to fall into line.

"I won't let you down." Clarkson offered a weak smile.

"I have faith in you." More than she had in Stone.

Full suits waited for the group. With practiced ease Cora stepped into the environmental suit, closing it up as she went along, but waited until the others were ready before she reached for one of the rifles, slid the energy pack in place and checked the weapon. The skin between her shoulder blades itched, and she didn't have to turn to know Stone had joined them. Meant she wouldn't have to drag him out. "There's a suit for you, should fit." She gestured to the remaining ones. "We're leaving in five."

He grunted but didn't argue.

The man was a problem. Sooner or later they would get into it, beyond a single thrown punch. As long as he waited until they were safe to throw his punch, she didn't care. The fight would settle things between them. But this wasn't the time, nor place, for a full out brawl. He wouldn't fight fair either, not that she planned on fighting anything but no holds barred. She was, after all, a marine, and there were always those who wanted to cause problems. Fighting by the book you kept to the ring. Any other time, you fought as if your life depended on it because one day it would.

"We stay alert. Any sign of alien life you alert me. We can't ever forget we're no longer alone. What they want with us, why they're here, none of it matters. We get to the Rooster, find the survivors, and bring them back. If we stumble across information, we can send back to Earth, great, but it's not our primary goal." She let her gaze move over the assembled men. What had happened to the other marines in the colony? Where they fighting back? Or dead? A hundred questions rolled through her mind. She pushed the voices away, locked down the questions, and refused to follow them down the dark alleyways such ideas always led to.

"Sergeant, if there's one group of survivors, there have to be others. Maybe at the base," said Walker.

"We don't know, and until we do, we act as if this group is the last knot of survivors in the colony. Got it?"

"Yes, Sergeant." His gaze flickered in Stone's direction, then away.

"All right, let's get this done. Stone, you're with me." She'd told him once, but he hadn't replied. Merely given her a hard glare.

"Understood," he **said**.

Grunts and obedience were safer than arguments.

"Keep low, keep tight, and no comm chatter. Emergency communications only." She pushed the helmet in place, slammed the face plate down and punched in the security code.

It was time.

"Wake up."

Small hands patted his cheeks. The same person who'd spoken? He didn't recognize the voice. Had he fallen asleep at his station again? He tried to ignore the voice. He didn't want to wake up, not even if being caught asleep would get him in trouble. Which it would if he was at work. And where else would he be?

"Mister, you need to wake up."

Zac groaned and opened his eyes. A pair of young pale blue eyes stared back at him. Soft brown curls added an air of innocent to the pre-teen, and he tried to remember what a kid was doing in the comm room. "I'm awake. Don't tell Laura, will you." Sleep, what was wrong with grabbing extra naps when he had the chance. Not as if anything happened out here. A few traders, new colonists, and the occasional asteroid. "Few more minutes, Laura doesn't need to know."

"Who?" The girl frowned.

"He's confused, give him a minute." An adult male, or at least one whose voice had broken. "Takes a bit to come around after a blow."

"Don't want them coming back before he's awake. Wouldn't want one of them to be the first thing you see." A second man

A voice he knew. No, not know exactly, but he'd heard it before. Where though? *Them?* Memory crashed back into being. The attack. Laura and Haden dead. The dome fractured. His hands moved to his chest. No suit. Where the hell was his environmental suit? He sat up, hands still patting at his chest and legs. "What happened to my suit?"

"They remove them when we're transferred from the cubes to this," the girl explained. "Charlie told me they stripped a few of us at first, then changed to taking only the suits and any tech."

"Charlie?"

"That would be me," the man who'd spoken before explained. "Kid is Iris. Other bloke is Matthew. He came in with you. You've been out for a while now. Couldn't tell you how long. They take anything tech from us."

"I'm stuck here because I tried to save his stupid ass instead of taking care of myself," Matthew replied. "Should have known better. Civilians don't know how to deal with all of this crap. Should have stayed hidden."

"You're outnumbered here, Marine," Charlie explained, his

voice steady.

"For now. There'll be others on their way. If they know there are survivors, they'll be working on a plan. We won't be left on our own. You watch, when the Marines kick ass, there's nothing of the enemy left in our way."

Zac rubbed his eyes and tried to ignore the banter. "Hazy." Did Matthew know what he was saying? No, nothing but bluster. He'd dealt with Marines before, often drunk after spending a few days leave trolling their way from one bar to another, most of them only quasi-legal at best.

"Will be, you were hit with a stunner. Least, I'm assuming it's what they used. Not like they explain anything to us. Energy. Knocked us out. Wake up sluggish and with a shadow across our vision. It fades though, in under an hour." Charlie sat on the plain white floor, his back to a matching wall. "You were in comm when this went down?"

"Yeah," he tried to see the man, but he was too far away to be more than a man-shaped blur. "We didn't stand a chance. One minute they were on the edge of the screen, the next they were close enough to hail."

"And did you?"

"Of course, but we got no response. By the time we realized they lacked transponders and were heading for us, it was already too late. They were on us. I swear, less than five minutes between them appearing on the scanners and launching their first strike." He turned his head, slowly, uncertain how his stomach would react to any sudden movements. A dozen other figures sat or leaned against a wall. One lay on the floor in the far left corner, and Iris sat close to the right. "Iris, where are your parents?"

"Don't know. I woke up and couldn't find them. Sirens woke me." Her bottom lip trembled.

No, he didn't need a crying kid. "They'll be fine. Maybe they're in another cell?" A cell with no entrance or exist. Only bare walls, floor, and ceiling. He strained to listen, hoping to hear signs of life from nearby cells. If there were any others close at hand. Shit, he didn't know. "Don't give up hope."

She chewed on the inside of her lip, then nodded. "I won't. Charlie said the same thing. Unless we see a body, they could still be alive."

"The Navy," asked Charlie.

"Hah, you want to rely on the flyboys? If they saw what was going on, they did nothing to help us. Not like the rest of the marines, if they are still alive, then they're fighting."

He struggled to recall what he'd seen. "One ship on the ground, not a big one. Wasn't on duty when it landed." He kept out of what the Navy was doing when he had the choice. Laura had been better at handling interactions with the Navy crews. "Another two vessels in close orbit. I didn't see what happened to them. We got the alert out, might be they caught it, or they were fighting the new arrivals. Three ships against one wouldn't be easy. Three against a ship they outmatch in speed and maybe weaponry? Odds aren't in our favor."

"Least we can hope the navy got the word out to the UTG."

"Marine, Navy, civilian. I don't care who got the word out, as long as Earth's been warned. These creatures took out the colony in less than what, two hours? If that? With what, three ships? Shit, they'll be able to do the same with the rest of the colonies, and then they'll turn their attention toward Earth. We better hope the UTG is ready for this because we weren't." Matthew scowled as he leaned against the wall. "They could take out the entire infrastructure back home before we have the manpower in place to strike back."

"Hope. Damn, you've been throwing that word around a lot."

Charlie shrugged. "It's all we've got. Might as well put it to use."

Stone kept his comments behind clenched teeth. Diving into it with Lawbook wasn't going to happen any time soon. No, they'd settle their differences when they were far away from Pluto and the aliens. If she died along the way, so be it. He'd win. Life, after all, was the biggest prize. Lawbook wouldn't survive long. She was military, they put themselves in danger in order to save the lives of others. And she no longer had Gunny to act as a sounding board, or pull her back from the brink. He wasn't going to take the dead man's place by trying to give her advise, not the type of mistake he would ever allow himself to make.

She wouldn't listen to him regardless.

No, instead he'd let the sergeant get away with hitting him. But the men he knew from the darker circles he moved in, wouldn't have left the matter at the first punch. Why hadn't she finished it? With the Gunny's death, she had to feel something about his loss and would need an outlet to clear her head and heart. God knows he would want to beat a target to a pulp if he'd lost a good friend. Or a man he respected.

Was she human?

Or one of those people who buried emotions until they had a safe outlet for it?

Not that he wanted to be around when she blew up. Tears. He couldn't stand a woman crying. They used it as a weapon.

He moved into position with Walker, silent as he allowed his mind to go over what had happened. His cheek ached, jaw complained, but he hadn't lost any teeth. More than could be said about the men he'd hit, most of them walked away with a mouthful of blood, blacked eye, couple of cracked ribs, and spitting teeth.

Women didn't give up after one blow. They came back, never let you forget what you'd done wrong. He'd been around enough of them to know you didn't assume everything was calm because they'd had the chance to say their piece. Which means he'd be the on the lookout for her next attack. Anything she might use to disrupt his life. It was how women worked and why he'd never married.

In twos, the group made their way through the airlock, then clambered one by one up the ladder. Moving in the suit wasn't as easy as it had been in the emergency suit he'd worn on the way down, but neither was he now worrying about the cold setting into his bones. His muscles no longer complained, the ache under control. The grey and green suits weren't bulky for the most part. His arms and legs, with the covering, felt wider, and the helmet had space in front of the mouth and nose to reduce the feeling of claustrophobia. He doubted the suit would cause a problem if they were in a tight space.

"Remember, once we're out of here, keep the comm chatter down. We don't know if they're listening. Don't worry about the suits, they'll stand up to scrapes and pressure. Projectile weapons will damage them, but unless it's a high velocity round, you should be fine. The suit will alert you if there's any damage."

If silence was this important, why hadn't either Lawbook or Gunny said something earlier? Had the chatter drawn the aliens to them? No, couldn't have. Or they'd be dead. Captured. Locked up in the box Lawbook claimed to have seen. Regardless, they wouldn't be able to fight back.

Only the sergeant had seen the box. What if she'd been wrong? Hadn't seen survivors in the grasp of the aliens at all. They hadn't been spotted, or if they had, the aliens hadn't deemed them worthy of attacking. It didn't make sense. Were the attacks focused on specific targets? High volume marks first? Take the large blocks of people, then hunt down the rest. He glanced at the woman ahead of him. No, whatever he believed, the woman didn't come across as a liar. More like a woman who could be too honest. Clung to old beliefs of being truthful even if it bit her in the ass.

The world before him, once they made their way to the front of the building, remained the same. A mass of rubble, broken buildings, discarded transport, and pieces of humanities existence.

Still, no survivors or bodies. Which suggested the aliens had grabbed anyone they could find, including the dear and injured. Perhaps they were the main course?

He shuddered.

Aliens. Unknown creatures with desires he had yet to fathom. Old dark tales of creatures living on the edge of the system, preying on humanity to fulfill their need for soft human flesh served on the dining table.

Horror stories.

Whatever had drawn the aliens to Pluto, he couldn't imagine it being the desire to feast on humans, alive or otherwise prepared.

Lawbook indicated she'd go first. Tapped her chosen partner on the shoulder, then turned away.

The first pairing headed out into the ruins, minutes later Stone and Walker did the same. He cast a quick glance at his companion, then focused on what they were doing. Booted feet carried him across to the next set of cover. Away from the safety offered by the supply dump. Only the insane would leave safety to head into the unknown, but he'd never believed anyone in the military could be called sane.

Now he was confident they were all lacking in the common sense department.

Moving from one set of cover to the next left little time to talk, but plenty of time to see the damage done to the colony. Few buildings remained intact. A couple were lightly damaged, but the majority had lost their upper floors, windows, and anything of a more delicate nature. More substantial buildings, ones built to withstand the loss of the dome, were in the center of the colony. Same with the base. Everything else had been constructed after the base. An odd arrangement for one who had grown up on earth and seen how the original cities had been created. Out here, beyond Earth, colonies had focused on the base, strong buildings, safe holds beneath in case domes broke, or unsuspected troubles waited for the colonists.

Hell's Own

The helmet reduced his peripheral vision but offered better protection from the zero oxygen environment. Dust hung above the more recent victims of the attack. Structures crumbled as he stared at them and in the distance, a figure on two legs, with an odd hump at the back where its wings lay folded, moved through the destruction in search of who knew what. He tapped Walker's shoulder then pointed in the direction of the alien. The young marine inclined his head, and passed the word to the sergeant.

Until the alien was out of sight, they waited.

Waited in silence.

The ground vibrated, not as violently as before. He frowned, trying to work out the direction it had come from.

The center of the colony. Near the Rooster.

And she was leading them into the heart of the problem.

Which gave him far too much time to think.

Small sounds filtered through into his awareness. The creaking of stone, plastiboard, and moisture working its way through the caves, it all combined into a low background noise Jakob could ignore unless he tried to rest. Then it changed, turning louder than he could cope with, as a nagging screech at the back of his mind formed. Nails on boards scraped across metal covered plastiboard. His jaw clenched as he tried to ignore the growing cacophony vibrated through his mind.

This wasn't going to work. Between the soft chatter of the others and the noise from the walls, sleep wasn't going to be a friend anytime soon. He rolled onto his side and tried again. He was exhausted, but his mind raced, ideas, and fears flitted through his mind in equal numbers. Random images of people he knew, men and women he'd seen over the past day, darted into the mix only to vanish before he had time to make sense of what was going on.

He stood and glanced around before moving through the

chamber.

"Giving up on the idea of resting?" Salla lifted her head as he walked past. "Don't blame you. A lot going on. Nerves, the background noise, every odd sound is enough to jerk you awake. Makes sense after what we've been through. Nerves are stretched to near breaking point. Sooner or later, one of this group will collapse into tears or hysterics. Maybe both." A small smile flickered across her face. "Come on, no point in hanging around trying to rest when we've both given up on it." She rose and rolled out her shoulders. "Hard to keep track of time down here. Weird, huh? We should be used to the way days work here, the shifts, or whatever."

"Yeah, I know." Was that a part of his problem? The issues with no evening light, no false daylight? The various other factors put in place to help the colonists adapt to the lack of standard morning, noon, and night. "Did you have any problems adapting to the colony? I know most do."

"No, it's the same as staying on a ship. The false rhythms." A shrug. "You get used to it after a time, use datapads and lighting to form a routine, but it can drive you insane if you don't have a sleep aid to deal with the worst of it."

"You were born on a ship?" She'd never spoken about her time before the colony. Few did. What had his dad said? It was easier to adapt if you didn't cling to the past.

"Yes, came here with the first colonists. Well, the first ones after the military. Dad used to tell stories about the military snagging all the best claims until he'd been here a couple of years. One of the only times I heard him admit he was wrong. Who in their right mind would want to dig for minerals when they get paid for sitting on their asses. Or they did. Guess it's all changed now. They're struggling, like the rest of us."

"Or dead."

"Yeah, there's that."

"They might be alive, you know. Could be those things have

taken prisoners." Why did he offer hope when they had no means of knowing what the invaders were up to. "The navy, once they're here, we'll be safe again."

"Lie to yourself if you want, but don't lie to me. We've no idea how many have been taken, or what else is going on out here. The navy, if they had a chance to fight back, were either destroyed or ran like hell."

"How do you know they ran?"

"Because it's what any sane man would do faced with an overwhelming force."

He wanted to argue, but it was pointless. Odds were she was right. They were dead or had fled. Either way, there was no help coming from the UTG unless they counted the marines heading their way. "I guess."

"Not something you want to think about."

"Would you?" Dumb question, she obviously had. "Sorry. It's a lot to take in. Not sure if this will ever make sense to me."

"Just because I've been thinking the situation through, doesn't mean it makes sense to me either." Salla smiled, though it didn't reach her eyes. "My dad, he didn't trust anyone not bound by blood. Eventhen, he didn't tell me everything."

"I didn't know your dad."

"No one did. Not especially me." Liquid glistened in her gaze. "And now I never will." She turned away, her eyes closed.

Was she crying? He reached for her shoulder only to draw back. Would she believe herself weak? Or be convinced he pitied her? Not a mistake he'd make. He knew Salla, in passing for the most part, and the young woman wore an invisible armor of confidence around her. At least until now. "We're going to get out of here."

"You might, I'm not going anywhere until I know what happened to my dad. He wouldn't leave me behind. I can't walk away from him now."

He didn't argue.

Chapter Twelve

Cora led the way through the remains of the colony. It didn't matter how many destroyed buildings she saw, they didn't fade into the background. Each one another scar through her memory of the families, friends, children playing in the squares; older men and women who had sat in the common areas, drinking tea, coffee, occasionally something stronger, as they relaxed with their neighbors. Small parks with brush, shrubs, trees, and grass, all designed to both please the colonists and help with the recycling of carbon dioxide. Now, nothing remained of the peace they had enjoyed.

Damn aliens.

They'd pay. One way or another, she'd make sure they'd pay for the damage they'd done, and the lives they'd ruined.

They'd been forced to stop and wait for the invaders to move three times before they made it to the Rooster. The building, with its distinct crest, sat on the edge of the main square, along with the government building.

Shadows moved through the square. All three alien types, if there were others, she hadn't seen them, mingled in the open area, close to the now dead remains of a familiar play area. One of the aliens gestured to a knot of three of the six-limbed creatures, mouth moving, arms waving. If they spoke, she couldn't hear them, but with the lack of atmosphere, there was nothing to conduct sound. No, that wasn't entirely right, the planet did, initially, have an atmosphere made up of nitrogen with trace amounts of methane and carbon dioxide. Three months ago the first of the terraforming engines, built by the colonist, had kicked into gear, but nothing except drawing in the gasses had yet taken place. What happened in the process she left to the scientists, as long as it didn't blow the world up when she was still on it.

Had they been destroyed?

She shook off the random question, her focus on the gathering of unwanted visitors.

Cora indicated for Lackey to stay on watch as she gathered the rest of the group to her, helmets touching. Like this, they could communicate without using the comms. It wasn't ideal, words could be lost, but it was better than risking the comms this close to the enemy.

"We have to get into the Rooster, but with the square in use, we've got two choices. Wait for them to leave, and we can't be certain they will, or find another way in," she said.

"Why don't we take them out? I mean, we're Marines. Shouldn't we be killing them?"

"If we had enough people, and there weren't civilians waiting for us, I'd say yes." Kill them, burn, destroy, get revenge for the friends she'd lost. Oh, the urge remained, nudging at her, telling her to give the word and go out in a blaze of glory. Her drill sergeant's voice sprang to life in the back of her mind. *Lawbook, you get yourself killed out here without good reason, and I'll drag your ass back from hell and make you run the gauntlet three times a day until the end of time.* "We don't have the people, weapons, or information to risk going in, guns blazing."

Walker ducked his head.

"Don't feel too bad, I'd love to kick their asses myself, but we have a job to do," she admitted. "And our time will come. Earth isn't going to sit back and let this happen without sending help. Once they join us, we'll get back to the important stuff and reclaim Pluto. They aren't arriving tomorrow though, might be weeks, could be months, and until then we're on our own."

Stone rolled his eyes. "Idealistic view. If they still think Pluto is worth the effort, then they'll send help. Eventhen it's going to be a while. Weeks before they get off their collective asses and decide who and what they're going to send. The UTG doesn't act quickly."

Unified Terran Government. She should have protested, stood, and defended the honor of serving the UTG, but why waste her breath. It would be a lie.

"This is different, it's not like one of their new regulations they're trying to push through. Pluto has a representative in the UTG, he'll speak for the colony." Walker said.

"If he finds out what's going on. I might not like it, Walker, but Stone is right. We could be out here, without back up, for weeks. Odds are they will send help, but they'll also try to negotiate, to keep the peace. They don't want to spiral into another war. The last one was centuries ago. And it doesn't help with the current situation. We still need to get into the Rooster, and soon."

"Tunnels?"

"They exist, but I don't know of the one which will get us in. I could bring up the data, but we don't know if they've hacked their way into the system I'd have to access." Too many unknowns. She swore under her breath, mind racing. There had to be a way which didn't include taking the open route across the square, right under the noses of the aliens. If they were collecting survivors, she wasn't going to offer them fresh meat.

The answer came from the one person she didn't want to lean on.

"I know the way."

Yeah, of course he does.

"They're coming." Iris whispered. "Don't let them see you're afraid. They've dragged out the ones who show fear. Not sure what happened to them." She nibbled on her bottom lip. "Maybe don't look at them at all, it's safer."

Zac frowned and glanced around. If the kid could handle them, so could he. Besides, he'd already had a ceiling fall down on him, and been knocked over by another alien, what did he have to be afraid of? *Three eyes, wings, scales.* He swallowed. Yeah, maybe not staring at the aliens would be the wisest thing until he became used to their presence. "Thanks for the heads up." He tried to smile, but at best he managed a weak grin.

"I peeked at them, through my hands," Iris admitted, her voice pitched low. "Still scared me though."

Doors opened and closed with a hiss of metal against metal, and he tensed. He lifted his chin, straightened his back, and he tried not to peek outside of the cell. He could do this, he wouldn't stare directly at them, no matter what his instincts demanded. His mouth dried as he sat and listened until the shadow fell across his seated form. *Don't look.*

Matthew stood, facing the alien. Or was it aliens? His head turned, and he stopped himself. He wasn't ready to meet their gaze. Not with the memory of the shadow the first time, the winged creature standing over him, weapon in hand ready to strike him. Cold sweat traced trickling lines down his back.

The noise, when it came, wasn't what he'd expected. Not words but chirps and clicks.

Of course, why would they speak English or any other old Earth language, when they were from God alone knew where?

The alien lifted one limb, gesturing with its digits and Zac turned to glance at the creature. His stomach protested, nerves running through his body as it threatened to void itself of anything not required to keep him alive. Tall, winged, though the scale-covered wings were folded behind its back. Three almond shaped eyes watched him from the other side of the clear wall. It tipped its head to the left and chirruped again.

"They think we can understand them," Iris whispered.

It turned its attention to the child and tapped one of the multi-jointed digits against the wall.

Iris ducked her head.

"Children should be seen and not heard, I think," Charles explained. "Anytime Iris speaks when they visit, they do the same thing. I don't believe they have any real experience with children outside of their own species."

"Oh, you can understand them?"

"Not really, more of an educated guess. Going by their reactions when we speak. Watch him, he's watching, head-turning any time one of us speaks."

"Him?"

"Sounds better than it, doesn't it?" Charles grinned.

"I guess." It wasn't human, assigning human genders to the creature made no sense.

The winged alien tapped the wall again, then pointed at Zac and gestured for him to approach.

"Oh, never seen them do that before."

Zac rose but didn't turn toward Charles. Maybe it was his civilian uniform? Or the fact he'd been caught with Matthew? *How the hell would I know what it's thinking?* Uncertain he took a step toward the creature, then stopped.

It made an odd zerrrrp noise and pointed to a spot. Gestured to Zac and indicated again.

"Alright, what is it you want?" Zac asked as he stood where the alien wanted him. "Not going to be a good conversation here. We don't know your language." Up close, the thing wasn't as scary as he first thought. "You're an ugly looking thing, but I'm guessing you'd say the same about us."

Iris giggled, though she tried to muffle the noise.

The alien inclined its head then moved to the left and gestured to Charles. This time they knew what he wanted, and the older man took his place. Matthew grunted but did as he was told when his time came, leaving only Iris behind.

"Maybe they're going to feed us?" Charles mused.

"Or they want to see our differences, height, weight, coloring," said Matthew.

A hiss was the only warning given before walls slid up from the floor, closing each man in his own cubicle. If the being had moved, Zac hadn't seen it, not with his attention caught between the others in the prison.

Hell's Own

Iris screamed as the wall behind her opened up, and an alien claw reached through to grab her by the back of the neck as Zac turned to glance at the girl. She struggled. He slammed his fists against the clear walls now holding him in place, but the structures remained in place. Iris kicked, twisted and sobbed as she was dragged out of the cell by the second alien until a loud zap silenced the child and she went limp in her captors grasp.

"Let her go." Matthew demanded as he lashed one clenched fist at the small cell. "You piece of shit, she's a child, no danger to you."

He wanted to protest, to scream at the aliens, but his throat threatened to close. This wasn't happening. What did they want with the child? With the rest of them?

"I'll kill you. If you hurt that girl, I'll hunt every last one of you down and kill you," snarled Matthew. "She's done nothing to you."

The alien made no sound but lifted it's left upper limb and touched a control on a small brown and green colored sheath on the limb. The front sections of their individual holding room moved, closing in on the men, forcing them to stand against the back wall.

They were going to die, all of them. Squashed for the amusement of a giant bug.

The material holding them in place shifted behind him as a cool liquid wrapped around his wrists, ankles and throat. It flowed into place, washing over his skin before it returned to solid form, creating bands around his limbs and throat.

"Fucking alien piece of shit. What do you think we are?"

They could coach it any way they wanted, but the collar said it all.

They were slaves.

Stone listened as the sergeant filled in the rest of the group, an idea forming as she continued. The tunnels. He knew the ones leading into the government building, and the ones connected to it. Including the turn off which should, in theory, get them into the Rooster building. He smiled. She needed him. He had the information she wanted. For a moment, he enjoyed the knowledge.

"I know the way in." He didn't hide his smile.

"We can't leave the kids trapped there. Sooner or later, their presence is going to be noticed."

"We won't," she replied, casting a glance at Walker. "Not if Stone is telling the truth."

"I have no reason to lie, not in this, sergeant." His jaw clenched. Was this how she planned on punishing him? How she would continue on with her vendetta against him? Anything he said brought into doubt until he eventually gave up? No, it didn't fit with what little he knew of the woman. This wasn't a vendetta, she was making her team aware of the doubts which lingered in regards to him.

"Glad to hear it, because if you do, I'll leave you to rot or be found by our new neighbors. Whatever happens first."

Not a threat, a promise. One he might have made himself if the roles had been reversed.

She didn't look at him, didn't need to with the way the helmets touched and assisted the transmission of their conversation. "Trust me, sergeant. I have no reason to lie, and every reason to speed up our escape. Hanging around here for any real length of time isn't on my to-do list." It didn't matter what she thought of him. He wasn't here in the name of the greater good. Business, but if he wanted to continue building his contacts, then it meant finding a way to stay alive.

"Then lead the way."

No thanks, no words of encouragement, nothing but another order. He didn't snap at the sergeant, no matter how he wanted to. It wouldn't help, and an argument out in the open would only draw the attention of the creatures hunting for them. "Keep low, keep close. Once we're in the tunnels, step where I step. A couple have protection installed, and there are turns you don't want to take. I don't know if we're going to run into problems, but it's best to be prepared."

"Got it. Walker, grab Lackey, we need to move out."

Lackey, Walker, Lawbook, names he hadn't known when he'd entered the bar. God, the bar. Jones and the others. He frowned. Why was he worried about them? They'd be safe enough; besides, it was his job to take care of himself, not allow concerns for others to get in the way. Business came first, it was the nature of the beast. The two men returned, and he waited to see if Lawbook would say anything else before he spoke.

A figure moved close to the hidden group. It lifted the weapon in hand then swept the area before it turned and fired at the remains of the structure twenty meters to the left. Shrapnel exploded outward, striking ground, buildings and rubble alike, but they didn't move. Didn't dare. The alien lifted the weapon above his head and turned back to join its friends.

Play? Letting off steam? He'd seen mercs behave in a similar fashion.

They waited, watching, listening for signs indicating the return of the enemy, but something else had caught their attention, and the small group continued their search on the far side of the rooster.

Lawbook lifted her left hand, her right resting on the rifle, parted her fingers to indicate a countdown.

He nodded. They were going to do this. He glanced at the other civilian, pointed at him, then to the left, indicating the man was to take position. His heart raced, mouth dried, adrenalin rushed into his system. When the five count finished, he broke into a run, bent low, gaze continually moving as he made his way into the rubble which covered the entrance into the tunnels. He didn't stop, didn't glance back as he slid to a halt and grabbed the edge of a large piece of plastiboard. The two men grabbed and shoved, clearing the section away. The second piece had four sets of hands working on it, and by the time they reached the entrance, the entire team was in place, silently working together.

He let his gaze flicker to the others and smiled. Maybe it wasn't so bad to be around the military in situations like this. They knew how to work together. Didn't ask too many questions unless they needed the information, and he had other bodies to hide behind if the invaders came after them.

No one spoke as he reached for the now cleared area and brushed the dust away from a small trap door. Not large enough for anyone to use, but it wasn't meant to be. He yanked the door open and punched in the code. To the right, a door clunked. He tensed from the vibration beneath him. If they were heard, it wouldn't be long before they had trouble breathing down their necks. He swallowed down his fear as the door dropped down five inches and slide out of sight.

Lawbook tapped his shoulder and indicated he should go first.

Fine by me. Staying out on the surface increased the chances of them being spotted. Stone leaned in, letting his helmet touch hers. "Left of the door, hit the red button to close it." He shifted position until he could put his foot on the top rung of the ladder and began the journey into the darkness. His mind raced, images of the passageway, the problems they'd face. He hadn't joked about booby traps. A few of the tunnels had been claimed by men like him, for tasks they wanted to complete in secret. Unless there was damage below, they'd be able to avoid most of the problems.

The trapdoor closed above him, vibrations playing through the ladder. Not enough to be dangerous, but he paused in his descent. He didn't look up, and continued down the ladder, jumping the last two steps and stepping aside to allow the others a place to stand.

One by one, the others joined him, the small group gathered in silence waiting for the last of them. For Lawbook.

The damn woman didn't understand; she placed herself in

danger by covering the rearguard. No, maybe she did understand, which only made it worse. Either she was convinced this was a part of her duty to the men under her command, or she didn't care if she died as long as her people remained alive. Marines. He'd never understood them.

She jumped the last two steps and glanced around as he switched on the small torches attached to his helmet. Her gaze caught and held his as she nodded.

He was still in charge. All right, he knew what to do. He beckoned for the others to follow him. Leading marines, not something he'd planned on, but they'd be able to survive unless by following him. No dead bodies.

Bodies he hadn't seen. Hadn't been able to get to the bottom of why the dead had vanished. He would. In time he'd get all the answers he needed, and be ready to part ways with the marines, and in doing so, he'd be able to get on with his life. His ship. His means of escape. He'd never have to deal with the damned military again. Not unless he ran into them elsewhere. It wouldn't be on Pluto, not with the aliens around.

He didn't waste time checking on the group and picked up the pace. He half ran, half jogged, down the tunnel, gaze ever moving, searching for signs the tunnel had been damaged or changed. Five minutes down the corridor, he paused, throwing up a hand to indicate the rest of the team needed to stop.

Team?

Oh, hell no, he wasn't about to start thinking of them as a team. Not his team. A group of men he'd been forced into working with, ones he'd be grateful to see the back of.

Light filtered down from above, pale, barely there, but enough to warn him what he was running into. A crack, wide enough to push an arm into, split the roof of the tunnel. Light, faint, delicate, seeped through from the colony. He peered at it. He strained to listen. Nothing. Only the occasional tremble of a pebble rattling its way from the surface.

Lawbook moved to his side and gestured to the crack, tipping her head to the left in a silent question.

He shrugged; he didn't have an answer to any of her questions. Nor could they stay here. The longer they remained in one position, the greater the chance they would be caught. Sooner they were on the move, the better it would be for all of them, and he could get away from this planet and the danger it presented.

He could do this.

Cora kept close to Stone now they were in the tunnels, her mind racing. The crack in the ceiling wasn't unexpected, not after the way the ground had trembled when they were in the bar. Shakes since had been rare, but still happened. Now she silently hoped the crack wouldn't spread, deepen any farther. She didn't need this to crumble in on them. Trusting Stone wasn't on the top of her list of things to do, but what other choice did she have if she wanted to get to the kids, and get them out without the aliens hearing them, tracking them down and then what?

What the hell did they do the survivors? The bodies?

Had she really witnessed the alien play, shoot a piece of wall for the hell of it, then celebrate, the way a drunken Marine might do? Damn, she had to talk with the pilot, find out what he'd been doing in the bar, and ply him for information. In all the times she'd spent in the bar, or others like it, she'd never seen a naval officer in the place. It was too rough for most officers. Which meant there had to be a reason why he'd been present.

She wasn't Navy, she understood ground combat, not flying through enemy controlled space. They handled boarding actions, shooting anything in their way, then letting others handle the cleanup, diplomacy or whatever else was needed.

If the ships are still in orbit, we're not getting off world anytime soon.

If leaving Pluto wasn't an option, then she had to find a way of getting the survivors and her Marines to a safe hideout and plan their attack when they were in a calmer situation. But no matter which way she turned the idea, one problem remained. She didn't have enough men. Enough people with weapon skills, and combat experience to defeat who knew how many aliens now stood in their way.

She pushed the ideas to the back of her mind. Find the kids first, plan later.

The small beams of light from the torches built into the helmet provided enough illumination to keep her from tripping up; still they took things slow. Silence. She was used to silence. Working with her squad, the full team, normally included low conversation through the private comm channel. This time they couldn't risk it. They had no clue what the invaders were up to, what level of tech were they dealing with, or anything more than there were at least three different types of aliens now on Pluto. Too many questions and no answers, nothing she could reach out for and build up the knowledge she could then share with the UTG.

She pulled up her scanner, checking ahead of them. The passive scan should fly under the radar, but she couldn't be certain. As soon as she had the information she needed, she shut it down and continued to follow Stone. The passages narrowed in places, widened in others, small pieces of rubble offered trip points, but she didn't expect her people to be caught out by them. The same as they had in the tunnels from the bar back to the colony.

Stone moved to her side, helmet touching. "Almost done, Sergeant. A few minutes more."

She wanted to say something, but he pulled away, the contact which would allow communication between them, broken. Civilians. They never understood what was needed unless it was drummed into them. She gestured to the rest of the group, keeping them tight, not spread out. They needed to be close enough to communicate, which went against her instinct to separate them out. If they were attacked, being bunched together offered two options, the ability to communicate and fight as a team, or be mowed down together.

Her leg ached as she walked, the reminder of the bruise she'd gained from the bar. The others had their own problems, scrapes, bruises, nothing which threatened their lives, but enough to remind them they hadn't come through unscathed. Despite the loss of Gunny, they'd been lucky. They hadn't been spotted, no other series injuries, and they would find the kids soon enough.

Stone paused after they'd taken a turn left, and rested one hand against a half-hidden door. He pointed to it as if he believed she wouldn't see what he was standing by. Her hand clenched, and she forced herself to relax. Whatever the man thought, she wasn't about to let her anger get the better of her. She gestured to the door. Did he have the code the way he had when he'd punched the right one in to gain access to the stairs?

The others waited behind her until the door opened. Airlock. Same as the one they'd used to gain entrance to the supply dump. Bigger airlock, enough for four people at a time. Fine, she didn't want to hang around waiting for one or two at a time to gain entrance to the safehold the kids had run to. Smart kids, she didn't know how many others would have thought of running in time.

But if there was one group of survivors, there would be others. And with those groups she'd find other fighters, or people willing to listen to her, follow orders and fight back. This was their home, and they'd want it back. Without the UTG sending help, it would be a long, hard struggle, but no one ever said joining the Marines would be an easy game.

She stepped into the airlock with the first group, waited for the system to run through its cycle and indicated she would be the first one out. The kids needed to know who was in charge, they were safe. Stone scowled but didn't try and push himself forward. She checked the readings before opening the helmet. Oxygen supply still working, fresh, without the background taste she'd come to associate with stale air. "We should be clear, readings are all in the green."

Helmets opened, the soft clicks and hisses filled the background as she stepped forward, moving deeper into the chamber. Large, grey walls, softly lit by emergency lights. Enough to allow them the ability to see what was going on. But no children. No adults. No survivors.

She activated her comm. "Sergeant Bloodlaw, we're here. Repeat, this is Sergeant Bloodlaw, I'm here with my team." If they could be called a team when she had an odd mix of Marines, civilians, and one representative from the UTG Navy.

A loud clunk at the far end of the room drew their attention.

"Didn't think they'd be waiting for us here, wouldn't make sense. They'd hide out in other rooms, give themselves space to run if need be." Stone grinned and walked past her in the direction of the door as it opened in front of them. "Wouldn't be sane to be where they would be spotted immediately."

The first two figures paused in the opening, outlined by the light behind them. She lifted one hand, allowing them to see she didn't have a weapon in her grasp now she'd shouldered the rifle. "You're safe with us, we won't hurt you."

Stone muttered under his breath, but she didn't look at him. Whatever he said, it wasn't important. Not now.

The final members of her group stepped out from the airlock, their steps enough to alert her even if the hiss and whoosh of the airlock hadn't. She didn't glance back for confirmation but kept her gaze on the group in front of them, still little more than dark forms presented against the lights behind them. "Do you understand? We won't hurt you. We're here to help."

"Speak for yourself," said Stone.

She tried to ignore him. Did the man have nothing better to do than aggravate the situation? "How many survivors do you have?" She walked, slowly, toward the now open door. "What are your supplies? Any with real suits or are you all working with emergency suits?"

Murmured sounds rose and fell within the survivors before one young, lanky, man stepped forward. "There are twenty-three of us, we all have emergency suits, but we found ten full suits in storage." He continued to approach, face pale and marked with dust. "We weren't certain you'd make it. Not with those things above us." He gestured to the ceiling.

Twenty-three survivors. More than she'd believed possible. "You've done well here. Why don't you show me what you've managed to pull together." She smiled, trying to appear welcoming. "We can talk about what you've seen, who is in charge, and what supplies you've gathered." How were they supposed to guide a group of this size back to the supply dump? Would everyone fit? The air supply, did they have enough? Questions rolled through her mind as she struggled to put the pieces together.

Gunny. She needed the Gunny's experience here, and the damn man had gone and died on her. *I'm on my own, and I've got this.* She told herself. She was a marine, not a civilian. She'd been trained. Had people with her who'd been through the same basic training She could, and would, do this.

"Sergeant Bloodlaw, I wasn't certain we..." The teenager took a deep breath and straightened. "We assumed we were on our own until you responded. No one else answered. Only you." He offered a hand. "Thank you."

"We're Marines, it's what we do." She softened her smile and took his hand. "You've done good here, more than in fact. So, let's get this part out of the way and see where we go from here." Ships, they'd need more than one. Or they'd need a bigger ship. One beyond her ability to pilot. Like most marines, she could handle a shuttle, a small hopper designed for traveling short distances, though they could be pushed for longer trips if enough supplies were on hand. "Lead the way."

Chapter Thirteen

Twenty-three survivors.

Mason Stone remained silent as the sergeant spoke with the teenager. His mind raced. His ship could take them, but it would be cramped unless he dropped his cargo. His stomach clenched. The last thing he wanted to do was leave his hard-won shipment behind. He silently swore. No point in raising his voice around kids and school teachers. He didn't need an uptight school ma'am telling him to watch his language.

"Lackey, you and Ready stay here. Keep your eyes and ears open, we need as much warning as possible if anything happens." Lawbook called out.

Ready. His eyes narrowed on the man. He didn't know anything about him, and little about Lackey. The entire group remained strangers to him, it was better that way. Getting friendly would only make matters worse, they wouldn't trust him no matter what he did. All the more reason why he needed to part ways with this company as soon as it was viable. He could get to his ship, escape, and keep his cargo. Dumping it only if there was no other choice. The Marines and these civilians could handle matters themselves. He didn't owe them a damn thing.

One ship might have a chance. If it ran silent, with every damn shield and damper in place, could slip away. But this lot? Multiple ships? No chance, not without help from the Navy and the damn cowards had left them to die down here. So much for the hero flyboys. Off drinking where it was safe, away from the coming battle. Making up stories of how brave they'd been before they were forced to retreat due to the difference in numbers and weapons. Lots of shiny medals and willing partners for the courageous men and women of the Navy.

His hands clenched. He glanced at them and forced his fingers to uncurl. No point in letting others see he was unsettled with what they'd found.

"Stone, you're with me." Lawbook indicated he should join her.

His lips sealed into a thin line. Did the woman believe he would ignore the request? Order. Whatever it had been? She didn't need to speak and gesture. Maybe it was how she kept her Marines in order. Hah, her Marines. She didn't own them. The gunnery sergeant was the man in charge, not Lawbook. Or he had been until he'd died. As for Lawbook, she had control of the current situation but lacked the experience to know when she should back down, take cover, and gather information before making a decision. No, this bright spark wanted to rush off, kill the monsters, and make a name for herself.

He didn't protest. He wouldn't be with them much longer. He'd leave her, and all this behind. It was the safest way to handle matters, and he had no cause to fight. Not once he had his ship back. If the aliens continued their conquest of Pluto, he'd be a fool to want to remain here.

"Mason Stone," Lawbook introduced him to the teenager. "He's a trader."

"What about the rest of the Marines? Are they with other survivors? Mounting an attack? What about the Navy? How many ships do we have?" The questions tumbled from the teen's lips. "We'll chase them off, won't we? The aliens? I mean, we're not going to sit here and let them pick us off one at a time? This is our home."

"Calm, you've had enough to deal with, and we'll talk once I've had a chance to check the rest of your group." She placed one hand on his shoulder. "We won't let you down, trust me, but first I need to find out about your group. Who's with you. The skills and supplies on offer here, before we plan our next move."

Trust? Was the woman insane, or was it a Marine thing? It didn't matter. He hadn't made the promise, offered these kids a sense of false hope. He didn't have to deal with the fallout, nor would he attempt to dig her out of the mess when it all went wrong. And it would. No doubt about it. Yet now he found himself next to Lawbook, leaning in as he spoke if a voice not designed to carry beyond the intended ears. "You're making a mistake. Be honest with them, it won't be as bad when we're left scrambling for answers."

She caught his gaze, grey eyes calm and relaxed. "I'm telling them the truth, Stone. I'm going to find a way to get them to safety. It won't be easy, but few things are in life."

Crazy Marine thing then. "Your funeral." He'd tried. No one could claim otherwise without lying. "Shouldn't have wasted my breath."

"Yet you did anyway. Says more about you than me." A small shrug. "You may not like it, but we're going to get these civilians out of here, get them off world along with anyone else we find, then come back for more. Marines don't leave a man behind."

"I was under the impression the code only applied to fellow Marines." Stone replied.

"Or those we're sworn to protect." Her jaw tightened, then eased. The irritation was gone in a moment. "You're either with us or against us, and if you're against us, you're with the aliens."

She didn't need to add to the threat. "Yeah, I get it." Did Marines go through regular mental health checks? Maybe she'd slipped through the cracks on her last checkup. This wasn't sane behavior. "Hope they have more suits than they've found. Or this is going to be impossible. With the dome cracked, and a hell of a lot of debris, the emergency suits won't be enough if we have to crawl through the colony. Too many risks for a basic suit to be damaged."

"If they have better suits, we can get them out." She followed the group into the next set of rooms. "It's not impossible with emergency suits, but it will make life harder."

He fell silent, knowing his words wouldn't be accepted, and let his gaze move over the room. Damaged, cracks in walls and ceiling both, not large enough to carry through to the surface, or spill a wall onto unsuspecting survivors, but too large to be dismissed as harmless after the way so many buildings had collapsed. Boxes, large and small, lay stacked along the walls. Cubes of unknown supplies, the boxes filled with who knew what. Had the survivors checked them for suits, food, water? Anything? Or had they remained hidden away in rooms deeper under the colony?

"Where are the others?" Lawbook asked as they walked through the chamber.

The teen paused to key in the code to open the door. "In here. It's one of the deepest rooms. Least, we think so. There are other doors, places we could explore, but we haven't taken the risk. Not after the first chamber. The cracks were starting to appear, and we moved before we lost the air. It's what sent us searching for a better place to hide, and we found this." The door opened, and he slipped through, followed by Lawbook.

Stone paused for a moment. One of the chambers had leaked? Made sense after what they'd seen. He glanced back, taking in the numbers with them, and entered the room.

Men, women, and children greeted him with silent, fearful stares. They didn't wear their masks, keeping them pushed back from their faces. But the room had enough air, and though chilled, it wasn't freezing.

A small whimper. The cry of a frightened child quickly soothed by an adult.

His gaze narrowed. A baby? He stared at the bundle clasped tight by a trembling woman. Fantastic. The last thing he needed to deal with was a blasted baby. And where there was one, there could be others. How did they expect to get kids out of here without being discovered?

"How many kids are here, little ones I mean." Stone turned his attention to the teen.

"Five too young to be in school. One of them a babe. Two are toddlers, half carried, half walking on their own, two old enough to keep up with help."

"Five. Right. And suits for them?"

"Only the emergency suits we all use." The teen replied.

"You have a name?"

"Jakob." A small smile flickered across his features as he ran one hand through shoulder length black hair, well marked with dust. Pale green eyes met his gaze, then turned away. "You're a smuggler."

"She didn't tell you that part." Stone didn't turn his gaze away from Jakob.

"No, it's easy enough to figure out, with what she did say. How she worded it. Besides, there's a look to men like you, so my Dad said."

Said, past tense. "He wasn't with you when this happened?"

"Pulled a shift at the medical center, I haven't seen him since." Jakob scuffed one hand across his face. "He might be safe. Could be he made it into one of the shelters, but I don't think he did. He's gone, same with Ma and the babe." He swallowed, his gaze shimmering with unshed tears.

"They might..." Stone let the words trail away. "I'm sorry." Offering the teen false hope would backfire sooner or later. "Lot of good people lost in this mess. Not something we can undo." A heavy weight settled across his chest, and he rubbed the heel of his hand into his sternum. What was going on with him? Too long spending time in the dark, making his way through tunnels and scrambling across the remains of the colony. "Where are the supplies? Your back up suits?" He had to get his mind back on track.

Women drew back away from them as he took the chance to do a visual sweep of the room and those within it. A handful of men, five who were adult. Mostly women and children, teens like his guide, younger ones stayed out of grabbing range, but none of them made the noise he had come to expect when dealing with children. No shrieks of joy, no loud noises, only frightened stares, and startled movements.

"Over there." Jakob nodded at the boxes along the left-hand side. "We haven't found a lot of usable items yet, only the ten suits. Might be a few extra emergency suits." He tapped the small pack on his belt which would have contained the transparent, emergency suit he and the others wore. Every man, woman, and child on the colony carried a suit with them. It took seconds to activate, which is why the colonists were expected to carry theirs with them at all times. And had back-ups in their living quarters. "Food and water, medical supplies. No, I know we have those, but I couldn't be sure about the rest. I've not been in charge of inventory. Salla is, she's the blond over in the corner."

"Thanks." He didn't wait for anything more the teen might say. Salla, interesting name, and it fit the woman. Older the Jakob, upper teens, maybe twenty. Legal, but too young for him, but he couldn't turn away from her. If she were a few years older, and they weren't hiding out from invaders, he might have other plans for them both. She was tall, willowy, sweet curves, a determined look on her heart-shaped face. Pretty with the ability to turn beautiful with the right touch. "Salla?"

She turned, long hair brushing her shoulders, green eyes meeting his gaze. "Yes?"

"I hear you're in charge of supplies and might have an inventory list." He relaxed. No point in frightening the girl.

"Something like that." Her full lips flattened. No smile of welcome. No warmth. Had he lost his touch? "But why would I hand it over to you?"

"Cocky aren't you?"

"Is there information you want to get off your chest?" She pushed one hip out, rested a hand on it, and shook her hair back from her face. "Go on, say it. Whatever it is."

Spirit. Strength. And this wasn't going anywhere. "Just need the list. The sergeant will want the information before she commits to a plan to get you out of here." Flirting wasn't workable with Salla, not in the current situation. She'd take it the wrong way. Hell, what other way could it be taken? Flirting to get information only worked if you put your heart into it.

And flirting with Salla, with a woman barely out of childhood and one he had to spend time with until he found a way of escaping, would be the biggest mistake of his life.

Cora ignored Stone as he moved away. The man was trouble, and she had no doubt Stone was searching for a means of escaping at the first chance. Jakob waved at Salla and walked over to the woman, leaving Cora with the third teenager who'd joined them. "I didn't catch your name."

"Lukas Vein," a small smile tugged at his lips only to vanish. "We weren't certain you'd find us. Once we realized the attackers might be listening in, we didn't dare reach out again."

"Lukas, you and the others have done amazing work here. You got people to safety."

"We worked together, but we at least two people on the way down." Lukas ducked his head. "Lily Hostlan, and Kevin Pride. Both college students helping out. They were snatched." He paused and paled as he turned away. "I was there. They pushed me out of the way. I should have been taken instead. I know others witnessed people being snatched. A child, Pippa, and another girl, Gail, was snatched up."

Taken? "What did you see?"

The teenager didn't respond.

"Lukas, this is important. The more information we have about these creatures, the easier it will be for all of us. Anything you remember will help. A small detail could be enough to turn the tide for everyone." Cora kept her voice low, calm and, she hoped, soothing. Kids weren't her thing, but the teenager was old enough to understand. "One of the things I have to do, in case no one else can do it, is send information back to the UTG."

He turned, eyes widening. "You think they might head for Earth? Shit, I hadn't thought of that. And I wasn't the only one who saw people taken. Jakob was with Gail, but Gail paused to grab one of the young ones, Pippa. Both were grabbed, and there was nothing we could do."

"I don't know if they'll head for Earth, but I can't rule it out. None of us can. They've come this far, it would be foolish to assume they won't attempt to strike the other colonies or hit Earth itself." Had the other colonies been hit, or were they focusing on Pluto first? Three ships, or a large fleet which they wouldn't stand a chance against? Too many questions and nowhere near enough answers. "Lukas, can you do this for me?" The other colonies. Jupiter, Mars, Saturn, Uranus, the stations, Earth's moon colony. Too many options and no answers to settle her mind.

"I'll try."

"It's all I'm asking."

Silence settled over Lukas, and she watched him closely, searching for any signs of panic as the teenager gathered his thoughts. He sighed and leaned against the wall, shoulders slumped. "We were at a school event. A lot of us had bunched up away from family, you know, the whole boring being around your parents, right? Yeah, I guess you do. The first ground shake came without warning, then the alert rang out. The get to a safe underground location alert. I'd never heard it, outside of routine test runs, but we all knew what it was."

She didn't speak, giving Lukas enough time and space to continue.

"I think I was halfway to the exit when I realized what I was doing. We all moved away from the danger, then we ran. Panic hit next, I think. It's where things become vague. I remember running, losing my friends for a time until there was a scream. More shakes, the buildings groaned, and a woman fell. I didn't see if she got back up. Then the second alert sounded, dome breech." He swallowed, his voice trembling. "I can't remember who grabbed me, but there was a hand on my shoulder, and I was yanked back. I think the same person must have activated my emergency suit because I don't remember doing it."

"You might have done it yourself, but it doesn't matter. It worked, and you're alive."

He nodded, eyes half closed. "Maybe." He licked his bottom lip. "It's all confusing for a time. It wasn't a quick trip, between people waiting for the elevators and the rest of us making for the stairs, it was packed. Then the ones at the 'vators remembered or realized they wouldn't work in an emergency like this one, and joined the crush. We hurried, but we were mindless, acting on instinct, but I guess it's why they run the drills, so our bodies know what to do even if our minds are elsewhere."

"Exactly, they do the same thing with the Marines. Lots of drills and exercises, especially during basic. Muscle memory."

"I remember being on the ground floor, then the doors into the rooster smashed open. Cries. Men, women, and children. Babies. Babies were screaming." He opened his eyes, brow furrowed. "I don't know how long it took for me to get to the ground floor, but there was a noise before the door blew in. It knocked people over. Several of them. Blood. Crushed bodies. It was like watching a holo, without the safety of it being entertainment. Am I making sense?"

"Yes, you are." What else could she say? Lukas had been through a lot, they all had, but unlike her and those others who worked for the UTG, he hadn't been trained for the situations.

"I wasn't sure." The frown deepened. "It was weird, a thing on four legs. Dark, mottled skin. It wasn't alone. There was a thing with six limbs, standing on its hind legs. It wore a suit, at least, I think it was a suit. A layer above the skin, thick enough to deflect anything we tried to throw at them."

"You fought back?"

"Kinda, we threw rubble at them before we made our way into

the tunnels."

"Brave."

"Stupid, all it did was anger them. The six-limbed one grabbed one of the kids, and her mother ran to try and free it, lease I think she was the mother. But the creature grabbed her and stepped outside. Another took its place, grabbing for us, and we realized we couldn't fight. A few of us did. We ran for it. A few of the adults stayed behind, I think there was at least one member of the Navy in the group. Maybe a Marine as well. Both wore uniforms, but it's hazy. When the lights went out, we couldn't tell who was a civilian and who was military."

"It will be, but you're doing wonderfully." Encouragement, the teen needed it, and they were being listened to. Six or more teenagers listened in, lingering close to Lukas. They wouldn't be able to catch every word, but enough to know what was being said.

"No, I'm missing a lot, and it's not there, no matter how hard I push."

"Don't push, let it come to you. Finish what you remember, the rest will return in time, and you can always add to it, find me and tell me what you missed, if anything." Would resting a hand on his shoulder work? He was old enough to be in basic if a parent signed off on it.

"Lily and Kevin were with me, I don't know when they found me, but they were there. They're both older than me, you know? Not that it matters now. They have to be dead."

"Maybe not, we've seen no bodies out there. No idea what the invaders want from us, or why they're collecting survivors and the dead, but I've seen prisoners. I couldn't get to them, not without being caught or killed, but there are prisoners."

Hope lit his features. "Which means Lily and Kevin could be prisoners?"

"Yes."

"Okay, it's something at least." Relief eased the tension in his shoulders. "Anyway, we ran, squashed at times, but we kept together. Then the wall on the left collapsed. The aliens were there, right there. I hadn't realized we were close to the outer walls, but we must have been because the rooster didn't collapse. Kevin pushed me through a doorway, and I was a few steps from the escape hatch when I felt a hand. Claw. Whatever. It grabbed me by the shoulder." He touched and rubbed the offending joint. "Still hurts there, ice cold no matter what I do. Thought I was dead when it had me, but Lily was there. She hit it, had a knife, though I don't know where she got it from."

Knife? "Did she cut the alien?"

"Yes, I think. There was fluid, purple, not red. Weird stuff, thicker than normal blood."

"Might not have been blood, but it tells us they can be injured."

"It howled, I think. I heard, experienced a sound, the vibrations. We hadn't lost all atmosphere then, and with suits, in place, any communication was muffled. We weren't thinking about using the comms." Unconsciously he touched the side of his face where the comm link was implanted. "Lily kept slashing at it, then Kevin was with her, a staff, pole, whatever in hand. I couldn't make it out. They pushed for me to run, to get through the hatch and I did. I got to it, halfway through, and looked back." Tears shimmered in his eyes, and he blinked. "It had them. They were still alive, still fighting. The purple liquid had spread, and Lily was screaming." His shoulders dropped. "I should have tried to help them."

"If you had, then their sacrifice would have been for nothing. You did what they wanted you to do. You got out in one piece." She rested one hand on his shoulder, the touch gentle. "You were unarmed."

"They're dead because of me."

"Or alive and prisoners. We'll find out." No matter how long it took, she'd find out what was going on, who these creatures were and what they wanted. Until then, she'd fight, hide, get the survivors out, then return to kick their purple blooded asses off her colony. "Don't give in to the guilt trips. Focus on the positive, what you've done, what all of you have done. Not many have escaped, and found a safe place to hide."

"But how long will it remain safe?" He lifted his gaze. "They're still out there, and we've no way of escaping off planet."

"Don't be so sure. There will be shuttles if we can get to them, we can get you and the rest of the group, off world."

"And the aliens? Their ships?"

"Leave it to us." *Because I've no clue, but I'll figure something out.* "You made your way down here?"

"Yeah, we kept closing hatches and airlocks behind us once we knew how many were in our group. A few of the adults wanted to go back out, find family members. You know?"

"I understand why. It's hard to leave people behind, doesn't matter if it's the safest thing for all concerned, we're still torn between saving ourselves or saving those we love." She squeezed his shoulder, then dropped her hand. "Anything else you can recall?"

"They gave up after we were down two levels. I don't know why, but they stopped trying to get past the doors, airlocks, or any other barriers."

Two levels. Useful to know, but only if they found it had been repeated elsewhere. "Useful to know, might be a reason, or they became distracted either way, it's useful."

Lukas took a deep breath and glanced around. "The adults will want to talk with you. One of them will remember, soon enough, that you're talking to a kid." He rolled his eyes.

"Thanks, Lukas. If there's anyone else you think I should talk with, let me know." It didn't hurt to let the kid believe he was equal with the adults. In age, he wasn't that much younger, and situations like this never only took age into account when there was a good reason. He'd done well and had been through more than enough for anyone to handle. "You've got this." Any minute now she'd find a set of pom-poms, but hell, a little cheering didn't do any harm, especially when she normally had to smack recruits into shape.

He smiled, a soft pink touching his cheeks.

Cora turned back to look on the group, spotting her people easily enough, except for Stone. Where had the man gone? Supplies, he'd mentioned them, hadn't he? She scanned the room as she walked toward a knot of people.

A baby's wail tore through the air.

Babies. Why did there have to be babies here? Kids, sticky-handed, whining children were bad enough, but keeping an infant quiet wouldn't be easy. Not unless they drugged the kid. Hard enough to keep older ones silent. Another problem to add to the list, but she'd be damned if she left anyone behind.

A movement caught her attention.

Stone. With a blonde teenager. Female. Salla.

Her hackles rose. If the man were trying to charm the teen, she'd have words. More than words if he attempted anything else. The damn female was too young for him, and they were in enough trouble. The thought burned in the back of her mind. He wouldn't be that foolish, and worrying about the teen would spend energy she didn't want to waste.

Gunny. Her throat tightened at the thought of the older man. Dying from crushing, or the injuries resulting from it, wasn't the way a man like him should have gone. Now she was left to handle the rest of this on her own.

Pull out of it. I can do this. I've never failed before.

Failure wasn't an option. Not when so many lives were on the line.

"Sergeant, we have a problem."

Just what she needed to hear.

He couldn't move. Not with the way, the separate cell held him, and the others in place. Iris' screams of terror faded into the background, but he couldn't turn to see what had happened. If the girl was still close enough to be seen through the transparent walls, he didn't know and wasn't in a position to check. "Iris? Can you hear me?"

"She's gone, they dragged her away," said Charles, his voice sharp, words clipped. "Bastards. If they've hurt her I'll--"

"You'll what? You're not combat trained," said Matthew. "Leave any revenge to those who know what to do with a weapon."

"I can still kill. If I get near enough."

The man was angry enough to manage it, regardless of skill or lack thereof, but it wouldn't be enough to stand against a combat trained Marine. Zac closed his eyes and let his mind run through the options. There weren't many available to him. To them. "As long as they keep us in these cages, we're helpless." Like this, he couldn't move not even to lift his hands and touch the collar now locked around his throat.

A prisoner.

A slave.

Owned meat.

The alien stood in front of them, watching the display. It's three eyes tracked each movement, however slight. And slight was all they could give. Their bodies locked in place, the need to move as he struggled against the restraints, and still, the alien observed them.

"What are you doing?" Zac demanded."What do you want with us?"

The alien stepped closer and tapped the clear confinement holding Zac in place. Once it had Zac's full attention, the creature brought its digits to its neck and touched where the collar would have been if there'd been one locked around the observer's throat.

"Yeah, you put it there. Your point?"

It didn't turn away from Zac and chirruped.

"I don't understand you. None of us do. We're not like you."

The alien inclined its head.

Zac frowned and pressed his face against the seethrough confines. "You understand us? Understand me?"

A small, but very clear shrug the only response.

It understood at least some words. Alright, this opened a small door. "What do you want with us?"

The alien touched his throat again.

"Slaves? Prisoners?"

It tipped its head to the left, eyes narrowed, then turned away from the small group. It walked with a clicking sound, each step marking its passage through the area until it was no longer in sight.

"Shit, they understand enough to cause a problem." Matthew leaned his head back against the cell. "Means we'll have to be careful how we plan an escape."

Zac rolled his eyes. "You really believe we're going to find a way out of this? Take a good look around you. We don't have a way of breaking out of the cell, have no clue where they've taken Iris and could be listening in on us. We can't break free when we're outnumbered, unarmed and held prisoner. Or didn't you notice the collar and manacles?" He tried to lift his hand but couldn't, not without bending his arm and twisting it through the small gap. If he managed to force his hand to his face, what was to say the aliens wouldn't tighten the confines of the cell until he couldn't move at all?

Or punished them.

Yeah, they could punish prisoners with ease, especially with the way they were being held in place.

"Iris, we have to find out what's happened to her." Charles insisted.

"I know, but there's nothing we can do from here. It's

ridiculous to believe we could." Zac took a deep breath and tried to force his thoughts back into a semblance of order. "But yes, we have to find Iris." The girl had to be terrified. Whatever happened to Iris, she was now facing it alone. He hadn't been able to help her. None of them had. "They can't keep us like this forever."

"Yes, they can." Charles sighed, shoulders slumped. "We could be kept on our feet for hours, days, however long they wish to keep us like this. And Iris, we'll find her. We'll get her and us out of this one way or another."

Zac wanted to ask how they were going to do it. What they needed to do to escape. It wasn't easy, nor were there any clues in front of them to led the way through to safety. What they needed to do to break free and find Iris. What happened to him, to the others, wasn't important, not unless it allowed them to rescue the girl.

Chapter Fourteen

This isn't going to work. Stone read through the notes on his datapad, the inventory list from here, and the supply dump. Too many people and items. They couldn't get them all out of here in one piece. Except if he dumped his load. Not going to happen. He'd worked too hard to leave it scattered on the surface of Pluto. His life, his entire life was in his ship. Not only the items gathered for sale, but the personal ones. Bottles of spirit. Pieces of... well, it didn't matter. He wasn't about to abandon it.

"You appear a little off." Salla set her own datapad down on one of the boxes. "Tired and other things. I've seen things like this before. In my dad. You remember him, right? The way he was able to tell things about people. You joked with him about superpowers. Nothing like it, of course. Impressive observation skills."

"It's nothing. Been up too long." When had he last enjoyed a decent sleep? He glanced at his datapad, eyes narrowed. Six hours since the first wave of vibrations had struck Jones' place. Yet his body ached, brain wanted to switch off, and the idea of a decent place to sleep continued to nag at him. He didn't comment about the observation skills. Whatever the man had been able to do, he wasn't here now, and if he'd shared the experience with his daughter, it didn't matter to him. "Exhausted. And I can't be the only one."

"Which is code for, you're a kid, keep out of it." She rolled her eyes and snatched up the pad. "Get over yourself, dude. You're nothing special. One of the lost, like the rest of us. We've all been there, running through the darkness and fighting to stay alive."

His hands clenched. "Hey, I didn't say it." What was going on here? "We've all been through shit. No one expected first contact to work this way. We were supposed to be, well, whatever." He growled, tension building along his spine. Why was he letting this kid get to him? *A kid I'd be all over if she were a few years older.* But she wasn't, and he didn't touch those who were underage. A body with all the right curves was one thing, the mind of an adult, one who knew how to please him, and herself at the same time, that was far more attractive than anything physical.

"You're like the rest of them. Nothing but another adult who thinks anyone under twenty-five is a child who needs to be controlled. Kept safe and out of the way. As if we don't know what's going on." She waved the datapad. "We've been fine down here. Most of the survivors are kids, older or younger than I am. We don't need a guy in an oh so last century trench coat looking down on us. On me. We lost friends, family, witnessed some of them torn out of our grasp. My mom, she was behind me one minute, then gone the next. Tully lost his sister, not even six years old. Who have you lost? What makes you any better than the rest of us? I'll tell you what. Nothing. You're one of us, and if you want to make it out of here **alive**, it's time you accepted it instead of lording it over the rest of us."

"Is that what I'm doing?" He hadn't, had he? No, she had to be wrong.

And why did it matter? She was a no one. Another annoying teenager, or however old she was.

"Yeah, typical *adult*." Sarcasm dripped from her words. "Doesn't even recognize when they're doing it. But we know, we see it, hear it, deal with it every damn day and--"

"Are you done?" Stone interrupted. "I mean, I know it's standard to allow the monologue, but it's taking time we don't have."

Her cheeks flamed. "Wow, you're one arrogant bastard, aren't you?"

"You expected something else? After all your righteous words?" He tugged on the edges of his trench coat. "There's a reason why I don't want kids. Have no desire to hang around with them, or talk about the fashion of the week."

"I'm not a kid. Sure, I'm younger than you, doesn't make me a child. I'm a legal adult, no matter what you believe." Salla lifted her chin as she spoke. Pride and anger sparked in her eyes, her stance filled with defiance. "Our lives have as much worth as yours, perhaps more as we have more years ahead of you, but you don't see us saying, hey, we know best."

"Because you don't have the life experiences to make that statement." Legal age. The knowledge he filed away, he wouldn't follow up on it except to reevaluate her actions and choices. "See here, ki-- Salla." He changed his means of address with a smile. "We're all under stress here, you, me, the Marines. But we're here, and we're forced to work together."

"Get over yourself, you're not a Marine." Her eyes narrowed. "You're a smuggler, trader, merc, maybe all three. Don't try and tell me you're not, I've seen you before. Know you have your hands in a dozen different schemes."

"Have I seen you before?" Did she appear familiar? Maybe it explained why he'd reacted to her earlier. The eyes, he knew those eyes. He flipped through the mental files he tried to keep in decent order. Eyes, set of the jaw, the defiance and strength, combined with the belief she was as strong as the adults. An image of the supply dump. A teen waiting in the shadows. "Duncan Prescott's kid?"

Her lips pressed into a tight, thin line as she folded her arms beneath her breasts. "Duncan's my father, yes."

"Where is he?"

"He didn't make it to the shelter." Her voice stripped of emotion.

His gaze flicked to the marines, then back to Salla. "I'm sorry." The words slipped free before he had a chance to prevent it.

"He's alive. I'm going to find him." Her features hardened.

Stone didn't turn away. "He wouldn't want you to risk yourself. He'd want you to remain safe, find a hole to hide up in until these bastards leave Pluto."

"You've no idea what my father would want, or not. You dealt with him on a business level, not personal. So don't try and pretend otherwise."

The words stung, all the more because they were true. "You really believe he'd want you to risk yourself? Put yourself out there and end up dead or captured? I know your dad enough to understand he'd be happier if you remained safe. I can't imagine he'd want you to go and find him." He studied the woman's face. Not a girl at this moment, but an adult who knew the risks if she attempted to find her father.

A small shrug. "I know he wouldn't be impressed if I ran without trying. I'll check the supply dump first, then--"

"He wasn't there." Stone explained. "I hit the dump on the way here. Assumed Duncan would be hold up with his stash, but when he hadn't found the man, he'd put his fate to the back of his mind. "Duncan told me about the dump years ago. Made it clear I'd have to pay for anything I took, and shared a guest code with me, so I could get into the dump." If Duncan couldn't escape, couldn't make it to a safe place, then what hope did the rest of them have?

Her shoulders slumped. "Which means when he was taken by them, he didn't break free. But it doesn't mean he's dead. If anyone could remain alive, it's my father. And your sergeant said she saw prisoners, didn't she? And she's smart, didn't panic when the Gunny died."

How the hell had the girl know that? They were on the other side of the room from Lawbook. It didn't make sense until realization sank in. "You have bugs scattered. Like father, like daughter. Never came away from a meeting with him without having to sweep for bugs. At least three of them every damned time. Told me he had to keep an edge on his rivals, and an eye on his friends." He gave her an assessing look. "I'll keep a close watch on you." And check himself for bugs. Shit, the girl was quick if she'd already managed to plant a few on him, but she'd had a fantastic teacher. "You didn't bug your father."

"Of course, I did." She rolled her eyes, taking no pains to hide her disgust. "But they block the signal, they blocked all outgoing communication. They would have swept him if they're smart. Not that it would matter with the communication dampers in place." Salla tapped the datapad on her belt. "I did a scan before you lot appeared, and it's obvious they have dampers in place."

More information he could use when the time came. "Anything at all, when you tried to reach him?"

"Crackles, static at first, then nothing. Went dead. Couldn't track a location."

Could be dead. The crackle caused by an energy burst. "Anything since?"

"What part of went dead, didn't you hear? Losing your senses in your old age?" Her lips curled into a sneer.

"Got a mouth on you."

"I'm Duncan's daughter, you expected anything different? He didn't keep his snark under control, or his opinions of people he worked with."

Not now he knew who had raised her. Damn, what had Duncan said about him? "No, I suppose not." He took a deep breath, sorting through the information he'd gathered. "I need to talk with the sergeant. She'll need the information concerning supplies before she decides what to do."

"Oh, I know what you'll try and do. Dump the rest of us, get to your ship, and get out."

Had her words carried? He didn't react, fearing one of the survivors would already be staring at him. "Is that right?"

"No skin off my nose, as I said, I'm not going anywhere without my Dad."

"And if it means dying?" Did the kid not understand the risks involved? "You haven't seen what it's like out there, the damage those creatures have done. The majority of the colony's been flattened." Except for the buildings in the center of the colony. Those had been intact, another piece of the puzzle, but without a picture to guide him, all he could do was grab the small shreds of information and file them away for another time.

"Mom's gone, years back. Dad's all I have. You think I'm going to walk away if there's a chance I can help him?" She took a step toward him. "Not going to happen. You can run if you want. You're a merc, no one expects you to hang around. Goes against the grain, doesn't it?" Salla didn't back down. "Go on, run for it. Make a break. No one will care. Mercs aren't expected to stand by other people unless there's money in it for them."

He bit back a growl. "If you were a man or an adult, I'd--"

"You'd what? Hit me?" She smiled, lifting her chin a touch more. "Go on, do it. One free punch, it's all you get."

Free shot? He'd expect this from an adult, not from this barely grown kid. A child he'd watched, in a way, grow up. "You think you'd be able to take it? No, never mind. If you believe I'd throw a punch at a kid, without good cause, you're insane. Which makes sense, considering who raised you. Your dad isn't exactly leaning on the sane side of the line. Now, you can have your temper tantrum, but don't involve me. I have enough to deal with." He shook his head as he turned away. Fighting with kids, as if he'd stoop that low without a damn important reason.

"Coward. Like every other merc, I've had the misfortune to run into."

No matter what Salla or anyone else believed, he had his reasons. Kids. There were reasons why he never wanted them and would take the first chance he could to part ways with the group. It didn't matter if Salla thought him a coward? The girl didn't know him, had no understanding of the life he lived. Her father might have shared a few stories, but had he mentioned the years he'd spent as a merc? *Not with the way she reacted.*

"Lawbook?"

The dark-haired woman glanced back at him before she ended

her conversation with one of the adults. "Is there a problem?"

He waited until he was close enough to talk in normal tones. "We have a problem."

"When don't we." A small smile flashed into life only to vanish a moment later. "What this time?"

"We can't get everyone to the base. Even if we could, it's where the invaders will have focused their attack. If there are survivors, they're in hiding. Odds are any ships on the ground will be hunks of smoldering metal, or under guard."

"I know." Her face smoothed into an emotionless mask.

"You have a plan?"

"There's your--"

"No, it's not large enough. We won't get everyone out. Choices, hard choices need to be made, sergeant. Who goes with us, and who's left behind."

"It's not going to happen. We all leave, or we all stay." She folded her arms beneath her breasts.

God, the woman was stubborn. "You're not being reasonable about this." He glanced back at the survivors. "We can't fit them all in one ship and the longer we stay here, the higher the chance we'll be found, and we don't know what they're doing with prisoners." Insane, she was nuts if she wanted to stay here. "I'm not going to die with the rest of them. If you want to risk your life, so be it. Not happening with me."

"Don't make me shoot you, Stone."

"Is that a threat?"

"It's a promise." She took a step toward him. "I warned you, back in the supply dump. You disobey or betray us, I'll shoot you myself. That hasn't changed."

Could he pull off killing her, without the others stopping him? No, it wasn't an option, they were watched. If he reached for a weapon, he'd be seen. Sure, he might get a shot off, but then what? "I'm not a soldier."

"Never said you were."

"I work for money, not glory, or a misguided sense of honor."

"Never claimed anything else."

Then what the hell was she thinking? "And I'm not good with kids."

"Then we actually have something in common. But we're not going to leave them to die. We'll find a way."

"What part of not possible are you failing to understand?"

"You're going to leave us here, aren't you?" The small voice, a sandy-haired girl, with a bruise on her temple, asked. "You're running out, and we'll be on our own." Ten, maybe younger, the girl lifted her soft brown gaze to peer at Stone and Lawbook. "I don't want to be left behind." She didn't cry, but her eyes shimmered, and bottom lip trembled.

"None of us do, Paula. It's why I'll make sure we get out of here, no matter what he says." Tall, striking, with jet black hair and a mocha cast to his skin, the man, barely old enough to be counted as an adult, rested his hands on Paula's shoulders. "We're all going to find a way out of here, and then the navy will deal with the invaders."

Zac bit back a cry of pain as he tried to shift his weight. His legs ached, knees throbbed, and the pressure beneath his feet increased as time passed. He closed his eyes and struggled, unable to relax. Any small movement only served to impress on him how he was held in place. He had no means of escape, and he no longer tried to talk, not even to keep his mind from sinking into despair.

Movement caught his attention out of the corner of his eye, but he couldn't turn his head enough to see what was going on. His neck ached with the weight of the collar, and the small shift of shoulder, neck, and head only added to his growing discomfort. Yet he couldn't ignore the flickering which continued to suggest they were no longer alone. If they'd ever been left unobserved, to begin with. How long they'd been held in place he couldn't tell, but his mind offered a dozen answers, ranging from an hour to days.

"Punishment?" Charles suggested.

"Huh? This? Maybe, I don't know." Zac replied, his eyes still closed. "It could be, or a means of breaking us down a bit. I'm not trained in escape and evade, or anything else which might help here. I'm a civilian contractor, working in Ops."

"E and E wouldn't apply here. You're talking about surviving interrogation," said Matthew. "Not the same thing."

"I'm not military, so excuse me for not remembering the right words," he snapped at the Marine.

"You should know them if you're Ops. Civies don't belong in a military job, don't know what the hell they were thinking of, signing up the likes of you." Matthew snarled.

"Maybe because they couldn't get enough serving military with more than one brain cell."

Matthew snorted. "Like it takes more than one to work in Ops. They keep the real brains out in the field, where they belong."

"Calm, he's not the enemy here."

Neither man replied to Charles.

A sound, soft, a whisper of movement, ended all conversation and drew the attention of all three men. Not the odd scrape-tap noise he'd come to expect from the aliens, but the footfall of a human being. At least, his instincts suggested human with a hopeful edge to the mental words.

The newcomer appeared a minute later, dressed in the simple garb of loose pants and a sleeveless tunic. His feet covered by slip on shoes, hair shoulder length and bound back with a black strip of cloth. A slender black collar was locked around the man's neck, but the oddest thing was the smile he offered the three trapped men. He inclined his head, arms folded in front of him as he paused a dozen pages in front of the prisoners. "Greetings, friends. Greetings. You're most welcome here and be at ease, you are among the chosen who will labor for the greater good of our masters."

Matthew growled, the warning low and dangerous. "We're not fucking slaves."

Confusion flickered across the newcomers' features. "I fail to see why you would be angry when you've been plucked from the dirt and raised to the status of the chosen." His gaze moved from one man to the other and back again. "We are the lucky ones. Fed, clothed, taught to serve, instead of sentenced to life on this rock, without the care and protection of our beloved masters." He sighed and closed his eyes, his lips moving, but if he spoke, the sound didn't reach Zac. "But I have jumped ahead." He smiled as he opened his eyes once more, the dark brown orbs alight with life and joy. "I am servant 5798, but I am also permitted the use name of Edward. Our masters have found human names have a calming effect on my fellow servants. A remnant of the past, no doubt, but you'll soon become used to life among the blessed masters."

Zac's mind raced. Did the man not understand what he was saying? He peered at Edward, why wasn't the newcomer able to fight his way free? He appeared to be calm, accepting his status in life, which meant he'd been a servant for a while. "How long have you been with them?"

"Them? Please remember to address our masters as either our masters or beloved ones. It is a matter of respect."

"Beloved Ones? Are you insane? What have they done to you?" Charles demanded. "They're fucking aliens, you weak-willed snot. The enemy. Nothing you say or do is going to change what they really are."

"How long, why all of my life. I was chosen when but a child to be trained as one of the trusted ones." Edward sighed and pointedly ignored Matthew's words. "I believe the young one who was sheltered with you has been handed over to those now in charge of her re-education. She will be a welcome addition to the ranks of the servants. It's been a long time since young born outside of the protection of the blessed masters was brought into the fold."

Trusted? Trustees? Zac struggled to recall what he'd learned about the penal system. The way some prisoners had extra duties and privileges. "A child? What of your parents?"

"I am told they died before the masters found me. They nurtured me, made certain I was taught all I need to know in this life. Over time I was given further training and skills so I may help the honored ones with their new servants."

"You can communicate with them?" Zac asked.

"Why, of course, and you will be able to do the same thing, once you have been prepared. But the work will take time, and I, among others, will teach you as we journey to the home of the masters. But first, we must attend to your bodies. You must be clean and rid of any bacteria or infections which may cause problems with the other servants."

"Not the masters?" He pressed.

"They are superior beings, and not susceptible to the same things which attack our weaker forms."

"Where did they find you?"

"Why, in the servant colony, of course. As all before you had come from. For the last fifty years, as you mark time, all servants have come from the colony of the pure ones." He waved a hand and dismissed their other questions. "Now, silence. The cleansing must begin before anything else takes place."

Zac tried to protest, but a thick white gas pumped into the chamber, stealing his ability to think or speak as it tugged him into the dark embrace of oblivion.

Cora stared at Stone as the young man spoke. She didn't turn away, refusing to break eye contact. "If you believe I'll leave a single survivor behind, then you're more stupid than I gave you credit for." She forced herself to continue. "And if escaping the colony, getting off world, isn't possible at this time, then we'll find a better place to hide up, keep the survivors safe and plan other options. I won't leave these people behind to be picked off one at a time. No matter what, sooner or later the UTG will be here, they aren't going to sit back and lose a colony, not when it's within the system. Pluto could be used as a staging area to launch a full-on attack on Earth, hitting each colony on the way to the final prize. They'll bring in either the Navy or try to establish a diplomatic resolution." The diplomatic option would be one they'd try first, right up until the point the aliens fired the first shot. Alright, maybe the second. Then all hell would break loose.

"You're insane. They sent three ships, not enough to take out Earth." Stone bristled his voice a sharp edge. "And if they have more than the initial three ships, it would be a mistake to take them on without more information. Look, if you want to die with the rest of these sheep, no skin off my nose, but I'm not going waste my life to be remembered three hundred years from now on a piece of cold stone if they allow us that much. Best we can hope for is to split up into small groups and find bolt holes as far away from the colony as possible."

She didn't reply, dismissing him without a word as she turned her attention to the two survivors. "It's not going to be easy, but we'll get you out of here. We have one ship, Stones, but if we can't get to the base, we're going to have to think of another way out." She kept her voice calm, it was the only way she could keep from losing her temper. Damn Stone, he was a problem. If she had to shoot him, then so be it. "We're going to need as many people as possible to get out in the first ship, and if anyone is left behind, which I don't plan on allowing to happen, it'll be me, and the rest of the Marines." Not the kids, never the kids.

"Right, then we leave you guys here, get the rest out. My ship, not yours. Think you can fly her without me?" Stone stepped closer, not enough to be classed as a full intimidation move, but close enough for government work.

She didn't flinch, refused to move, and forced her voice to remain level. "We haven't made any decisions except the fact we're not leaving the civilians behind. If you want to be involved in the plans, you'd be wise to remember the agreement to follow my orders. Unless you want a second bruise to match the first." She shouldn't have hit him, no matter the provocation.

Stone unconsciously reached up and touched the bruise on his cheek. "Lucky shot."

Did he want to be drawn into the middle of a fight, in front of the others? "Arrogant asshole. We've got enough work to deal with here, and you want to pick another fight? Waste energy which would be better used to plan out our route, and get the kids out of here."

"Hey, you're the one who brought up hitting me again. I'm just taking you up on the offer."

"He's pissed because I called him out," a woman in her early twenties wandered over.

Cora tried to place the face. She'd seen this one before, not among the survivors but before the attack. She hunted through the information, details she'd stored away in the back of her mind. A store, dealing in an interesting mix of supplies. A few legal, others not so much. "Duncan's daughter? Salla?"

A smile brightened her face. "Yes."

"Duncan?"

"Taken, but this one told me there's a chance he might be alive. You've seen prisoners?"

"In a cage, I couldn't make out features, but by the shapes, it held men, women, and children, all alive and still moving in the confinement cell." Had Duncan or anyone else she knew been in it? Or were they among the dead? Her heart sank at the thought. *Snap out of it, Sergeant. This is work, grieve later.* "We'll get them back. All of them, but first we have to focus on getting you and the others to safety. We can't risk a rescue mission until you, and the rest of the survivors are far away from here." If such a thing as safety existed, she'd find it. But they were still facing more trouble than she was willing to admit to in front of the group. Who knew how many ships were out there? The information shared by Stone had been vague, and since the initial attack, there'd been no means of communication between themselves and the base. If anyone still lived, they'd either be fighting for their lives or in hiding.

Stone didn't speak, but his dark gaze followed her every move.

Damn man, if he didn't accept how things worked sooner or later, she'd be forced to teach him a lesson the hard way. If they had the time. Which they didn't.

She swore under her breath before she allowed herself a moment to meet his gaze. "Did you get the supply lists?"

"No. She decided not to hand it over after our talk."

"So, you were being your normal charming self. Got it." rolling her eyes was such a teen thing to do, yet the urge nagged at her as she chained it away in its box. "Salla? You have a copy for me?"

"For you, sure. That one, no chance. Only reason he'd want one is to see if there's anything he can steal."

"Trade."

"Same thing," Salla replied.

She ignored the protest. "Appreciated." Cora transferred the list to her datapad. "I'll need time to go through this, and we've got to locate other possible forms of transport to get us all off this rock." If it was possible. Remaining on Pluto when the colony had been all but destroyed, wasn't an option she wanted to investigate.

"And if you don't find anything else, you're planning on sacrificing yourself and your men to allow this lot a chance at survival. Well, I hope they have another pilot among them. Otherwise, they're stuck even if you do find another ship."

Her jaw set. "You forget, we have Harvard."

"And you'll need more than that Navy waste of space."

"I can pilot for them," Salla suggested.

"You're a kid," Stone growled.

"I'm twenty-two. My Dad had me in the co-pilot's seat ten years ago." Her eyes narrowed as she shot Stone a disgusted glare. "I can pilot the Ajax. But I'm not leaving until I find out about my Dad. He could be alive."

The Ajax. Where did she know the name from? "Understandable." Damnit, they needed another pilot. The Ajax was a big ship, and she'd already mentally assigned Harvard to Stone's vessel, in case the man decided to do a runner, or worse. "Anyone else you know, who can do the job?"

"The Ajax? Where the hell did your Dad pick that hunk of junk up?"

"Does it matter? And it might have been a junker once, but he's repaired it. Looks like new. Or close to it." Salla shot a smug look at Stone. "And this one doesn't know it all. He doesn't claim the colony as home. Doesn't claim a real home anywhere except his blasted ship."

Cora filed the detail away. People without a home had little to fight for.

"There are a couple here who could handle it, they're younger than me but skilled. Not my Dad's level of ability. Enough to get you off planet."

But could they avoid being shot down, or boarded? It was a risk she had to take. "Who are they?"

"Lukas and Dianne," she gestured in the direction of a knot of teenagers. "Lukas is the better pilot on a technical level. Dianne has sharper instincts. Put the two together, and you'll have it covered."

Kids. Flying the escape craft. Why was she thinking of doing this? They were barely more than children, and shouldn't have the pressure of escaping Pluto on their shoulders. But what other option did she have?

"How big is it?"

"The Ajax? Should be able to hold twenty people in comfort. Thirty at a push... Decent shields, if we stay close to the surface, we should scrape under their sensors."

"You mean hug the planet? A kid like you?" Stone shook his head. "You're not old enough to have enough practice with something as dangerous as planet skimming. I doubt there are a dozen pilots on the edge who know how to skim Pluto without painting their remains across this rock."

"Not like you haven't done it before. And Dad taught me how to avoid most scans, and put me through enough practice runs to be certain I could handle any situation where I'd need to slide under the radar."

"Alright. Skimming the surface is a possibility." Not a good one, but she'd take what they could get. Cora mentally counted the men, women, and children in the group. Too many, unless they used Stone's ship they'd never be able to get everyone off planet. If they found more survivors, then the problem would increase. Last thing she wanted was to lose any of the current survivors, bad enough they'd said goodbye to Gunny, at least the man had died doing something he loved. This lot, they were civilians, lost, frightened, but willing to act together as a unit.

She scrubbed one and through her hair, grateful she kept it short. "It's an idea, and better than nothing. Thanks. I'll talk with them, and Stone, see what we can put together."

Stone grunted, and she refused to turn toward him. If the man had a problem, they'd discuss it later. Away from the others. Perhaps he was right about the planet skimming, but it was another option, and there were mines, small settlements, and tunnels with bolt holes, away from the main colony. Had they been hit? If not, would the aliens continue to ignore them due to the lack of heavy weapons? Information, never enough at hand in a situation like this.

A heavy rumble rolled through the ground. Vibrations shocked a path up her legs as more than a dozen survivors reached for a handhold or post to keep them upright. Rock and plastiboard cracked above, around and beneath them.

"Mama!" A child's trembling scream split the air. "Mama." Dust filled the air, small pieces of debris clattered down, and the ground shuddered. "MAMA."

Cora struggled to remain on her feet. The child, she had to find a way to help the toddler. Without thinking, she darted across the room, her gaze sweeping the area for signs of damage. The crack overhead widened, but not enough to open the room to the eyes of the aliens. If they had eyes. She hadn't been close enough to them to be certain.

One arm wrapped around the tousle-headed toddler as the ceiling continued to whine its protest against the trembling earth. She hugged the child to her chest and rolled out of the way moments before a slab hit the floor where the toddler had stood crying for her mother.

"Ursula?" A fearful voice called out from the door leading out of the chamber. "Has anyone seen Ursula?"

Cora pushed to her feet, still holding the toddler who now squirmed in her arms. The trembles eased, slowly, until she was able to find her balance without falling over.

"Mama?"

"Think I have her," she looked down into the pale blue-green eyes of the dust-smeared child. "Ursula?"

"Want Mama." She stuck her thumb in her mouth, eyes wide as she wriggled.

"Oh, my God. Ursula, you weren't supposed to wander off." The woman hurried over and snatched the child from Cora's arms.

She didn't object.

"Mama," said Ursula as she wrapped her arms around the woman's neck.

"Silly silly girl. You need to stay with me, understand? You stay with me no matter what."

Ursula's bottom lip curled in a pout. "Sworrie,"

"Thank you, I felt everything begin to shake, turned to grab her and she'd gone." The mother smiled and ran one hand over Ursula's back. "I didn't know what to do, then I heard her cry out and--"

"It's fine, she's unhurt, no harm done." Cora dusted herself off. At least the kid hadn't thrown up on her, or one of the other less than pleasant reactions children of this age was capable of. "But we can't stay here much longer. The way things are going the ceiling is going to crash in on us before the end of the day." Sooner if the aliens attempted another strike,

Her mind raced. What had they attacked this time?

Had they found more survivors?

"We'll know if they try to break in here. The sensors will trigger an alarm." Ursula's mother explained.

"Maybe, unless they've been damaged by the attacks." How many more could the structure take before it collapsed in on itself? "We need to get out of here before it's too late." Which meant Stone had to make a decision. Either he was with them, or against them. "Get your things together, and I'll get the rest of this group moving."

Salla hurried over. "Part of the tunnel has collapsed. The one you and your people came through. We won't be able to evacuate that way."

Cora cursed in three different languages before she took a deep breath and brought her emotions under control. "Then we find another way." There had to be other tunnels, and she couldn't be sure if the direction they needed to travel remained accessible with the passageways or not. "And a map of the passages here. See what options we have for getting the hell out of here before there's nothing left to hold up the ceiling."

Ceiling, walls, the entire thing could collapse, caving in on the survivors and marines both.

"I'll see what I can find." Salla paused long enough to take in the chamber before she darted out of sight.

Hell's Own

"You still believe you can get them all out of here?" Stone leaned in, keeping his voice pitched low. "Don't get me wrong, I admire your strength, but in this, you're being foolish. I could get you and your boys out easily enough. My ship's one of the fastest, and it's armed. The Ajax, last I heard, didn't have weapons. Even if those kids can pilot it, they'd be outclassed."

Hitting him would solve nothing, but damn if she didn't want to knock him into the middle of next week. "We take what options we can."

"Right, which means you're still stuck on this plan of yours. Save them all. Be the goddamn hero people remember when the dust settles. About time you saw sense. You know what happens to heroes? They die. Oh, sure, it can be a glorious death, but you're dead all the same when they start toasting your honor."

Cora forced her face to remain a mask of calm. No matter what the man said to her, she wasn't going to lose her temper. "Marines don't leave people behind."

"They don't leave one of their own behind." Stone leaned against the wall. "Doesn't say the same about civilians and kids. You can walk away from them without a problem."

"Then you don't know how the marine's work, do you?" An edge entered her words, and she struggled not to lose her grip on her emotions. Her gaze narrowed. Was he pushing her deliberately to reduce her ability to command both the remaining marines and the survivors?

If so, it wasn't going to work.

"I've seen your kind walk away from the dead and dying before."

"Then they had a reason to walk away." Cora turned her attention away from Stone. "Get your gear together, Mr. Stone. We leave in the next thirty minutes. You either leave with us or stay, your choice."

"You need me," he said. Stone pushed away from the wall and stalked toward her. "You and your people won't get out alive without me and my ship."

"With the Ajax, we'll be fine."

"You can't all fit on the blasted Ajax. You'll get the rest of your original group on board, but anyone else? No, you need a second ship."

"Are you offering to take a few of the kids?" She knew the answer before voicing the question.

"Hell no, I'm offering to take you and your people."

"No deal." A merc and smuggler, he'd have his ship locked down so no one without the codes could pilot her, and they wouldn't have the time needed to break into the system, not if the aliens glanced their way.

"Then get out of my way, and let me do my job."

"You really think those boys will follow you? That the corporal will accept your decision about fighting and dying to give a bunch of kids the chance to make it out, only to be blown up or captured before they break orbit?"

And there it was, the sticking point. She hadn't talked it through with Lackey, or any of the others. As Marines, they should follow orders, and be ready to protect the civilians until they were out of the reach of the aliens. But after all, they'd been through, she couldn't depend on them doing the right thing. "They will."

"Let's test your theory. Hey, Walker!"

The marine turned from the entrance into the tunnel, the damage enough to have sent the men in from keeping watch on the corridor.

Cora frowned. What the hell was he up to now?

"Yes?"

"Come here a minute, will you? Need to talk with you and the other uniforms."

"About?"

"About your sergeant's ridiculous plan on getting you all killed."

Chapter Fifteen

Stone didn't look at Lawbook. "You knew about this, right?"

"No," said Walker as he made his way across the room, his gaze flicking from Stone to the sergeant and back again. "Sergeant? What's he going on about?"

"This civilian seems to think we should turn our backs on the others and leave them to die." Lawbook shot him a glare then turned her attention on the youngest member of the team. "He's suggested we run with him, live and let the rest of them die, be taken prisoner, and used for whatever the aliens have in mind."

The young marine blanched, his gaze narrowed. "Is that allowed? I mean, I always believed we had a duty to civilians in situations like this."

"No one here to tell you otherwise, except this stubborn sergeant of yours. Think she's taking Gunny's death to heart. Wants you all to go out in a blaze of glory." Stone indicated Lawbook with a jerk of his head. "Me, I think we should live to fight another day. Better for all of us."

"Except for the civies, most of which are kids who should still be in school," Lawbook added.

"Why can't we all get out?"

"Not enough room in my ship."

"What he's not telling you is there's a second ship, Walker. One we already have both a pilot and co-pilot for. We need to split the survivors up. Most on the Ajax, the rest on Stone's ship. Or the fact we may not be able to leave Pluto and could be forced to find another base of operations. We don't know if the alien ships are still in orbit, but the odds are at least one of the three vessels we know were a part of the attack."

Walker nodded, his brow furrowed. "Sounds fair on the surface of it. I mean, I don't want to leave a bunch of kids here. Be a douche move. And hadn't thought about the other ships, what we'd be facing."

"It's why we need to have the second option. We both know there are bolt holes, supplies, and mining settlements scattered across Pluto, away from the main colony. If we can't get any information about the fight we'd be facing if we tried to escape the planet, then we head for the outer settlements. We get away from the colony and hope the outer claims haven't been targeted yet. If not, they'll already be on alert with the block on communications."

"You hope they'll be on alert. For all, we know they're asleep, or drunk. Miners. Can't trust them to think of anyone but themselves."

"You should be right at home with them, Stone," Lawbook smirked.

Stone shot a glance at Lawbook. What the hell was going on with these people? Didn't they understand the danger they were in? Mining settlements? Had she ever dealt with the bastards running those things? They cared about one thing, themselves. No strangers allowed. Not unless you had the right trade goods to offer them. Items like the ones he had stored away in the belly of his ship. "You telling me you'd give up your life for them?" He gestured at the nearest group of civilians. "For a bunch of whining men, women, and children who'll do nothing for you in the long term, and could get you killed?"

"It's what we agreed to do when we joined up." The young marine explained. "We all know there is a risk. Not like they hide anything from us. Okay, fine we all know they lie to get you to sign up, but the majority of what they tell you these days is the truth."

"Glory hound," Stone grunted.

"Hell no, I want to serve my time and maybe go into one of the private security firms out on the other colonies. I can do it if I serve for ten years." Walker grinned, his eyes bright. "I'll jump the ladder if I have service under my belt. Maybe more so now there are aliens involved." A shadow passed across his eyes. "If I make it back. But if I don't, I knew this when I joined up."

He pounced on the moment of doubt. "You could get out of here with me. You and the others. Then you'd be able to apply for those jobs when the time comes."

"Yeah, but I don't think I'd be able to live with myself if I walked out. I'd be a coward. I mean, how could I talk to anyone, claim to be a Marine if I acted like a coward? What if I met a relative of one the people I'd left behind?"

"You know the odds of that happening are slim."

"But it could still happen. Doesn't matter, I'd know what I'd done. No, it's not cool, man. Not cool at all. Don't know why you'd think of doing it. It's not like you're a coward or something, You're a merc, you have to have been in tough situations before now?"

"Yeah, but I was paid, and I didn't take on a job guaranteed to get me killed. Not my idea of a sane work environment." Why couldn't the man see the issue? It was one thing to sign up, another to agree to die for strangers. Even if they recognized some of the men and women among the survivors, they weren't family or friends. Not going by what he'd seen. No one had reacted to them as if they were related, or close.

Idiots.

If things continued this way, he'd be the only survivor, then questions would be asked. Like how he, out of everyone, survived and escaped the attack. No, he didn't like where that line of reasoning took him.

"You're either with us, Stone. Or against us. It's time to make a choice."

"And if I choose to walk away?"

"We won't stop you. But try to steal anything, and I'll kill you," said Lawbook.

She was right, though he wasn't about to tell her. Getting out of here wasn't going to be easy, not with the dangers waiting for them. No matter how he wanted to run, leaving the kids behind wasn't an option. "What can you offer me to work with this lot? I'm a businessman, better place a decent offer on the table, or I'll walk away."

Salla, still close enough to hear them, laughed. "Dad always said a merc will want payment. Fine, the Marine's don't have the funds. I do. I'll give you ten percent of my father's business."

"Deal." The look of pure shock on Lawbook's face was worth more than any money Salla could offer him. If he'd wanted to rub Lawbook's nose in the offer, he didn't get the chance as an alarm rang out, piercing and undeniable.

"They're coming. Masks in place, seal your suits. We just ran out of time."

"Get the civilians moving, we can't stay here." The Sergeant called out.

Jakob turned, grabbing Salla by one arm as he half hurried, half dragged Salla to one side. "We have to find a way to get everyone out of here. Is there anything, a memory, a conversation with your father, which might help?" A fresh set of violent shudders worked their way through the ceiling, forcing a wide crack into existence even as the vibrations moved down the walls and into the floor. "Much more of this and we'll have a full cave in. We can't stay here and wait for those things to show up."

Salla half closed her eyes, the orbs moving beneath the lids. "I think -- yes, a minute." She grabbed the data pad she wore and tapped instructions in. "Yes, here. We can escape this way. It connects to one of the passageways leading to the edge of the colony and where Dad put the Ajax."

"Alright." He lifted his head and searched for Bloodlaw. "Sergeant, we've got a way out here."

"Harvard, you go with them," the woman said as she strode across the chamber, ushering survivors in their direction. "Don't look back. Don't stop, no matter what you hear. Harvard, use secure nine to get a message to me. Salla, I need a copy of the route." She offered her datapad to Salla.

"On it." The girl grabbed the pad and got to work, her fingers scurrying over the screen.

"Grab what you need, what you can, and go with Salla and Jakob." Sergeant Bloodlaw announced, her voice carrying easily through the cavern. "Harvard is in charge and will be keeping you safe. If something happens to him, you listen to Jakob and Salla. No arguments. Stone, you're with me, same with the rest of the Marines. All civilians with Harvard."

Jakob didn't think, he reacted. He refused to let his mind wander, knowing it would allow him the chance to dwell on the dangers, the problems facing them, and the monsters out there. Creatures who'd destroyed his home perhaps killed his friends and family. He'd seen the things if only glimpses. They weren't human. Could never be regarded as human. And they were here to hurt them, to take what humanity had built, laid claim to and created. "Salla?"

"Ready." She snagged a bag and slipped it on his back.

Men, women, children, chaos in the making.

Cora Bloodlaw gathered her people and gestured for them to take position. The crack widened and the shadows moving across the opening confirmed they were coming. "Keep it covered, and don't let them get past you. Doesn't matter how you do it, we aren't going to let these things get to the kids." More than kids now. Adults. But they were civilians, men, and women who didn't know how to fight. Except for the two of the three who'd chosen to travel with her from the bar.

Liam and Virgil. The third civilian she'd sent with Harvard. She needed fighting men, people who wouldn't flinch at the first round of fire. Not men who would freeze and get not only themselves but others killed in the process.

"I said all civilians go with Harvard."

Liam gestured to the small group. "Don't see any civies here, do you, Virgil?"

"Only fighters," Virgil replied.

Not Marines, but fighters.

"Besides, if you'd meant all civies, you'd have sent me with them," Stone added a rifle in hand, one he'd taken from Duncan's storage.

"How are you going to get paid if you don't go with them?" Lackey grinned at the Merc.

"Oh, I'll get paid. Unlike you lot, I'm going to make it out of this mess in one piece."

Strange, the man joked as if he were one of her Marines. *He is, for now.* She could accept the situation, his change in how he handled things. When they were safe, he'd revert to the asshole she'd become used to dealing with, but until then they were all on the same side. She could deal with this, handle the man fighting alongside her people, same as she would with Liam and Virgil.

"Incoming," Ready called out.

She lifted her gaze, eyes narrowed as she searched for the sign Ready must have spotted, rifle shouldered. Her breathing and heart rate remained calm, steady. No matter what she faced, she wouldn't give into panic. It might not work, she could die here, but disgracing her fellow Marines wasn't a part of the plan. "Don't shoot until you have a clear shot and make each one count."

No one responded they didn't need to. Not when they all understood what they needed to do, who they were here to protect, and the dangers presented by the invaders.

The first shape appeared, not distinct from the mass behind it. Too far away to make out a clean target. She relaxed, refusing to give into the fear niggling away in the back of her mind. Fear kept you sharp unless you allowed it to take control.

Limbs. The shapes she'd come to expect from the handful of sightings she'd had of the invaders. Wings. Beings with four limbs, ones with six. But no sign of beasts of burden. She allowed her gaze to focus on the first of the creatures before she squeezed the trigger. A firm caress but not the jerk pull which might damage her aim. She didn't wait to see if she'd hit her target, but did as she'd been trained, fired a second shot at the same mass of alien life, then move to the next outline.

Harvard tapped Jakob's shoulder. "Let me take point."

Jakob wanted to argue, but the older man was the only member of the military with them, and Bloodlaw knew what she was doing. Didn't she? He didn't ask but nodded to let the Navy pilot know he agreed.

"You'll stay with me," Salla insisted, her face calm despite the situation. "Can't take point if you don't know the way to go."

Jakob smiled. It didn't matter who they faced, what dangers lay ahead, Salla would never allow them to treat her as a child. Lessons he needed to take to heart. Physical age didn't matter, he was taking the role of an adult, leading and working with Salla and Harvard. Offering suggestions, keeping the others safe, and, like Salla, he was prepared to fight. Age no longer played a part in how he reacted. He had his own life ahead of him, one he planned on living to the fullest extent, but that meant he had to survive whatever was headed their way.

Noise. Gunfire rang out behind him. Jakob turned before he could prevent the reaction.

"Stay alert and keep focused on moving forward," Harvard instructed. "Watching over your shoulder will only slow us down."

"Yeah, I know."

"Could have fooled me." The older man grunted and kept close to Salla. "Which way?"

"Here, we need to move this part of the wall, then we can slip through into the tunnel." Salla gestured to a vast expanse of blank wall. "Should be a way of opening it here." She ran one hand over the smooth rock, her brow furrowed. "It has to be around here... got it." She pressed in, two fingers digging into the wall as it moved beneath her touch. Dust rolled down from the top of the rock formation, a low whine and the grey expanse opened at a snail's pace.

They would make it out. No matter what, he had to believe they'd all make it out of here in one piece.

Stone fired, using the rifle instead of his sidearm, his gaze fixed on the opening. The Marines and the two civilians all shot at the same time. Flachettes struck targets, but the energy weapons did more damage. Either way, bodies fell, and more came to take their place. He didn't need to switch weapons, the rifle an energy weapon which allowed him to cause more damage than the standard weapons customarily used within the confines of a ship, or dome. He didn't need to be careful here. He simply needed to kill as many of the damn things as possible.

Wings snapped out to either side of one of the aliens as it dropped down, landing on its hind limbs, mouth open in a snarl that bared fangs. No suits, no sign of the thin covering he'd witnessed earlier, or Lawbook had mentioned.

Ugly buggers.

Teeth, claws, scales, wings. Whatever they were, he knew one thing.

He'd kill every last one of them if he had to.

Energy bolts sliced through the air, striking the winged alien. Each blow knocked it back a step. Liquid oozed from its chest and neck, and still, it didn't fall. It hissed, the sound carried through the cavern, confirming oxygen remained in the tunnel. A shriek followed sounds carried through the chamber as the crack overhead spilled out three more winged aliens. With more behind them. A never-ending line of aliens, each one ready to strike out at the humans defending their hiding place until the last rifle ran out of energy.

And they had enough energy mags to last a long time.

He smiled as the first winged creature fell under a barrage of fire and shifted his attention to the next target.

Chapter Sixteen

"They're not stopping," Lackey called out. "Sergeant, there's too many of them."

"Keep firing, and keep calm," she replied without looking at the man. Each new alien arrival only added to the chaos. The crack remained small enough to prevent a full-scale attack, and it was the only thing in their favor. She kept firing, picking a target and double tapping before she began her search for the next one, always aware of the previous mark in case it continued to move. She fired and made sure they went down and moved on. It was up to the others to be sure they did the same with their own shots.

Shapes fell from the crack in the ceiling, one landing on top of another as they continued to enter the cavern. The numbers increased at a slow, steady pace instead of the rush of attackers they would otherwise have faced. Yet they knocked each other to the floor with how they landed, turning to snap at their companions, especially those with wings if they were hit by one without wings. She filed the information away for another time as she picked out the next target. Sergeant Cora Bloodlaw fired, again and again, aware of the others around her. The Marines. Her Marines. All fighting, willing to keep shooting until they were overrun and had no means of escaping.

"We can't keep this up," declared Ready. "We've got to back up."

"Not yet." She snapped. "We're going to give the kids as much time as we can. Hold position until I saw otherwise."

"Sergeant's right. We break position now, and they'll gain ground. We're holding our own. Don't need to move." The reassurance came from the one source she'd never expected. Stone.

They could do this. Hold the line. "We move when I say, not

before."

"You're going to get us all killed," Ready snapped. "Sergeant, we're outnumbered."

"Tell me something I don't know. And if you keep whining like a wet behind the ears officer who thinks his experience is worth something, I'll kill you myself."

A cry. A voice she recognized. One of her own people. She wanted to look to check on the man, but it wasn't possible. Not with the numbers attacking them, the creatures which continued to approach them. Bolts of energy. She'd seen that from the start. Their weapons weren't designed to protect a dome or a ship. The bolts of energy enough to damage walls, buildings, and now people.

"Walker's hit," Lackey called out.

"Cover him." She didn't shift her attention away from the aliens. She couldn't. Whatever happened, she had to keep her focus on the attackers. Each new squeeze of the trigger resulted in an alien body jerking from the impact. "We can't give them time to get their balance once they land." The winged aliens were recovering from the drop faster than the ones without wings. "Aim for the wings if you can't hit anything else." Delicate compared to the other parts of their body's.

Keep firing.

They had to keep firing.

No matter what.

Jakob glanced back over his shoulder. Shots. The distinctive noise of bolts slicing through the air before they struck their intended targets.

"Don't look back, it won't help." Keevar grabbed his arm and kept them both moving. "The Marines wouldn't want us involved."

"I can use a rifle."

"We all can, but they're trained to do something we aren't.

Stand." Keevar released his grip on Jakob. "Don't know about you but I'd be scared shitless back there."

He didn't argue. Jakob took a deep breath and kept pace with the men and women behind him, his steps keeping him close to Salla and Harvard. "Salla, how much farther?"

"Half a klick before we take the split," Salla called back.

A loud rumble rolled through the passageway, shaking the ground beneath his feet. He stumbled, one hand smacked a wall as his left knee struck the floor. Pain, bright and burning, shot through his leg. A dozen cries of protest rang out behind him. Salla twisted, holding the datapad close, protecting it as she struck a wall. Dust filled the air. Small pieces broke away from the walls, ceiling, and floor.

He scrambled to protect his face from the rain of dirt.

It was going to collapse. The entire tunnel would collapse on him. On them.

They weren't going to make it.

Stone growled, the sound vibrating in the back of his throat. His focus moving from one target to the next, always tracking more than one alien at a time. They fell, beneath the barrage of shots, but still kept coming. Like insects swarming from a hive or mound, they continued to appear, creatures out of nightmares with wings, strange limbs, and weapons he'd never seen before this day. Sweat beaded and dripped into his eyes beneath the mask, and he blinked it away. Bastards kept coming, no matter how many he killed or injured enough, so they didn't claw their way back up, the numbers continued to grow.

As did the number of bodies.

Bodies.

The word flashed through his mind; his shots still finding targets.

An explosion ripped through the ceiling, tossing dust and

debris into the cavern. He flinched and dropped down, one hand covering his face. Around him, the Marines did the same, protecting themselves as best they could. He clung to his rifle, aware it was the one thing which had the chance of keeping him alive. Dead he'd do nothing. Alive he'd collect the money Salla offered, and he could barter this story for drinks until the end of his days. That alone was worth fighting for.

"Shit, don't let them past us."

Lawbook?

He twisted, shaking off the dirt, clearing his mask with a swipe of hand as he looked up. The crack had widened. The small trickle of aliens now turned from a dripping tap to a full shower.

"Well, fuck."

"We're not going to make it," said Ready, his voice trembling.

"Yes, we are. We're not giving up. We're Marines. We fight as Marines. We don't run away like scared children." Lawbook pushed to her feet, firing as she moved. "Fight and die. Or run and die. Your choice, but I know which one I'm choosing."

"You're one stubborn bitch, Lawbook." He grinned, though he didn't turn to look at her as he moved to her side, firing, picking targets along the way.

"I'll take that as a compliment."

"It was meant as one." Marine or not, he'd fight with her and share the occasional drink with her. This was a woman he could respect. "Where the hell are these things coming from?"

"Same ship they arrived in, I assume." Her voice ragged, a hitch behind the words. "We've still got this. This is all about time. We have to do is keep them back from the kids a little longer."

He wanted to agree with her, but the ability to speak vanished as a sharp pain struck him in the stomach. He gasped, stumbling back onto his ass, one hand pressed against his now aching body.

Now I'm screwed.

He moved with her, fighting, picking out targets with the skill she'd associate with a Marine. The other two civilians, Liam and Virgil, fought with equal ability. It didn't matter what they had been before this attack, at this point, the three civilians were a part of her Marines. Men she'd fight and if need be, die with. Cora grinned, teeth bared, jaw tight as she fought. Bolts of energy struck the enemy, often before the aliens had a chance to fire back. But the widening crack changed the odds.

More aliens. Far more than she wanted to face, but she wouldn't run. No matter the cost, she wouldn't damn well run.

Her limbs ached, joints throbbed, each time the ground shook it only added to the pain, aggravating bruised flesh, but she didn't stop, nor did Stone or the rest of her people.

Stone cried out and fell back on his ass, one hand pressed against the core of his body. She moved, without thinking, placing herself in front of the now downed man. It made sense, she was the nearest one to him as she took a stance over his body, standing across his ankles, feet parted enough to allow him to move if required. "How bad?"

"Don't know. Bloody hurts."

Walker and now Stone. They weren't getting out of this. "Get to the tunnel, go. Follow the kids. You and Walker, if you can both move."

"Not leaving," Stone grunted.

Stubborn man. "Your choice, asshole."

"Ah, tell me how you really feel." He coughed and shifted back, the sound of his heels dragging on the ground enough to let her know what he was doing.

The crack, now a full-blown entrance spilled ten aliens, or more at a time, into the cavern. Outnumbered. Outgunned would follow soon enough, but the kids had a chance to escape, find a place to hold up and be safe from the aliens until someone else came to help them. There had to be a way of closing off the gaps, reducing the chances of the beasts following them.

"Start backing up toward the tunnel. Three covering, the rest helping with the injured. Virgil, help Stone. Ready, take Walker." Leaving herself, Lackey, and Liam to cover the retreating men and their injured companions. Her mind raced. There had to be a way to block the attackers from following them. From getting to the civilians. Her gaze lifted to the gap in the cavern. How long had they been working on the hole to get to them? They'd avoided setting off any early alarms, perhaps by blocking the signals?

No time to think about it now.

Stone grunted as Virgil helped him to his feet.

"We've got to bring the rest of the ceiling down." The answer hit her a second before she spoke. "Get everyone back to the tunnel." They could do this. Buy the kids more time, but only if they brought the cavern in on itself, shutting off all the tunnels long enough to buy time to reach a safe hold. "Move. Now!"

*****

"Salla?" Jakob pushed himself free of the debris. Others moved behind him, and the rest of civilians shook off the dirt and dust. He glanced up and checked the tunnel. Cracks. Small ones, debris, small pebbles clung to hair and clothing, but no one appeared to be hurt beyond bumps and bruises. "Salla? Harvard?"

"Here." The man replied as he pulled Salla to her feet. "We're fine. Everyone in one piece?"

A couple replied, but most grunted or started to move toward Salla.

"We're good, don't think anyone was seriously hurt. A few bumps and scratches. Nothing more." Jakob replied.

Echoes of the fight rippled through the corridor, growing distant as the group hurried toward the hope of salvation. He glanced back and did a quick headcount. He couldn't see them all, but enough to be sure the majority of the group remained intact. If there were severe injuries, no one alerted him to the fact.

Salla flashed a weak smile, her face marked with dirt. A small series of scratches marred her neck, but he couldn't see any other sign of damage.

"We need to hurry." Salla checked her datapad and picked up the pace, her steps slapped against the floor in a rapid tempo. "Run, before the rest of the corridor falls in on us." It was all she needed to say to hurry the rest of the group along.

Time had no meaning as they traveled. The lights they carried enough to allow them the chance to see where they were going. Small cracks and movement of rock showed the tunnel had suffered from the last shake, damage which grew less noticeable the longer they jogged through the semi-darkness.

Salla turned a corner and stopped a dozen paces later, her gaze moving over the expanse of rock in front of them. "No, this shouldn't be here. Damnit. I know this shouldn't be here." She lifted the datapad. "I don't understand. It's right here, there should be a tunnel splitting off in two directions, but there's nothing."

Jakob stared at the wall. Rugged, not smoothed out by the tools used to create the corridors. No, this was the natural appearance of the rock wall.

They were trapped.

Stone hurt. Each breath triggered waves of pain up from his abdomen and into his ribs. He groaned but refused to lean on Virgil. "I can bloody walk," he snapped.

"Sure you can, but it's easier with help." Virgil tightened his grip on Stone. "She wants to bring the whole place in."

"Might be an idea." Yeah. He could see where she was going with the idea. Block the main cavern, kill a mess of aliens, and buy time to escape. "Might take some of us out with the insect demons."

"Insect demons?"

"What else would you call them?"

"Dead."

He grinned. "I think I could grow to like you, Virgil."

"Mutual." Virgil set him down three meters into the tunnel. "Check yourself out, I'll be up front with the rest of them." He gestured to Walker as Ready set him down next to Stone. "Might want to give the young'un a look over, if you're up to it. Ready, they're going to want you up with the Sergeant."

The young one. The description fitted Walker. "I'll be able to fight soon enough." But it wouldn't prevent him from checking in on Walker. "Go, I've got this."

Walker's eyes remained closed, his face pale. Stone reached to check a pulse and found himself relieved when the man's pulse throbbed beneath his fingers. "Good, you're still alive. I won't have to kick your ass for dying without permission." Except he didn't hold a rank in this unity. Still, it had been the right thing to say. His eyes narrowed on the wounded man. How bad was it though? Blood sluggishly pulsed from Walker's left shoulder. "Not good." He grumbled as he pulled the small med scanner from a pocket. It wasn't as advanced as the one Lawbook had used on the Gunny, but enough to do what he needed. "Well, shit, kid. You've got a mess in there." One he couldn't fix now. A few things to ease the pain, but that was it. He wasn't a healer, had little more than the basics, first aid, but nothing more. And because of that lack, Walker might die.

Eyes opened, a shudder ran through the Marine. "Stone?" A whispered word, but he heard it clear enough.

"Here. You don't need to move around. Not now. Give your body time to adapt."

"Hurts."

"Shoulder is in pieces. You've turned it into a jigsaw. You'll need a medic to patch you up." If they ever found one or caught up with the survivors. The kids had found several medical kits, and if there were even one person who knew their way around the human body, then Walker would have a chance.

"Figured."

Shots rang out. The noise of battle as the rest of the Marines took position in the entrance of the tunnel. Bolts slammed through the air over his head, and he ducked in. "Keep your head down. Can't guarantee the bolts won't find you if you try and sit up. You don't need another injury on top of the first. Unless you want to be greedy and build up more scars to impress the women back on Earth."

"Chicks dig scars." Walker shuddered, his face a sickly grey-green. "No thanks, one's enough. Should be spectacular though, if the pain is anything to go by."

"Wise man." He edged away from Walker. "I'll be right back. Don't want to miss out on all the fun."

"You're insane."

"I know, but don't go telling everyone."

"Secret's safe with me," Walker sighed and closed his eyes. "Think I'll take a nap. Yeah, sleep sounds good about now."

Stone blinked, a haze covering his eyes as he turned away from the injured man. Dust, yeah, that was it. He had dust in his eyes. Wouldn't stop him from killing a few more of their unwanted guests, not this time.

Chapter Seventeen

"There has to be a way." Jakob pushed past Harvard. "You didn't make a mistake, Salla. I know you. This isn't your fault."

Salla nodded once, sharply. "Alright. But it doesn't change reality. We're trapped here. Maybe they didn't update the data, or -- no, Dad checked. He came down here and mapped this out himself. He wouldn't have missed a solid wall."

Jakob touched the wall, searching for a sign of a hidden level, a press point, buttons, control panel, or anything they could use. "Has to be something here."

"No, Dad didn't add notations for a wall." She tapped the pad. "I'm missing information, or I've forgotten what he taught me."

Harvard walked along the wall, facing the stone as he searched. His left heel caught, half vanished into the ground as he stumbled back, barely righting himself in time.

"Not a door, a trap door." Salla dropped to her knees and scuffed her fingers along the small dip which had caused Harvard to fall. "Here, it's here. Help me clear it."

Jakob and Harvard joined her, but the others stayed back when Salla snapped at them. Too many people would make the work confusing, but with three of them working together, it didn't take long to find the outline of the door and the panel next to it. Salla glanced at her datapad again, then keyed in a code.

Metal and stone scraped against each other as the trapdoor shifted, dropping down before it slid underneath the floor. Lights glowed in the tunnel beneath them, and Salla grinned as she looked up and caught the eyes of a dozen onlookers. "Down the ladder, then follow the corridor. It only goes one way, you won't get lost."

"One at a time, people. Salla, you go first, Harvard, stay with me." Jakob organized the group, only realizing he'd given the pilot an order when the first of the civilians began their climb into the lower tunnel.

"And if I decide I'm in charge?"

"You won't," he replied, watching as Salla disappeared from view. "Or you'd have sorted that out with the Sergeant earlier on. Wouldn't leave it this late to get into an argument about leadership.

"Smart." Harvard's eyes narrowed. "Why did you want to keep me back?"

"Keep her safe." Jakob indicated after Salla.

"Always," said Harvard. A moment later, he was gone.

"Anything we can use to bring the roof down?" Cora called out. If the aliens understood her words, it wouldn't matter, the odds of them being overheard with the noise of bolts slicing dangerous lines through the cavern, were slim.

"Give me a minute, Sergeant. Think I might... yes. Virgil, your rifle. It one of the adapted?" Ready asked.

"Yes."

"Swap." He tossed his rifle to Virgil, catching the other man's in return. "Lackey, yours is the same, I think."

"Yep, don't know where Duncan picked these up but they're sweet."

"You don't know how much. These are capable of handling explosive rounds, not just energy bolts."

"Yeah, if we had any."

Ready tapped a pouch on his belt. "I may have relieved the supply dump of a round or two."

Cora laughed as she picked the next target, dropping one of the nearest aliens, then picked out her next two, firing as soon as she had an opening. "Two rounds be enough?"

"Be better if we use two or three each, but we can do it. It'll make a mess." Ready explained as he passed a handful of rounds to Lackey. "We need to hit the weak points." He pointed out the areas in the ceiling. "We hit those, and it should come down on the rest of those bastards." He fingered the rounds before loading them. "Keep targeting the new arrivals until you run out of ammo, or the job is done."

"Covering fire. Let's keep these critters from going after these two." She didn't need to say their names for the rest of the team to know what they needed to do.

A figure lumbered his way behind her and dropped to one knee, rifle in hand. Without a word, Stone began to pick his own targets and fired.

Bodies fell. Shots fired. Grunts, the shudder of explosive rounds striking the rock overhead. A combination of fear and the drive to survive ruled her actions, tempered only by the voice of her trainer. No, not the trainer. Gunny's voice. She smiled, though she doubted it would be a pleasant one. Not with teeth bared and the need to kill the creatures firing at them, running in their direction, and trying to destroy everything she held dear.

Her Marines.

Stone winced, each time the rifle fired his abdomen protested, bruises awakened from the shock running through his system. He didn't know how badly he was injured, hadn't taken the time to run a scan, but it didn't matter. His teeth gritted. He wasn't going to whine about a few scrapes. Not when there were other people at risk. People he hadn't wanted anything to do with when he'd first been forced into working with them, but now, somehow, had become important to him.

He fired again and again, not missing, not daring to miss. Time. All they had to do was buy enough time and space for Ready and Lackey to bring the ceiling down. He smiled, anger building as he continued to fight. He'd kill them. Kill all of them. Every single foul creature now charging toward him with death in their eyes. "Come and get me." The words escaped before he had time to stop them. He laughed as the aliens fell. Thick purple blood, or goo, whatever they called it, splattered across stone and plastiboard. Death. He was death to them. A walking, breathing, laughing grim reaper ready to send them back to hell.

Had he spoken, not just thought the words?

It didn't matter.

"Grim reaper here, your time is up. Go back to hell where you belong."

"Not here, you don't belong here. This is our hell, not yours. It belongs to us. Not you." Lawbook screamed her defiance at the oncoming horde. "Hear me, you warped bastards? We're Hell's Own, not you."

Explosions rang out. Rock, dust, debris, and bodies tumbled down. Cracks widened, the second wave of explosive rounds struck the roof of the cavern. The ability to hear what was happening in the chamber died with the loss of the remaining air. The bolts, explosions, the cries of human and aliens alike, all now muffled and lost with the stolen oxygen.

Hell's Own. Yeah, the name fit both the fighters and circumstances.

They were all insane, and he no longer cared.

Jakob remained silent as the last of the group made their way down the ladder, leaving him on his own. He wasn't moving. Not until he knew if the Marines were following them. He couldn't abandon them. Not after all they had done, all they continued to do to keep his friends safe.

A muffled sound, then nothing but the rumble beneath his feet. Dust shook from floor and ceiling alike, but the sounds were gone. He checked his datapad. No oxygen. They'd expected this, it had been one of the reasons they'd all pulled on their suits before they'd made their way through the tunnel. His friends were safe or would be. If he had to, he'd close the trapdoor and cover it so the aliens would be delayed in finding the survivors. If they couldn't find the door, then they'd be unable to track the men and women who'd vanished down the ladder.

The Marines. Where they alive? Had they died to protect him and the others?

He frowned and took a step toward the entrance. No, he wouldn't make that mistake. He had to wait. Find out if there were survivors, then follow Salla into the deeper tunnels. Ones he hadn't known existed until Salla had shared the information.

He pressed one hand against the wall, letting the trickle of energy from the explosions vibrate into his fingers.

He'd wait.

A few more minutes.

It wasn't too much to risk when they now fought to keep him safe.

They'd make it.

They had to.

He couldn't accept any other outcome.

"It's coming down. All of it. We've done it," Virgil's voice carried across the comm.

Cora allowed herself a moment, a split second, to look up and assess the situation, only to smile as she realized he was right. Large cracks, open areas of sky above them, the distant lights from the few sources still intact in the colony did little to illuminate the now exposed cavern.

"Move, in the tunnel, move now. Ready, you have two more of those shells?" She gestured for the group to get into the passageway. "Liam, Virgil, get Stone and Walker to the civies. Don't want them slowing us down."

"On it."

"Six left for me. Lackey has four."

"More than enough. Fire one more each to bring down the rest of the roof." Cora took a deep breath as the last two shots were fired up at the slender remains of the ceiling. "Rest of you, move. Into the tunnel. Pick up the pace." The shudder and crack of stone played through her feet as the last part of the ceiling came down with a silent crash. Bodies, black, brown, touches of purple from the liquid in their bodies, all mingled with dust, rock, debris, and pieces of equipment. How much more of the cavern would cave in, she didn't know, nor was she about to wait around to find out. The floor split beneath her and she jumped, hitting the ground close to the tunnel entrance.

No more time to waste. The entire thing was going.

"Go. Now." She gave the order.

Like the others, she ran, stopping only long enough to snap the order out to Ready. "Bring down the entrance. One shot each."

The two men turned, dropped to one knee, and fired.

Dust, the movement beneath his feet, it all built up and still, Jakob continued to watch and wait for the Marines. Explosions, he couldn't ignore them, not with the way his body reacted to them. He pressed one hand against the wall, holding himself in place. They weren't coming. He couldn't expect them to survive. Not after this.

He had to leave, join the others. Find Salla and Harvard.

He didn't move.

Could he hear anything on the comm? He tapped it into life and listened, half praying, half pleading with the voices within to allow the Marines a chance to find him.

If they were dead, what then?

They still had Harvard, the man was military even if he was Navy, not a Marine. He knew how to fight. Would be able to help them, and Salla wasn't a wilting flower. She was a fighter, knew how to handle weapons and situations, she'd have to with a father like Duncan.

A hand touched him on the shoulder, and he turned, eyes wide, not expecting anyone to approach from behind him.

"I couldn't leave you alone out here." Salla leaned in, her helmet touching his enough to allow communication without activating the comm. The short range comm would be harder to listen in on, but it was still possible if you knew which signals to look for. "No sign of them?"

"No, not yet." Soon, they wouldn't be much longer.

"They might not make it. Not after those explosions."

"They have to." A prayer, a hope, it didn't matter. He wouldn't allow himself to believe otherwise.

The Marines would join him, they wouldn't let him down.

Chapter Eighteen

"Move it. Don't make me shoot you." Lawbook warned her voice carrying across the comm channel.

"You wouldn't waste the ammo or energy packs," Stone replied as she caught up with the main group. "Glad you made it, Sergeant."

She nodded her thanks but wasted no time in small talk. Her interest focused on the members of her group, she checked in with each of them, and he turned away. Watching the woman do her job wasn't a good use of his time, especially as walking continued to be a problem. His abdomen continued to complain, the bruises ones he would complain about later. When they were safe. Away from the aliens.

If any of them had dared to follow their now dead companions into the cavern. Nor would they be able to easily track the group now. The idea was a damn fine one, and the tunnel had collapsed behind them thanks to the final two shots. Where there any other explosive rounds left? He'd heard Lawbook ask, but couldn't remember the answer. Didn't have a way of finding out without sounding like an idiot, and he didn't need the information at this point.

"Keep moving," Lawbook ordered.

What other choice did they have?

He pressed one hand to his aching flesh and grunted. Moving hurt, but at least he was on his feet. Unlike Walker, who couldn't walk on his own. Two men half walked with him, half carried Walker and the injured man groaned, though there was no atmosphere to carry the sound, the look on the Marine's face said it all. He was hurting. Badly. The damaged shoulder could be healed, but not unless they found a medic, a healer, doctor, hell, he'd take a vet. Not that he expected there to be one on Pluto, to his knowledge, no one had been allowed to bring pets.

Why anyone would want to transport animals here was beyond him, but there was no accounting for taste.

He frowned, the hairs lifting on the back of his neck as he turned toward the entrance, weapon in hand.

They weren't alone.

Not possible. The entrance was closed, collapsed. They couldn't be followed.

Cora turned at the same time as Stone, sidearm in her right hand, eyes narrowed as she searched through the darkness. Her jaw clenched, tension building across her back. Something was there. She could feel it in her gut. No matter what was going on, what else they fought, she wasn't going to ignore her instincts.

A movement. Small. Tiny compared to what she'd seen before. Impossibly small compared to the aliens they'd already seen. It crawled across the ceiling, no bigger than the length of her arm.

She didn't think she reacted. Cora took aim, one hand cradling the butt of her sidearm. She cupped it, lifted the weapon, tracing the pattern of the creature's movement. It darted, not keeping to the zig-zag or straight route. It moved, seemingly at random. But there was a pattern there, one she had to find. She forced herself to relax, her mind finding the numbers until she squeezed the trigger.

She wasn't the only one.

Four shots struck the black and grey creature, tearing the thing apart.

"If there's one, there'll be others. Keep moving. Virgil, with me. Need backup in-case more of these things show up." She wouldn't let the aliens find the civilians. If she had to stay here until her air ran out, she'd make damned sure they never located the kids.

No matter what it cost her.

*****

Jakob wrapped his arms around Salla, holding her tight, her muscles tight beneath his embrace. "It's alright, this isn't sexual. A friends hug, nothing more."

She relaxed and leaned into his touch. "We can't stay here any longer. I've told Harvard the route, but they're going to close and lock the doors behind us, and we'll be trapped here."

He knew the words made sense, but he didn't like it. "I don't want to leave them."

"I know, I don't either, but we have to. They wouldn't want us to die, waiting for them. You know that. It would be tossing their sacrifice away, making it as if it didn't matter. Their lives, the fight, they're back there to save us, not to let us join them."

He sighed and stepped back from the hug. "Alright, I know, we have to leave." He took a deep breath and glanced back down the corridor.

A shadow moved over the walls, then two, three or four of them. Human shapes, running, weapons in hand.

His heart raced, hope burst into life. "They're coming. They've made it." At least some of them had. "Get the door open, we're running out of time, we have to get them down into the lower tunnel." Away from here. Where the aliens couldn't find them.

And then what?

Interlude Four
Unified Terran Government: Alpha Comms.

"Cavanor," Grant snapped the single word.

Sheila tensed but shifted her gaze away from the screen. "Yes, Captain."

"A word. Now."

"Captain, I'm still trying to reach the colony on Triton, and there's no reply from any vessels in the area." It didn't make sense, the ships should have received the message by now.

"Now, Cavanor."

She glanced back over her shoulder but didn't move from her station. "Sir, I have to get this message through, we need a reply."

"Captain Grant, is there a reason you're trying to distract Cavanor from her work?"

She turned fully, unable to ignore the command in the man's voice; one she'd only heard twice before, but it was one she'd never forget. Standing on the observation platform Admiral Roger Stirling held position, back straight, hands at his sides, jaw set, his grey hair cut into the familiar high and tight, his pale green gaze fixed on Grant.

"Admiral, I-- it's a matter of protocol."

"And you believe protocol is more important than finding out what's going on with the Pluto colony? With our two silent ships? And now, apparently, problems forming around Triton?" Stirling curled one hand on the railing.

A light flickered on her panel. Despite her desire to continue the watch the play between Stirling and Grant, the job came first. "Sir, incoming message from Triton."

"And?"

"Text, not voice. Bringing it up now." Words flickered across the screen. Ones she'd hoped never to read. Her mouth dried, throat tightened as she swallowed and tried to make sense of the message. To understand what she was seeing. "Pluto's been attacked, sir. Alien ships. Three ships. Both of our vessels are down. Triton and the other colonies are readying for an attack."

"Cavanor, send a message to all stations, ships, and colonies. Pluto is under attack. All hands are to report to their stations and await further instructions."

"Yes, Admiral."

First contact, in her lifetime.

Aliens.

They were no longer alone in the universe.

Epilogue

Sergeant Cora Bloodlaw took a deep breath and let her gaze move over the small group. No one had been lost, not in the civilians she'd met. Her own people had taken a few bumps and bruises. Walker, in time his shoulder would heal if she could get him to a medic. If not, he'd still improve but his shoulder injury would cause more problems in the years to come. But sooner or later the Navy would return and get them off this rock. Away from the aliens and life...

Fooling myself.

Normal. It would never be that again. Not for those who called Pluto home, not for the people of Earth or anyone in between. They couldn't shove the genie back into the bottle. Not this time. The aliens were here, and she had a lot of work ahead of her. They all did. A brief glance at the map Salla had provided told her all she needed to know. A handful of mines, passages with ground vehicles large enough to, in a convoy, transport all of the survivors to the outposts far beyond the colony. For now, they were deep enough underground to buy them time. With the trapdoor shut and covered, the odds of them being traced immediately were slim. But the odds still existed, and she'd learned not to take safety for granted.

"So, now what?" Stone, one hand pressed against his injured abdomen, his face drawn and pale.

"We get them out of here, to the mining settlements, pick up transportation along the way, and gather information."

"I see."

"You don't approve?"

"I didn't say that."

"You didn't have to." She turned her attention away from Stone.

"No, I don't suppose I do. Short time together, but you're smart enough to figure out what else is going on. Those things aren't going to give up, and from the way they struck, it's clear the Navy got their asses kicked up there, or they'd have sent help long before now."

"I know." Cora rubbed her chin, giving herself a moment to think. If the word had reached Earth, they had hope, but right now they were in the dark, and it wasn't going to change anytime soon. "It's not going to be easy, but keeping these people safe, getting them out of the colony, it has to be our priority. Once we're in a better position, we can regroup and find out how many guns we have on our side." It was a plan, not much of one, but it was all she had to work with.

"And I'm with you until the skies are clear and I can get to my ship. I don't think they've found it, but there's no way of knowing without getting eyes on it." He shrugged. "Besides, it was becoming interesting around here, and I wouldn't want to vanish before Salla pays me. Bad for my reputation."

Cora shook her head. "Then welcome aboard, Stone. But remember one thing, you disobey my orders, and we'll have another discussion."

"Would that be like the one we had down in the supply dump?"

"A good starting point, but yes."

"Well, at least I know where I stand."

Where they both stood. This was their world, their home, their colony. If they had to fight to take back their slice in hell, so be it. After all, it's what she was a Marine and this was what she signed up for.

Watch for Hell's Children, coming August 2019 from T.S. Weaver.

Want sneak peeks, first looks at covers, snippets and behind the scenes information?
Sign up for the private Facebook Group dedicated to System Wars.

https://www.facebook.com/groups/TSWeaverSystemWars/

Author's Bio

T.S. Weaver is one of the alter-ego's of Terri Pray.

Originally from England, she now lives in Minnesota with the love of her life, her knight in battered, tarnished armor, and their youngest son. The household also consists of fellow gamers and creatives, Rage and Scott. Along with two service dogs, two cats, and a horde of random ideas which insist on waking people up at 4am.